Also by Heather Sappenfield

The View From Who I Was

HEATHER SAPPENFIELD

LIFE AT THE SPEED OF US

flux
®
Woodbury, Minnesota

First Edition
First Printing, 2016

Book design by Bob Gaul
Cover design by Lisa Novak
Cover image by iStockphoto.com/58414132/©shansekala

Flux, an imprint of Llewellyn Worldwide Ltd.

Library of Congress Cataloging-in-Publication Data
Sappenfield, Heather.
  Life at the speed of us/Heather Sappenfield.—First edition.
      pages cm
  Summary: After surviving a snowboarding accident, eighteen-year-old Sovern Briggs, still grieving over the death of her mother, experiences uncanny insights into new realms of perception.
  ISBN 978-0-7387-4730-9
  [1. Space and time—Fiction. 2. Grief—Fiction. 3. Mothers—Fiction.]
  I. Title.
  PZ7.S27Li 2016
  [Fic]—dc23

                                                                    2015028594

Flux
Llewellyn Worldwide Ltd.
2143 Wooddale Drive
Woodbury, MN 55125-2989
www.fluxnow.com

Printed in the United States of America

*For the unperceived histories
that moment by moment surround and influence us.*

O

The swirled texture of my bedroom ceiling reminded me of ice. My blanket weighed a thousand pounds and flattened my body against my bed. The equation for the rhythmic *ting* of the baseboard heater whispered in my head. The fridge whirred in the kitchen downstairs with that high-pitched squeak marking every cruel second. From outside came the muffled scrape of a plow pushing heavy snow. February 22: 2/22. I took a calming breath and threw back the covers.

My bedroom window looked out across the garage roof layered with a foot of new white. A storm had pummeled Crystal Village overnight, and fat flakes still fell. I pressed my temple against an ice bloom on the glass and gained a view up Crystal Mountain. The gondola cars moved uphill from the village center, slow as the lift's engine warmed. I pictured the powder-hungry skiers and boarders already lined up in the maze, ready to climb into those suspended glass boxes, hooting and laughing and so psyched for the 8:30 opening while the liftics shoveled clear the loading areas. Clouds obscured the mountain's top, but I still sagged with longing to be up there.

Dad was already in those clouds, no doubt, supervising ski-patrol crews heading out for avalanche control. It wasn't fair that he still spent most of his time up there while I was a prisoner down here. But then, life didn't play fair. Least of all school.

2/22.

I forced myself away from the window but paused to press dots around where my temple had melted the frost— one, two, three, four, five toes to make a cheery footprint on the glass. I pressed my hand there and obliterated it.

I shuffled to yesterday's clothes on the floor at the end of my bed. I strapped on the bra, walked to my dresser, and drew out a fresh pair of days-of-the-week underwear. I slid on *Saturday*, though it was Tuesday. Anymore, I didn't care what day it was. Life was a rotten movie looping in slow motion. As I tugged on the jeans and T-shirt from the floor, that handprint on the window caught my eye; it seemed like someone waving from beyond the glass. I didn't bother to wash my face, but I did brush my shoulder-length hair and my teeth.

2/22.

On the kitchen counter lay a note from Dad: *Let's eat out.* I crumpled it.

Last night, Dad had come home with a new crew cut. I'd almost choked at seeing his chin-length hair gone. Time was, Mom pushed back that hair before she'd kiss him. My eyes had met Dad's—the first time in ages—and we could have said hurtful things. Instead, I'd wrapped myself in silence and turned on a movie.

Tonight, I wouldn't be at dinner, I'd be with Gage. Fate may have screwed me royally, but it had granted me Gage. He always had pot or booze—cigarettes at the least—and nicotine-flavored kisses. Those kisses were best in rule-breaking places, like school, or a coffee shop, or in plain view of lifthouses. Places where news would get back to Dad. Gage grinned at my fury, respected my silence, and was always ready to ditch. Today, I'd need all of the above.

Lately, though, I'd gotten so wild I'd scared even him.

There was this clothing store where I'd go sometimes with Mom. I despised that store, but Mom loved it. She'd run her fingers over the sweaters or jeans and sigh. Sometimes she'd even try on stuff, but she'd always put it back. Only once did she buy something—a measly scarf—and only because it was on sale.

Over the past two weeks, I'd gone into that shop three times, chosen something Mom would have loved, and stuffed it into my parka.

Each time, Gage had waited outside, and I'd strode past him, headed straight for Crystal Creek. I'd yanked the sweater, the jeans, the dress out of my parka, crouched on the bank at a stretch of open churning water, and fed them in. I liked watching their colors get sucked under the ice.

The first time, Gage had leaned against a tree and said, "Jesus, Sovern, *I'll* buy stuff for you." His family was eight-digit rich. I'd stood, pressed him against the bark, and kissed him. The second time, he'd stepped away from that tree, toward me, and said, "What the hell, Sovern?" The third time, he'd just leaned against that trunk with his arms crossed and watched me with a weird flicker in his eyes.

He knew exactly what was going on. Everybody knew. A year ago, our accident, Mom's death, and her memorial service had twice been on the front page of the local newspaper. It didn't take rocket science to figure out my equation. *Sovern Briggs + 2/22 = implosion.*

That crunched Honda had actually groaned as the Jaws of Life forced it open. Amid that whirl of sirens and flashing lights, I'd committed myself to silence. In silence, I couldn't hurt anyone else. In silence, I was safe. Every now and then a word slipped out or a situation forced me to speak, but mostly, I stayed mute. Now I leaned on the kitchen counter and traced my lips.

2/22 = the anniversary of the day my voice killed Mom.

I walked to the entry, shrugged on my parka, and checked that my snowboard gear was ready to lug to Gage's car. I watched out the narrow window beside the door for his BMW SUV. I blinked back the sensation of the Honda sliding, then flipping, and flipping. The equation for that slide's velocity whispered through me.

I'd thought about ditching the whole day, but I needed distraction. I needed the adrenaline rush of smoking a joint with Gage on the way to school and of walking into Crystal High knowing I reeked of marijuana. I needed his defiant kisses in the halls—in front of teachers and everyone—to make me feel alive. I didn't have a first period, so I'd endure three classes—Spanish, English, Calc—and then ditch. Fifth period was just Art and sixth was P.E. I'd be snowboarding; that was physical activity, right?

Fifteen minutes passed, but Gage didn't arrive. I texted him: WHERE R U?

He didn't answer.

I leaned my head against the window's frame. My unworthy pulse throbbed in my ears.

After half an hour, I considered ditching after all. Yet I was pissed. Had Gage blown me off? On this of all days? I had to know, so I stormed out the door for the twenty-minute walk to Crystal High.

Even though I didn't have class first period, I was still late to Spanish, partly because before entering the school, I'd taken the time to find Gage's BMW parked in the lot.

Usually, he met me in the halls between classes, and we'd end our rendezvous with smoldering kisses aimed to make people squirm, but he wasn't at our meeting places. In third period, Lindholm looked at me with concern as she led a discussion I did not hear. My mind was focused on confronting Gage in Calculus. As a rule, we never ditched math.

2/22.

I didn't even go to lunch, just waited at my locker till I could head to class. I sat in my desk in front of Gage's— looking like an idiot—and waited. And waited. The bell rang and class started. No Gage.

I couldn't think straight. I kept picturing his car parked in the lot. Had he ditched just this class? Was he avoiding me? I felt Kenowitz's gaze on me several times, like Lindholm's had been in English, but he never said anything. I wondered if the teachers had gotten a memo: *Sovern Briggs + 2/22 = flammable.* The bell rang and I bolted for Gage's locker.

I found him in the Student Union, hanging with his fellow seniors. His back was to the room, but his buddies spotted me. They inspected me as I approached on legs moving some other body. One of them said something, and Gage glanced over his shoulder, then back at his friends like I was nothing.

I felt like an idiot, like the lowly junior I was, which was ridiculous really since he and I were the same age. School's stupid hierarchies. I studied the drape of Gage's gray T-shirt over his muscled back, his black skullcap, and his brown hair brushing his shoulders. No wonder half the girls in the school were in love with him. I arrived beside his chair, and his buddies stopped talking. "Later," they said, smirking as they rose.

Gage scooted back his chair and looked up at me with an indifferent expression. "Got something to say?"

Knowing me like he did, it was mean. Especially because he'd always said he liked my silence.

2/22.

I forced out, "What's going on?"

His eyebrows rose. "She speaks!" He stood, and I forced myself not to step back. There were maybe six inches between us. "Listen, Sovern..." He scratched the back of his head the way he did when faced with a puzzle. For one instant, I saw panic in his gaze, but it turned hard again. "We're done."

It was all I could do not to slug him. Or kiss him. How could he break up with me? On this of all days?

He shrugged, then grabbed his history book from the table, slid his pencil behind his ear, and strolled away. Even after he'd disappeared down the hall toward class, I stared after him.

I noticed other students watching, and my pulse amplified. I spun on my heel and headed to my locker. I needed elevation.

1

I rose from the chairlift's seat and rode my snowboard away from the lifthouse, front boot buckled in and back boot free for maneuvering. I stopped, and skiers and boarders streamed past. My cigarette burned warm between my fingers. I sucked a long drag as I squinted at the view.

White smothered everything—the pines and aspens, the lifthouse, the ground. Last night's storm had moved on, and the sky was so blue the contrast stung my eyes. Don't you cry, I scolded myself. But I'd already lost the battle.

Usually this air comforted me. Up here I felt closest to Mom. Today, my problems magnified till they were like the images on a movie screen, and the foam that lined my goggles was a soggy cold mask.

Most afternoons, Gage and I had stood right here, buckling up after ditching sixth period. When we'd ditched fifth period, it was even better. I'd kiss him and scan around, daring any of Dad's ski patrol to report me. Even now, I felt the thrill of when one of them recognized me. I'd look directly at him, or her, and take a purposeful drag on my cigarette. Most of them would look away, the dilemma of whether to tell Dad already scrawled on their faces.

I remembered that blank look Gage had given me an hour ago and flung my cigarette to the snow. It sank beneath the surface. I could relate. No doubt my rage had scared off even him.

2/22.

Failing. I was always failing.

"I hate tests!" My voice charged out at the postcard world. I willed it down to the valley floor till it bashed into that interstate snaking along the river, into houses, restaurants, hotels, shops, and stupid school. Idiots had stopped around me, staring. I traced my lips. Had that yell really passed through them?

Disgusted with myself, I tugged on my glove, leaned over, and buckled in my rear boot. I rocked onto that foot, then my front, inching into the fall line. As gravity kicked in, I spun myself around in a 180 so my right leg was forward. I followed a narrow catwalk, leaning toeside to hold the board's uphill edge. I arced onto a run called Last Chance, spraying a rooster tail of snow on a group standing around an instructor. Their cries blurred as I sliced to the run's far side and ducked beneath the yellow-black striped ropes marking the ski-area boundary. This was our favorite powder stash. Gage and I poached it virtually every time we rode. We called it Shangri-La.

I pictured Gage gliding along before me, brown hair ribboning against his helmet. I smelled Mom's honeysuckle shampoo, sobbed, and waited for speed to build. I needed its thrill. Daily. Another source of adrenaline that relieved life's pain. I accelerated to that point where panic fluttered my innards and everything—the dull tick of time, Gage, even Mom—subsided beneath instinct and survival.

At the edge of my vision rushed a white blur. I looked directly into a snow whirlwind just as it batted me onto my heels.

When a snowboard's broad edge catches, there's no controlling its physics, and I shot into the forest. Snowy branches cracked and raked across my cheeks before I got my arms up. I veered straight at a trunk, hit it elbow first, and yelped in pain. A sound like a plucked cello string—bones breaking, no doubt—vibrated through me as I fell backward into the void of snow surrounding the trunk.

As I was falling into that three-foot well, the spruce shuddered, and snow—lots of it—avalanched off its branches, onto me. That fall and the snow hitting me hurt like hell. I wriggled my face free, gasping, but the snow had become white cement that immobilized the rest of my body. My elbow and ribs pounded like someone was slugging them.

I started to yell *Help!* but "Coward!" came out. A word meant for Gage, yet when it touched air, it was for Dad. "Coward!" I yelled again. This time for me.

My toes and a thin line of my snowboard weren't buried.

My pigtails were stuck in the snow and tugged when I tried to move my head more than an inch. Itchy blood dribbled down my face. I laughed at the irony of my helmet's protection.

A crow landed in a neighboring tree, loosed a squawk, and lurched into flight. The sound of its wingbeats stretched across the emptiness. I was trapped, out of bounds, with no chance of anyone hearing me even if I screamed. I'd only whimpered once in my life. During the accident that killed Mom. I whimpered now.

All I could do was stare up through that tree. I rocked my head, the little I could, to the rhythm of *2/22, 2/22, 2/22*, and the branches and sky became a green, brown, turquoise, and white kaleidoscope. After a while, I noticed I was humming "Blackbird," the Beatles tune Mom sang to me when I was little, and to herself as I got older. I spied a brown-gray lump of the wrong texture: a porcupine staring down. He shifted on his branch, pissed.

"Don't like my music?" I croaked.

He fumbled to a closer branch, so he could peer straight down at me. Company, at least.

I had no idea about time, but the sky turned dusky. It was freezing. Sleep was a drug, and my body turned numb, even my arm's and ribs' throb. This was how I'd felt at Mom's memorial, except smothered by the clingy smell of gardenias as Dad's sad mouth formed words in slow motion: *It's a test, Sov. If we survive it, we'll be stronger.* Uh-huh. Like he'd even tried. That was the last time we spoke, in words at least. Both stubborn as hell, we used to butt heads daily.

Mom would say, *If I wasn't around, you two would kill each other.* Mom. Always right.

This weird thing happened then. Maybe *cold + pain = hallucination.* All I know is that the porcupine's pelt transformed to Dad's new crew cut, and its beady eyes became Dad's. He shifted on his branch, and I saw his fear. "Dad," I said. "Don't be scared. I won't hurt you."

Like he understood, he started coming down. Not graceful at all. Claws scraping. Fumbling from branch to branch. I sighed in relief: Dad was finally here.

He reached the last branch, directly above my face, and I smelled him. My gaze focused hard, and he was no longer Dad. Quills up, that porcupine was coming down. I screamed.

The porcupine freaked, scrabbled around, and fell. He landed next to my face, loosing a grunt of pain and sending a white wave across me as quills pierced my cheek and one side of my nose. A stretched wail erupted from me and hung in the air. My second loud sound. It felt like a taunt.

The porcupine's quills, the ones not in my face, clacked gently as it waddled away. Then it was just me and pain and landscape.

Had Mom felt this lonely? I saw her as I had a million times: her skin masking a crushed back. She couldn't even move her head to look at me. I took her limp hand, an odd grip with my fingertips resting over her wrist's pulse. I felt her heartbeat grow fainter, fainter, fainter. Then her eyes fluttered shut and her pulse disappeared. "Hang on, Mom! You can!" I shouted, then and now. If only I hadn't been whining. If only she hadn't taken her hand from the steering wheel to pat my leg in that rhythm that promised the world would be okay. *Me + anyone I loved = disaster.*

Sleepiness ruled. I heard Mom humming "Blackbird," Paul McCartney harmonizing now. I relaxed, mind reaching for her again. My future would end with my past.

"There's a track!" a guy shouted. "It went straight at that tree. Look! I *knew* that was a scream!"

Damn. It sounded like Wash.

"Ah, shite!"

Figures, I thought. Of all my possible rescuers, it was Wash. Relief and guilt pressed down on me harder than the snow.

I pretended to be unconscious and pictured the two ski patrollers as they glided up and snapped off their skis. There was radio static. A post-holing step. The swish of red Gore-Tex.

Wash leaned over the tree well. "Briggs! It's Sovern! Are those quills? Sov, what happened?"

Come on, Dad, I thought and pretended to struggle for consciousness so I could see his reaction through my lashes. But he just hovered behind Wash. Hunk with a moustache, a heart sliced open, and no clue what to do. I shut my eyes as Wash radioed for a sled.

They called Dad "Beautiful Briggs." Even the guys. He was six foot three, cut from lifting weights for his job—always Mr. Ski Patrol—and big-screen handsome. He used to smirk at that nickname. Now it made him clamp his lips and look away. Mom had coined it, back when he'd hired her as a patroller. Ever since third grade, I'd loved imagining them on the ski lift—Dad trying to be Mr. Professional Boss while attraction drove them nuts.

I opened my eyes a millimeter. Ice clung to Dad's moustache as his gloves dug out my body. He was in the tree well with me, and Wash leaned over the edge, scooping out snow along my other side. Dad maneuvered around the trunk, leaning against it, and plowed back most of the heavy stuff across my middle. He stopped and looked at me. Through his goggles' lens, his eyes narrowed, just as I realized I was still humming Mom's song.

"Where are you hurt?" he said.

I barked a laugh. Hurt? It was 2/22. I'd been hemorrhaging a year. To the day.

"Sovern," Wash scolded.

I couldn't look at them. I forced my mouth to say, "Arm. Ribs." The quills were self-explanatory.

"The right?" Dad said.

"Right," I said, like *whatever*, and then willed my mouth shut.

There was the bump and click of moving metal and fiberglass. Wash became framed by a third ski patrolman hauling an orange sled.

"Backboard," Wash said, and straps whizzed as they were pulled from their ratchets. Dad knelt and studied his knees.

"Briggs," Wash said.

Dad looked up, and Wash handed down a backboard. Wash slid down beside Dad in the well. Dad burrowed an arm under my helmet and one below my butt. Wash did the same for my legs and feet, and they maneuvered the board underneath. I sucked air through my teeth at the pain. They strapped me down. The tree made lifting me out a puzzle, but they finally turned me, gloves swishing against the sled, so the third patroller had my head.

"Hey, Sov."

Great. Tucker, who was twenty-two and totally gorgeous. He pulled as Dad and Wash shunted me up. They all breathed like trains. Little veils rose from their mouths and merged with the sky.

A snowmobile's growl echoed across the emptiness, and I imagined a patroller driving it down Last Chance, then U-turning and waiting on the groomed run for me to arrive so he could haul out my sled. Through the trees I could just see Phantom Peak in the distance, cast in twilight's orangey-purple. I concentrated on it to push down the humiliation of this predicament. How could this be happening right now? When I was little, Mom always told me to watch for the first star and make a wish, that it would come true, and I believed her. Uh huh. This was when she died. In fact, we were approaching the very minute of her last breath.

Fate. Always working against me. Like that snow whirl-wind? What was the probability of that? And that porcupine making me scream? Wash and Dad would have continued their sweep of this area, never knowing I was trapped here. And Mom? Laughing, patting my leg, me laughing too just as the Honda's tires licked ice? Yet I felt relief at this rescue, and that brought bile to my mouth. How could I live when Mom did not? Each quill piercing my face grew in potency. I screamed. Against their piercing, against the throb in my arm and ribs, against the humiliation of this moment, against the ache of Mom's death turning Dad and me to hushed cowards. Against knowing that probability meant zero because fate ruled life. I could not stop screaming.

The men flinched back from strapping me into the sled. Wash put a hand on Dad's arm. Agony filled Dad's face.

"Hurt?" I said to him, as mean as I could.

Tucker made this raspy sound.

"Sovern!" Wash said.

Dad studied Phantom Peak. "I deserve it."

Tucker finished strapping me in. He layered a hot-pack across my chest, below the blankets and tarp, and its warmth seeped through me. Wash and Dad stepped into their skis' bindings as Tucker strapped my snowboard along my side. The sound of two more snowmobiles bit the air, come to haul Wash, Dad, and Tucker out of this bowl too since the lifts had closed. Three patrolmen driving snow mobiles. Three here with me. Six witnesses to my shame.

"I got her," Wash said.

Dad just studied that lit peak.

Tucker shaped the tarp so it framed my face. Canvas smell swallowed me. I could see Wash only from the waist up as he took my sled's handles, but I knew he was stepping his skis into the fall-line, that Tucker was pushing the sled from behind. We took off.

I'd never ridden in a sled. Fine powder sprayed across the tarp's frame like a contrail. Pines were shadows against that twilight sky. That snowfield was so smooth it was like riding on air. There was the centrifugal force of a right turn, and we passed under the yellow-black boundary ropes and back onto Last Chance.

The snowmobiles were U-turned to face uphill, just like I'd imagined. The three ski patrollers who drove them lunged to my sled, relieving Wash. I'd have to endure being hauled up out of the bowl and then down the front side. I rolled my eyes.

They slid me to the back of a snowmobile, folded down its hitch, and connected the sled's handles to it. I lifted my head, and, because we were facing uphill, I could see a patroller straddle the snowmobile and start it up. Wash stepped to him and said something. The patroller's chin dropped. Wash put a hand on his shoulder. The patroller nodded after a minute, and his gloves moved to the snow-mobile's handlebars. A flick of his wrist put it in gear, and we started the journey back.

Which of the ski patrollers who'd visited infant me in the hospital, watched me grow up, surrounded Dad and me at Mom's memorial, hauled me uphill now? How many of them here now had I taunted as I'd stood near lifthouses, daring them, willing them, to tell Dad about my bad behavior?

The other two snowmobiles roared to life, and I knew they would follow. Each snowmobile could haul two people, and there were five guys, so someone would be towed behind. Probably Dad. Ever since Mom died, he was all about being alone.

Though the guy drove slow, my sled bucked over Last Chance's small moguls and the quills in my cheek swayed. I gnawed my lip against the pain. We passed the spot where I'd sprayed the class. We hit the flat of the road, and the patroller accelerated up it. A snowmobile sped past, Dad towed at the end of its rope.

Through the air's crystalline mist, the first star winked on, but no way was I making a wish.

2

We reached the gondola that ferried people in heated cars with Wi-Fi from Crystal Village to the mountaintop. It arrived in the first floor of a big log lodge. Next to where the gondola arrived was a ski-patrol station. Over its door hung a white "+" sign on red background: ski patrol's emblem. Until last year, it had always represented *Mom + Dad = me*. Someone unhitched my sled from the snowmobile.

Crystal Mountain Resort was a metropolis of hurtling bodies strewn seven miles over three peaks that rose from one long ridge. It had three treeless bowls on the back and regular runs through thick forest on the front. It had one gondola from Crystal Village, plus eleven more four-person chairlifts—two of these from either end of the village. The rest of the chairlifts originated from either mid-mountain or the back bowls.

At the top of each of the three peaks perched a lodge and a ski-patrol station. We were at the westernmost peak, called Emerald West. The middle, highest peak was called City Center and had a small lodge that housed ski patrol's headquarters. The third peak was called Sapphire East. Tourists always expected the gondola from the center of Crystal Village to go to City Center. Mountains aren't symmetrical, though, so it ended here, at Emerald West, and the whole ski mountain reached east of town. Every ski patrolman wore a radio, but usually those radios were spread out over the resort's vast terrain. Now, together, they crackled in an eerie stereo. Tucker yanked his from his belt and said, "We're at Emerald West. Ten-four."

All the other guys heard him, knew what his words meant, and if I hadn't been the director's daughter, he'd have knelt down and told me, *We're going to ski you down the front side now to an ambulance waiting at the base. The ride is about fifteen minutes.* Instead, he eyed me like a horse about to shy away. I wished they could just shove me into a gondola car and send me down alone. But a sled didn't fit.

I heard Wash draw his skis out of the snowmobile's rack. They blurred to the snow beside me. He stepped over them.

"I got her, Wash." It was Dad, though I couldn't see him.

Lines appeared on Wash's cheek as the side of his mouth curved up. Tucker's gaze flickered. Big John grinned. Of course, Big John had driven my snowmobile. How could I not have recognized a giant?

"I'll take caboose," Wash said. Caboose meant he'd follow my sled. Protocol.

A voice shot out of the radios. "Hey, Crispy here. Send

updates on Sov, will you?" Crispy worked City Center. Moments later, "Ditto that." Sarge, in Sapphire East.

Dad moved into my vision, straight-shouldered like I hadn't seen for a year. He lifted my sled's handles. He glanced at me, but I looked away. He took two skating steps, and we took off. Dad at the helm, mountain closed, no skiers to avoid: we'd make this 2300-foot descent in record time. It'd become lore. All of this would, I supposed.

More stars blinked on. I glimpsed town below, all soft golden lights, even the cars zinging along the interstate. Finally, I couldn't avoid watching Dad. The tarp's lip hid his legs, but that emblem on his back was front and center. The twilight translated his jacket purple, and its "+" sign glowed. His helmet was still black. I could just make out six letters across his goggles' strap: *Dargon*. I corrected my reading to the brand I knew they were: *Dragon*. Wash followed, no doubt, and I pictured a serious expression on his usually grinning mouth. With each of the sled's undulations, the quills yanked my cheek.

Pines soared by. The ropes around the Pay to Race arena flew by, and I knew Dad skied onto a run called Pride. We were halfway. Record time, for sure.

We passed a snowcat rumbling up. Through its driver's-side window, Tara waved, her pageboy blond hair swinging forward. Sinewy even in her jaws, she'd been driving cats for as long as I could remember. Snowcats are basically tractors, with rollers behind them made for pressing snow into perfect corduroy, and Tara was the only woman driver. Second in command when it came to grooming, she was one of my idols. She'd also been one of Mom's best friends. She was part of what I'd always thought of as my ski-patrol family. As Dad steered into her groomed track, I cringed at the thought of Tara's reaction when she heard about this.

My ride smoothed, and we picked up speed. I heard the four other snowcats that I knew were following her in a staggered line across the run's width. I smelled their diesel. The facing ridgeline jutted just above the tarp's frame.

A splintering crack sounded.

"Briggs, look out!" Wash shouted. "Falling tree!"

Dad's shoulders twisted. He threw his skis sideways to stop, and their scraping edges launched a blizzard. I smelled sap and shut my eyes as branches raked my face. Again.

"Shite!" Wash shouted.

Dad disappeared in a grunt of pain and the sled bucked over him. Its handles, the ones he should have held, banged down at my sides.

"Daaaaaad!" I screamed.

I knew Pride well. Ahead, a steep, quarter-mile face dove down the mountain till it became a gentle grade that merged with the beginner's route. The beginner's route wound its way through the easiest sections of all the runs on this part of the mountain. Dad no doubt planned to follow it around this steep face. Now, I jetted over Pride's knoll, airborne—one, two, three, four, five—and my innards took flight. But the sled touched down gently beneath my head, and though I expected another crash, the front landed like a caress.

I moved so fast the handles barely clattered, and I heard the snowcats above. Wind pressed the tarp into my chin. I could see ahead. See how Pride curved right as it gentled. But gravity would keep me hurtling straight off that edge into the pines. I tried to calculate my speed, the height of the lip, the distance I'd sail.

I shot over the run's groomed edge, mimicking that scream from the porcupine's fall as I counted—one, two, three, four, five, six—and landed. Like landing in a pillow. White smothered me. I still slid, but slower, slower, slower, till my sled tapped a trunk. A trickle of snow sifted from its branches. Tears burst out—I'm talking a river of tears. They pooled along my goggles. I was too worn out to care.

Dad appeared and kicked out of his ski's bindings. He was leaning hard to the right with that arm pressed against his stomach, glove limp. His goggles dangled from the strap at his helmet's back, lens cracked. Across his helmet ran an orange gash from my sled.

"Sov? Sov! I'm so sorry! I'm so sorry. I'm so..." He whimpered. And then he cried. He carefully lifted my goggles till they rested on my helmet, and he watched my tears slalom through those quills.

Above, Wash was frantic on the radio. We were near the base; help would swarm us in minutes. But just then, we were two blubbering dorks. My arms were strapped down near the elbows, stuck beneath that damn tarp. I lifted my left hand, made this little nub. Dad covered it with his glove.

3

When I was little, our neighbors were clouds. We lived in this cabin at City Center. It was part of Dad's job. They needed someone to trudge out pre-dawn, dip a yard-stick, and phone in each night's snowfall amount. This was 1998, before the world became addicted to websites and smart phones. A brassy-voiced woman would record the snow report, and TV, radio, and thousands of people would call the hotline. I'm not kidding. Skiing is big business. Crystal Mountain's guest capacity is 24,000. Dad was the guy in charge of safety.

Life in the clouds was heaven. Two chairlifts surged up to City Center from front-side and Gold Bowl, but our cabin was nestled away from them, behind a cupped hand of pines. It had one main room, a bedroom only an arm's length bigger than its queen bed, and an elbow-banger of a bathroom. My white crib was in the main room. When I got sleepy, Mom would lay me down in my footie pajamas, humming "Blackbird." I'd suck my thumb, watching, as she and Dad read or played a game or snuggled on the couch till I slept. *Mom + Dad = me.*

Mornings, pre-dawn, Dad would shuffle from the bedroom and stuff on his boots. He'd come back in from measuring the snow, cold stuck to him, and lift me out, carrying me on his hip as he made that call. I'd stretch to grab the phone's curly black cord, big in my small hand—our narrow link to the world. Things change.

Days, Mom and I built snowmen or forts or explored nature. I'd toddle around and she'd say, "A is for *avalanche*. B is for *bear*. C is for *cornice*. H is for *hawk*. L is for *lodge*. P is for *powder*. S is for *ski*. T is for *tree*." Like it helped.

We had no TV. We'd cuddle on the couch, and Mom would read and read and read to me. Book after book after book. We'd practice matching sounds with letters, Mom saying, *You can do it,* over and over and over. Her gifts to me: a deceptive vocabulary and the patterns of stories etched in my bones. Just don't ask me to write them down.

Beyond that cupped hand of pines, a gliding city teemed around us. Sometimes, a friend visited while her mom skied. A couple days a week, Mom would fire up our snowmobile and we'd descend to town for music or dance class, story hour at the library, or play group. We'd haul groceries and books home in a little ski trailer.

Mom always bought flowers. I'd sit in front of her on the snowmobile and shelter those flowers as we ascended the runs' edges, skiers and boarders streaming down. Those blooms would color our table. I'd stand on a chair and run my fingertip along a tulip, a rose, a daisy, and feel ridiculously proud.

Most days, Dad joined us for lunch. It always began with Mom and Dad kissing. Always kissing. Dad would bring Wash or Sarge or Crispy or Big John. Never two at once. Somebody had to work. Back then, "Uncle" came before their names, and I knew the balance of each of their knees. Wash, a bachelor always, would stay with us some nights. His snores would wake me, and I'd study his sprawled self on the couch and understand, even then, that our equation was really *Mom + Dad + our ski-patrol family = me.*

Dad was always out early to check snow safety. If there was accumulation, or if the night wind had howled, he'd be dynamiting cornices or avalanche areas. We'd hear the distant booms and I'd say, *Daddy*. Dad read snow like other people read the newspaper.

Evenings were golden. The lifts closed. The patrollers finished sweep. The only humans were us and maybe Wash. Tara would usually stop by. Mom would fill her travel mug with coffee before she rumbled away in her snowcat, headed on her nightly journeys. Deer, elk, fox, ermine, lynx, mountain lion, and bear would emerge.

Summers were best, though. We'd see only the occasional hikers or mountain bikers, but even they weren't around till the Fourth of July. Forest Service closures for elk calving kept Crystal Mountain's outer reaches off-limits till then, so the action stayed at Emerald West and front-side.

One lazy summer afternoon, a moose strolled right past

the cabin's deck. Dad and Mom sat in comfy patio chairs, listening to insects buzz while I colored with markers between them. I was at Dad's chair in a second, and we froze, Dad's hand firm against my hip.

"He's a long way from marshland," Mom said.

"He's headed to Secret Lake," Dad said.

Secret Lake was a retention pond just down the ridge that held water for snowmaking. There, Dad taught me to skip rocks. He was an amazing rock skipper, and he taught me to lean and cock back my arm, flick my wrist last for extra momentum. I got pretty good but could never match Dad's forty-six skips along that mirrored surface, the rock stopping just shy of the pond's far edge. I used to love to watch the rings of those skips merge, forming a new wave pattern till it rolled against the shore. Even then, patterns whispered to me.

Another time, Dad reclined in a patio chair and I reclined against him, watching twilight gild Phantom Peak while Mom sizzled something oniony on the stove. She called, "Watch for the first star!" just as a rangy scrap of gray streaked between the patches of late-spring snow in the open stretch in front of the pines. Dad and I shot forward, peering.

"Wolf!" Dad said. "I'd swear it." He wrapped protective arms around me and leaned back.

Every night, coyotes would yip in the dark. Some nights, we'd hear the mewl of a mountain lion. Or the similar mewling bark of a bear cub, and a mothering grunt. Foxes made a coughing noise. In fall, elk called for mates in squeaking threads that rode the crisp air. We never heard the raccoons, but they wreaked havoc if we left anything out, and porcupines consumed shoes, coats, helmets—anything with salt from sweat. Skunks we avoided by smell.

And then once, as Mom ran in for a snack, I spied a guy standing at the forest's edge with long black hair and a sleeveless deerskin shirt, pants, and moccasins. A bow was slung over his shoulder, and a knife rode his hip. I was playing with a kitty camp I'd gotten for my fifth birthday. I rose on pudgy legs. Yearning filled his face. Yearning for me. I backed toward the door, saying, "Momma?" Mom came out carrying a plate of cheese and crackers, and the guy vanished into the trees.

"What, Sov?"

I pointed. "Ute!"

"Ute?" She scanned where I pointed. "There aren't Utes here anymore, silly."

My chin quivered.

"Come here and have a snack. Should we read our book about Utes before our nap?"

I nodded and sniffled, but my boogieman had taken root. Sometimes, I dreamed about him, and I'd wake screaming. In them, he watched me from anywhere forests edged my life.

Calves, fawns, cubs, me—all us babies in heaven. Mom gave me one extra year. Then I turned six, and school's predatory world yanked me from those clouds and into a living nightmare.

4

I limped from Wash's geriatric truck to our condo's garage
door, still groggy from a night in the hospital. My arm's
humerus bone had a compound fracture, three of my ribs
were cracked, and my cheek was shiny with antibiotic
cream. They'd had to put me under to extract those quills.
In my parka's pocket was a urine-sample cup holding all
eighteen. They were long as my index finger, black on one
end, white on the other. Each had two dashes of white with
black in-between, like some kind of code.

My arm was immobilized in a brace, plus a sling made
of two wide straps that connected to my wrist. You'd think
that big arm bone would command my attention, but those
ribs didn't play fair. Every tiny movement, every breath,
translated as not one, not two, but three stabs of pain.

Wash, baseball cap backward like always, pressed our code

into the keypad next to the garage door. His name was actually Darragh Washington, but nobody could ever pronounce his Irish first name, so everyone called him Wash. His other hand balanced a foil-covered plate of cookies from Crispy.

Dad stood behind him, right wrist in a cast. Tuesdays were his day off. Lucky timing, I guess. Dad never took sick days—hadn't taken one since Mom died, and none for as long as I could remember before that. Now he squinted down the row of repeating condo garage doors, harsh and bright in the morning light. Side-by-side everything. Outside and in. Horizontal and perpendicular as graph paper. My prison.

Dad, Wash, and I entered the laundry/mud room from the garage. A long hall to the front door ran along the wall inside. This hall led to the kitchen too, then to the dining room, and finally to the family room with its bank of sliding glass doors and a stubby deck that overlooked narrow Pearl Creek on its burbling path to Crystal Creek. I salivated to duck back there and smoke.

Our dining room table and chairs were the cabin ones. Till Mom died, fresh flowers always colored their center. Pots and pans hung from an iron rack above the breakfast bar between the kitchen and dining room. Mom had haggled the lot from a garage sale, but it was really nice.

Upstairs was another corridor. My bedroom and bath, then Mom and Dad's. Their room looked out on the creek and tourist condos beyond. My bedroom looked across half the garage's roof, a few hundred yards to the next mountain, scraggy with sage.

This was Affordable Housing. Put up by Crystal Village

to keep real working folks living in town. It was where we'd moved when I'd turned six, so I could get to school easy. I called it "the Condo." Never "home." When Mom lived, we were a two-ski-patrol family, always scraping by. A year ago, we'd become a one-ski-patrol family.

Even so, Mom had made the Condo comfy. A few years back, the Facet, Crystal Village's priciest hotel, had remodeled. Our hotels remodel about every ten years, Crystal Village being one of the swankiest resorts in the world. When they do this, they have a furniture sale, and regular folks flock to it. Mom bought an emerald-green velvet couch, leather armchairs, and a coffee table. She also bought my pine bedroom set.

Dad eased his strained back into an armchair. I settled on the couch and itched to turn on a movie. Mom had rarely allowed TV or movies, but in her void, they'd become my third addiction. Gage, cigarettes, movies—each an escape. Wash set the cookies on the counter, opened the fridge, and peered inside.

"This is sorrier than mine!" He pulled out something mold-blue in Tupperware and tossed it in the trash. "Looks like I'm headed to City Market. Any requests?" He opened the cookies and held them out to Dad and me. We shook our heads. He took one, bit in, and studied it, chewing loud. "How does a man who lives to bake burn every damn thing he makes?" He moved behind the couch and looked from Dad to me. "Well, you're a pitiful lot."

I remembered my wail, saw the agony I'd put in Dad's face. How he'd stared at Phantom Peak. That loneliness—just snowscape and me—swept in.

Dad webbed his hand across his face, ran his middle finger and thumb from the outsides of his eyes in, till they met at his nose. "You're a good man, Wash."

Wash snorted. "Tell that to the ladies." He had this expression where the left side of his top lip curled up, creasing his cheek, while his left brow pressed way down. Even in the roughest times, it cracked me up.

Dad and I smiled. Wash must've said that a million times, yet he'd never gone on a date that I could recall. It was as if our ski-patrol family was enough. It wasn't like he was ugly. He had a shrubby head of dust-brown hair seasoned gray, a twinkling gaze, constant stubble on his cheeks, and a smile that invited company. His features seemed squashed, as if someone had pressed on his head and chin, compressing things about an inch. It made his smile seem extra-wide. I thought it improved him.

"Later," Wash said, keys jangling. We listened to the garage door clank down. I pictured our garage, empty but for bikes, skis, snowshoes, and camping gear. Once, we'd employed that gear every weekend. But then that crunched Honda was towed away and never replaced, and everything stopped.

What equation represented the Briggs family now? *Dad − Mom = x? Me + Dad = y?* We were variables, and I couldn't fathom this simple math.

Dad and I hadn't been alone since he'd rested his hand over that nub I'd made in the sled. Now, alone pressed on us. He studied his cast. Pain had taught us habits that needed unlearning. Yesterday had been as low as a person could go. I shoved back the fury that hounded me. My mouth opened, but no sound came.

"You don't have to explain, Sov." He laughed sadly. "Hmm, *explain*? As if you'll talk." He shook his head on a sigh. "I've considered ending things myself. Every day."

My mouth sagged. Never once that whole hospital night had anyone asked what happened. Least of all Dad. I had to force words. "I just needed speed."

Dad tilted his head. His eyebrows rose. "*Speed*? Well, that's a relief." He scrubbed his face with his hands.

A vast distance seemed to stretch between us, and it felt like if I didn't do something, it would double, triple, quadruple. I winced on a deep breath and I blurted this noise like a frustrated animal.

"Sovern?"

I eased my phone out of my pocket and speed-dialed Wash.

"'Sup?" Wash's crappy truck radio played '80s rock in the background.

"Get some flowers?" Each word triggered my ribs' stabs, and I forced myself not to wince for Dad's sake.

"That's my girl," Wash said. "Any particular kind?"

"No thorns."

Wash's chuckle always ended high. "Gotcha."

I hung up.

Dad + *me* = *y*. Time to start solving for *y*.

"I'm sorry about Gage," I said.

Dad's eyebrows rose.

My gaze fell to my jeans' frayed knees. Beside me, the

couch dipped with Dad's bulk, and his un-casted hand tugged my shoulder. "Come here, kiddo."

He leaned back against the couch's arm, and I leaned against him. We were like a couple of statues.

"You could have been killed." He shook his head, and I thought he was scolding me about what happened in Shangri-La till he said, "A tree falling like that, and me losing you."

Poor Dad. Our ski down the mountain would be legend in the worst way. He sighed. Something seemed to release within him, and he relaxed. I searched the air for what he'd sighed out. I blew at the thing as if exhaling cigarette smoke, hoping to send it to oblivion. We listened to the fridge whir. The baseboard heater ticked. He spread his left hand on his leg, and I could feel him looking at his silver and turquoise wedding band.

"How about we work on being *us* again?" He petted my hair the way he used to when I was a kid, and that just about killed me. I sat up, ran my palm over his crew cut. It resembled the long summer grass in the back bowls as it yielded to the wind.

He snorted. "Like I said, we haven't been ourselves."

I lay back against him and remembered that porcupine peering from his branch. How he'd transformed to Dad. How I'd pleaded with him to come down. My arm in its sling had settled slightly forward. As I mentally traced that tree's bruise perimeter along my arm and ribs, I thought I felt a tingling there.

5

The wind banged Crystal High's doors shut behind me. Until I'd started riding here with Gage—using it to make Dad crazy—I'd always walked to school. Despite resembling a giraffe, I loved walking. Craved it, actually. Even in a blizzard.

I nudged back my hood and shook a tiny bank of snow from my hair. School smelled like four hundred wet jackets and had the unreal sense of shelter that happens when nature rages outside.

Dr. Bell, the principal, stood before two giant stairs that stretched the entry's length. The immigrant girls from Mexico or South America, most hauled here so their parents could work as maids or dishwashers or carpenters, huddled on those stairs with tear-striped faces. They still wore their jackets, and snow melted on their shoulders. Dr. Bell spoke slowly to them in mangled Spanish. They definitely had it hard, but they always seemed to have each other as they hung out there, loud with laughter or tears that seemed to press against my silence.

Crystal Village had so many Spanish-speaking immigrants that my elementary school was bilingual, and I'd emerged fluent. Still, I resented those immigrant girls. In third grade, I'd come to understand that although they arrived in the U.S. stumbling over English, within a year they could read it better than I ever would. Ask me to write it down? No way. Believe me, in this world a person is defined by how well she reads. Can't read? You must be dumb. Or lazy. Probably both.

I drifted to the stairs' far side. Dr. Bell was shorter than half the guys in the school, so maybe he wouldn't spot me against the wall. We'd seen way too much of each other lately.

"Sovern!" he called. "Glad you're back!"

I only missed one day, I thought and fought an urge to roll my eyes. I swallowed back my nicotine craving and studied the scuffed toes of my wet Converse. Mom would have been all over me for not wearing boots.

A corridor of banging lockers and shouts waited at the top of the stairs. Freshmen and sophomores were in this first, bustling hall. I always marveled at that, since juniors and seniors, who had their lockers in the secluded back halls, were more likely to snag on mischief. People assessed my sling. Nobody talked to me. No doubt, I'd become the joke of the school after how Gage had broken up with me. Plus, in the last year, I'd earned a dangerous reputation.

At the Student Union I cut through tables and chairs

toward my locker's hall. Handler, the school counselor, was talking to three wrestlers, coffee mug in hand. He saw me, said bye to the guys, and caught me on the diagonal.

This time I did roll my eyes.

"Heard you had a run-in with a tree." He took a sip.

"Uh-huh."

Handler wore dorky golf shirts with little logos every day. Mom used to be in his office weekly, plotting with him to ensure I had fair opportunities. I'd done testing and all, had dyslexia's written proof. He'd encouraged her to get me into special education, so I could have "modifications."

"I know how that works." Mom had shaken her head. "Sov's brilliant. You know that. Once you're labeled, you're done."

"Times have changed, Taylor," Handler said.

Mom looked him straight in the eye. "How many dyslexic doctors or lawyers do you know? They keep their dyslexia a secret."

Handler had pressed his hands on his desk and his lips in a line. I stared at the beckoning door, open a crack. Mom would know. Dyslexia was hereditary, and Dad didn't have it.

Since she'd died, Handler'd been on me like glue. End of sophomore year, I'd pretty much walked around in a stupor. But in junior year, I'd plummeted, and every time I ditched, he'd text Dad. After a while, I used that to my advantage.

Come December, Handler had caught me at my locker. "I know what you're doing, Sovern, and I don't believe you're that cruel."

I'd started to walk away, even though I hadn't gotten my

books, and he'd stepped in front of me. His gold shirt had the logo of a big-antlered buck with *Deer Hollow Golf Club* embroidered beside it.

"Life's dealt you some difficult stuff. Don't let it beat you. Think of your mom."

What do you say to something like that?

Now he said, "Things okay?" and waved at Bonstuber, who stepped into the hall from his Bio room.

"Uh-huh." Left-handed, I opened my locker easy.

Handler leaned against the lockers next to mine. "How's your dad?"

I shrugged. For some reason lying to Handler was hard. Maybe because he'd been Mom's ally. He knew Dad from tragedies. Once a year, a Crystal High student would have an accident or incident on the mountain. Afterward, Dad, Crystal Mountain Resort bigwigs, the police, and the school hunkered together. They always worried students would flip out and start a bad-behavior epidemic.

"If you ever need to talk, you know where I am," Handler said.

"*No problemo.*"

He threw back his head and laughed because *I'd actually spoken + I'd tossed Mom's battle to get me excused from the foreign language requirement right there between us.*

Mom alive, my Spanish grade had been crutched into a C-. Current grade: D-. Like I said, I'm fluent, but I'd hardly talked the last year, so class participation was *cero*. And writing Spanish down? Not happening.

Handler patted my shoulder and left.

I drew out my Spanish folder, slid a pencil behind my ear, slammed shut my locker, and headed, sighing, toward the classroom in the opposite hall. I entered the Student Union. Before a bank of windows with a Crystal Creek view, Gage stood, taller than all the other guys, hands in his jeans pockets. Muscular in a way meant for anything but sitting, he wore his black skullcap like always, his brown hair brushing his shoulders. I stared ahead and forced back the fire in my cheeks as his gaze stalked me.

I'm five feet ten inches of mostly loping legs. The summer before Mom died, a New York guy approached us in Crystal Village and gave her his business card, saying I could model if I rolled back my shoulders. For three weeks, I found Mom staring at that card. We needed the money. No clue what happened to it. What a joke that she even considered it.

Sovern Briggs ≠ fashion. Without Mom to guide me, I wore musty jeans and gray Converse every day. Only my T-shirt changed. And my days-of-the-week underwear. A long-standing joke between Mom and me, she'd first bought them when I was little, to help me memorize the spelling of each day. The tradition had continued, partly because on bad days *Tuesday* still got me.

––––––––

In second period, Literature and Culture, I slumped into my smack-in-the-middle seat. This class was social studies and English rolled into one for underachieving upperclassmen. I'd deduced that the middle seat, in any class, attracted the least attention. I was the underachiever of the under-achievers. The lowest ratio.

Lindholm stood at the back, adjacent to her desk, talking with Jenny Fowler. Jenny had made the U.S. ski team and was constantly gone to Chile or France or Italy. As the tardy bell rang, I tried to imagine a life with such purpose, and Jenny, tall as me but one-hundred-percent muscle, hurried to her front-row seat.

Lindholm touched my shoulder lightly—*welcome back*—as she walked up the aisle. A thin paperback book occupied her hands. I shrugged at the ghost of her touch on that shoulder, Handler's on the other.

Lindholm held up the book: an orangey-red background with a sun setting or rising, I couldn't tell. Books sped my heart rate. Across it stretched the silhouette of a bird, beak to the sky in flight.

"We're studying the African-American experience next. This is *I Know Why the Caged Bird Sings*. It's a memoir by Maya Angelou, one of our most famous African-American writers and poets. She died on May 28, 2014. In December 2014, NASA sent a copy of her poem 'A Brave and Startling Truth' on the Orion, a spaceship that went farther into outer space than man has ever gone."

Poetry didn't usually do it for me, but that got my attention.

"She was only the second African-American poet," Lindholm continued, "ever to read a poem at a presidential inauguration. President Clinton's in 1993. It was titled 'On the Pulse of Morning.'"

Catchy, that: a morning having life's rhythm. I brought my free hand to my sling hand and pressed my thumb to my own unworthy pulse. I swallowed back that nicotine craving.

Lindholm would have us up to our elbows in African-American everything, like she had with Native Americans before this. Ask me anything about the Utes in the Rocky Mountain region. According to her syllabus, Asian-Americans were next. Though Crystal High was forty-eight percent Latino, hardly any African- or Asian-American students graced its halls. Lindholm seemed to be compensating for that.

She turned and wrote blue-ink facts about Maya Angelou on the SMART Board: *Born 1928 in St. Louis, Missouri.* I pulled out paper and started my usual mangled notes. Time was, a voice recorder rested on the front of my desk. Time was, Mom found audio versions of every book we read. My writing stopped as memory took over: me winging that voice recorder against my bedroom wall. Hearing it clunk to the floor behind my dresser. Grief had blocked me from noticing I'd stopped doing those things. I slouched back in my desk, ribs complaining, and traced my mind over the perimeter of who I'd been for the last year.

———————

Crystal High was an open campus. At lunch, upperclassmen could leave school. I had first lunch at 11:00, so I was rarely hungry. I usually just bought an apple from City Market. Despite the storm, I decided to brave the five-minute walk. Though I despised cars, I missed Gage's heated leather seats as I tugged up my parka's hood. The recreation path had a direct spur, so driving and walking took the same amount of time, but walking wasn't considered cool.

When entering City Market, the floral section was right there on the left. For the first time since Mom had died, I wandered through it. I traced a yellow tulip's curved petal, a daisy's circumference. I bent and inhaled a faceted rose. I decided to treat myself and buy something from the deli. As I approached, Gage was standing there with two buddies, so I retreated into the bakery. Camouflaged behind a rack of fancy breads, I watched them stroll toward the doors, deli packages in their hands, headed for his car, no doubt. Gage always ate in his car, and he usually ate chimichangas. *I'm attracted to anything bad for me*, he'd say, then smirk and pull me close.

Gage was wicked smart. Made Bs and Cs even though he ditched constantly and never cracked open a book. If he sensed an A was near, he'd botch a test or skip a paper. School for him was a boring game. He hated the thought of college, but his parents were forcing him to go. The first two times, he sat through his entire SAT test, arms crossed. *Meditating*, he said. Then his dad took away his BMW SUV, so he finally tried and earned two points shy of a perfect score. His dad designed software for Microsoft. Gage lived in a slope-side house on Crystal Mountain and vacationed on their yacht in the British Virgin Islands.

I don't want anybody telling me how to think, he'd say about college. When he saw in my expression that I agreed, he'd get this sheepish smile, say *Come here*, and kiss me. *Except maybe you*, he'd add. A joke, of course, since I rarely talked.

He adored my name. My birth certificate reads *S-O-V-E-R-E-I-G-N*. I can spell it now, if I concentrate, but it was way too much for a kid with dyslexia, so Mom shortened it to *S-O-V-E-R-N*.

On our first date, Gage had said, "Sovereign, like autonomous? Like self-governing? Like free? That's fucking cool!" Most folks had no clue what "sovereign" meant. Gage and Mom might have been chummy if they'd met.

I ordered a Reuben, which took forever because they had to toast the rye bread and melt the Swiss cheese, but it was my favorite. The tables in the deli area were full, so I headed around the building's side, to this delivery area with a portico high enough for semis. Snow pelted down. My ribs' stabs made me smooth my pace to a lope, blinking against white. I entered the shelter, flakes weighing on my lashes.

Gage and his buddies looked up. He blew out cigarette smoke and nodded to me through its haze. His buddies glanced between us. Gage tossed them his keys.

"See you in the car," they said. Their gazes trained on me in challenge as they walked past. Gage and me, we'd hung out full-time, so they hadn't seen much of him the last few months.

"Hit a tree, huh?" Gage said.

I moved to the stucco wall and leaned against it.

"You do it for me? That's romantic." He took a long draw of his cigarette, its end flaring. He reached out and ran his fingers along my healing cheek. I stared at my sandwich to keep from slugging him.

"I miss you," he said, smoke streaming out with his words.

"Why aren't you in your car?" I said.

He lifted his brows. "Since when are you a talker?" He squinted at me, then shrugged. "I needed a change." He looked out at the pelting snow. "I got used to you in that passenger seat." He pressed his lips together and tapped them with the fingertips of the hand holding the cigarette. Then he offered the cigarette to me.

I shook my head. I wanted to blurt a million cruel things, but I didn't trust words.

He shrugged, took a draw, stepped forward, and exhaled in my face, all sexy. "I miss you, Sovern. But you're so pissed all the time."

My body craved that cigarette down to my toes. My lips craved him more. He took a long draw, leaned forward, and kissed me.

"Tastes good, doesn't it?"

I forced myself to match his stare.

"Want a ride?"

I longed to say yes, but I thought of Dad and shook my head.

His brows rose in surprise. "See you in Calc." He strolled around City Market's corner toward the parking lot.

I studied the sandwich in my hands. Its delicate cellophane reflected my unlucky face, and I covered it with my thumbs.

6

I slumped on the curb, burning from Gage's kiss. I tore open the sandwich, determined to be good, but on the third bite, I exploded up and headed into the snow. With no idea where I was going, I ended up on the recreation path that snakes along the river and through town. There's a short stretch between Crystal Village and school that hugs the banks beneath an arch of regal spruce. It feels protected, safe.

Four inches of snow had covered the path since they'd plowed that morning, and my knees lifted high. At each stab of my ribs, I said, "I can." I *can* stay in control. I *can* hang on to that thread of goodness. I *can* remember Dad holding me on the couch, holding my hand through the sled's tarp. I *can* resist Gage. *Gage = smoking, drinking, drugs.* "I can. I can. I can."

I tried to summon Mom's voice from memory, saying *You can* right with me, but it wouldn't come.

Snow raced at my eyes. Hair escaped from my hood and

pestered my cheeks. I blinked back tears, stumbled on the path's edge, and slammed against a tree before I hit ground.

"Dammit!" I rolled to my knees and pulled my feet beneath me, left palm against bark for balance. A sound— like a plucked-cello-string—vibrated through me. Eighteen vibrations seemed to shimmer out my quill-pocked cheek.

Soft sun. New-green grass. A fly's zzzzzz.

I lifted my head, blinking. Mom and I strolled toward me on the path. Mom's arm curved around my waist, and the Sovern in front of me listened as she spoke.

"See?" Mom said. "Always believe *you can.*"

I blinked. I'd gone insane. The Sovern looked my age, but content. She smiled a little and wore black slacks and a pale blue blouse. A blouse I'd never owned. Her hair weaved a French braid. Mom's flowery dress billowed against a breeze that brushed warm on my face. A butterfly flitted behind them. Yet this was nothing like images on a movie screen. This was 3-D. Real.

"Mom?" I said.

Her eyes leapt to me, her brown gaze more piercing, more determined, more alive than ever.

Do people really gasp? That's the only way to describe the sound I made. I stepped toward her, hand reaching.

White blur. Stinging snow. Biting wind.

"No!" I rushed to where Mom and I had stood. Of course there were no footprints. But they'd been so real!

I imagined Mom's arm around my waist, its comforting friction of embrace. That vision-me seemed to be my opposite. Not just because of the blouse and slacks. Not just because of my tidily braided hair. No, the difference lay in how she held her body. The ease of her step, the suspension of her arms from un-hunched shoulders, and the confident tilt of her chin. On that Sov, these aspects of me were unified and relaxed.

I ran my fingers across my brow. If someone had taken a thousand photos of me over the past year, that brow would be furrowed in 999 of them. Now those furrows were deeper than ever.

Mom had looked right at me. She'd *heard* me. I considered my wet Converse, my dirty jeans, my empty-sleeved parka, the bulge of my sling, and the scraggly ends of my hair. No doubt my cheeks were chafed from cold, like my hand now stuffing my hair into my hood. I studied my lone tracks, followed them with my gaze to the tree and the matted circle where I'd fallen, and then back down the recreation path till they disappeared around a curve. Each step was long, since I'd lifted my knees. Each footprint solitary. Snow pelted my back, and it seemed the loneliest trail in the world.

I sensed motion and my pulse sped. "Mom?"

Nothing.

A familiar shuffling drew my gaze to the tree's middle branches. I discerned a different texture: a brown-gray lump peering down at me. I traced the quill-pricks on my frosty cheek.

7

I pressed the code on the Condo's garage keypad—0501, my birthday—and stormed in. I toed off my soaked Converse and yanked off my socks. My feet were cold red. I hung my parka from its hook. I marched upstairs to Mom and Dad's room. To their wedding photo on their dresser. In it, they faced one another and held hands with their heads steepled close. They stood a few hundred yards from Emerald West's ski-patrol office, where I'd waited in my sled for Dad to ski me down.

In the picture's background loomed Phantom Peak. It was named for how its ridge cast an afternoon shadow on itself that resembled a face. According to legend, that face used to hold a distinct willful expression, but these days, it was open to interpretation. Chuck Murphy, Justice of the Peace, stood before Mom and Dad, holding their vows. Those vows now hung, framed, on the wall beside the dresser.

I studied Chuck Murphy's jolly face and longed to gouge my fingernails into whatever face—God, fate—had stolen Mom.

Mom's wedding dress was creamy and knee-length, and matching roses lined the fold of her hair's French twist. I pressed my thumbnail against the thin crescent of scar on her left eyebrow. She'd gotten it tree-skiing with Dad on her first day of ski-patrol training. According to Mom, it had bled a ton, and as Dad applied the bandage, she'd felt an actual spark at his touch.

Even on this wedding day, Mom was just pretty. *Thank God you got your father's looks*, she always joked. Yet Mom's personality gilded her lovely, and at times she stole my breath. She stole Dad's, no doubt, and it was obvious from the way he looked at her in the photo. He was stunningly handsome in a black tux. The photo didn't show the two hundred guests watching them speak these vows. I'd have given anything to have sat among them.

I took the photo to Mom's side of the bed and lay down in her place. I ran my finger over her image. Just half an hour ago, the vision of her had seemed so real.

"Help, Mom. Are you out there?"

Insanity. That's what was going on. *Gage + nicotine withdrawal = me over the edge.* I felt myself soar over Pride's edge, counted—one, two, three, four, five, six—and laughed that desperate kind of non-laugh.

The picture fell to my chest. My left hand was tired from doing everything. I tilted up my palm and scanned its lines. Was my life's path graphed out there? Did a hash mark show where Mom died? Could there be another hash marking her return? I turned my head into Mom's pillow and sniffed, but a year of laundry had erased her honeysuckle scent.

"Help, Mom. Anything?"

It felt like my ears bled, I listened so hard. I heard Gage instead: *I miss you.* I shook my head. Gage represented all the wrong things I'd done over the last year. *Gage + me = hurting Dad.* I had to move on. I concentrated on the photo again till Mom and Dad turned blurry and sleep took me.

My sophomore year, Handler told Mom he thought I was gifted in math. All I knew was that right after Mom died, the patterns I'd seen my whole life turned intense. As a junior, I was taking Advanced Placement Calculus, which was the equivalent of Calc 1 and 2 in college. The next year I'd take an online Calc 3 class Handler found at Stanford.

"You could have eight college credits," Mom had said when he'd first laid out the plan.

I'd scowled at her. Just the word "college" summoned a vision of me flailing through a maze of books. But I took Calc after all because, well, math was my thing. It structured life into vivid sense. I hoped, wherever Mom was now, this one talent made her grin.

The first day I walked into Calc, Gage had already claimed my seat in the middle. Only two open seats remained: the first row, or directly in front of him. No way was I sitting in the first row, so I slid into that dangerous desk. His scrutiny singed my back, but I was too proud to move.

The first month, we didn't talk, but each day Gage turned me molten. In reality, I was probably just a narrow back with unbrushed hair. Then Kenowitz caught me doodling as he solved a problem on the SMART Board. Handler had sent out word to keep an eye on me, for sure. All my teachers were watching me close.

"Sovern, are you getting this?" Kenowitz said.

Mom's absence had been practically pulling me under that day, so I glowered and nodded. I'd already gone through the entire book the first week of class.

"You can solve this problem, then?"

I shrugged.

"Will you show us?" Disbelief laced Kenowitz's smile. He was a cool teacher, really; I just have this way of confounding people. Of catching them off-guard and making them act ways they don't usually act. Ways they're ashamed of later. I don't mean to, and it's kind of hard to watch. Friendships are a struggle. I avoid people mostly.

Kenowitz handed me the black marker, and I stepped to the SMART Board. About two minutes later, I'd solved the problem, skipping a step by using a different approach than the clunky one taught in the book. When I turned around, Kenowitz's mouth hung open. In fact, fifteen zero-shaped mouths faced me. And one smirk: Gage.

The quest over, I lost my composure. My cheeks flamed. I sat down.

Kenowitz stepped to the board, considering me. He pressed his lips and scanned the room. "Well, people," he said. "Let's try the next problem using the method Sovern has shown us."

He turned to the board. Everyone started writing. I felt a pencil—a finger maybe—rustle my hair's ends along my back.

"Genius," Gage whispered.

The next day, when I sat down, he said, "Briggs. You're named for a two-masted ship. Me, Brogan, I'm named for work boots. The lace-up kind."

I turned in my desk, disbelief all over my face.

"Yeah, a 'brig' is a jail, but it's also a wind-driven ship. A beauty." For once, he wasn't wearing his hat, and his blunt fingers tucked his shoulder-length hair behind his ear. A lock of it fell forward, showing his ear's tip, and something about that blunt-fingered movement and that sliver of ear was so alluring I actually salivated. My zigzag smile must have looked ridiculous. *A sliver of ear + agility with words = I don't have a chance.*

The doorbell woke me with Mom and Dad's wedding photo a rectangle weight on my chest. I rubbed my face. The clock read 3:02 p.m. I knuckled my eyes as I descended the stairs. Big John filled the skinny window beside the front door. I blew out my breath and opened it.

"Hey, Sov."

Silence.

"Your dad sent me to check on you."

Handler must have texted Dad that I'd ditched. Again. I swallowed against what Dad must have thought. If I hadn't seen Gage, I'd have gone back to school after lunch. This wasn't his fault. But then I considered the vision—seeing Mom—and I couldn't regret ditching.

Big John watched my face with interest. I spun on my heel and walked down the hall. He closed the door and eased off his boots and jacket. I drew a glass of water in the kitchen. He entered the room and stood across from me, the breakfast bar a thick line between us. I avoided looking at his good-natured face. We listened to liquid rush down my throat.

"Your cheek looks good."

I shrugged.

"I wonder how many folks in the world have had a jowl full of quills. Dogs, sure. But humans?" He grinned. "How the hell'd that happen, anyway?"

Nobody had asked me that. It seemed like the sort of thing a person would want to know.

I shrugged.

"Still not talking? Word is, you're saying a *little*." Big John sounded hurt. He was like that, always wearing his heart on his sleeve.

"An impasse." I shrugged.

He chuckled. "With a porcupine?" He scanned the room. "Haven't been here much lately." He focused on the yellow tulips in the table's center, and he smiled sadly. I thought how he had twin sons in kindergarten. Big, grinning, tow-headed boys I hadn't seen in a while. I pictured them towering over the other kids.

"Time was," Big John said, "I'd come over here and you'd

be at that table with headphones on. Or the couch. Those things were pretty near part of your head. Remember?"

I nodded. Before Big John had fallen in love and married—all in about a month—he'd been here almost as much as Wash. Those big headphones had etched the patterns and vocabularies of stories in me, and that made people believe I was smart. Till they saw me write or heard me read, that is. I hadn't worn those headphones in years—earbuds had replaced them—so I knew he was remembering me little, like his boys. Placing himself in Dad's position.

"Thanks." I said it like *Please go,* and then wished I could rewind the word.

"Talking, indeed." He looked at his hands, turned, and lumbered back down the hall. The set of his shoulders was like a mirror of all my faults. He scuffed on his boots and shrugged on his jacket. "How 'bout you call your dad?"

I nodded.

"Maybe next time, tell him before you leave school. He's not your mom, but he loves you just the same." Big John stepped onto the narrow porch. "We all love you, Sov."

Shame pressed my chin to my chest as I shut the door. I slumped on the stairs. If this was a movie, the audience would itch to slap me. I pictured myself in those headphones like Big John had. Where had they gone?

I trudged upstairs and searched through my desk, under my bed, on my closet's top shelf. No headphones.

Inspiration hit, and I walked to Mom and Dad's room. My body's indent on Mom's side of the bed stopped me cold. It looked like she'd just taken a nap. That Mom/me vision came right back, but I shook my head. I opened Mom's top dresser drawer, leaning back a little like something might jump out. There, right at the front, lay those headphones.

I slid them on, saw my kindergarten self in the mirror over the dresser, and bit back a laugh. I reached out to that young reflection, but when my fingers touched the cool glass, it was me. I ground the freckle that rode my upper lip. The only one on my face, and I hated it. I drew the cord from the drawer, coiling it around my hand, and there was that business card from the New York guy who'd said I could model. I shut the drawer.

Still wearing the headphones, I smoothed the covers on Mom's side of the bed, fluffed my head's dent from the pillow, and put back the wedding photo. In my bedroom, I smashed my cheek against the wall to see along my dresser's back. I got a broom from the kitchen pantry and retrieved my voice recorder. Coated with dust, its corner had a blue scrape that matched my bedroom wall, but I put in new batteries, pressed the play button, and it worked.

Like Mom had shown me a thousand times, I turned on my laptop and opened the library's website. I meticulously typed *I Know Why the Caged Bird Sings* into the catalog's search engine. It didn't work. I looked closer, dove my fingers into my hair, and tried to fix the spellings.

I was in luck: the library owned an audio version, read by Angelou herself. I downloaded it onto my phone, and downloaded the visual book onto my Kindle so I could read it with bigger font. Then I headed for the kitchen table, to sit where Big John had seen the kindergarten me, and realized I still hadn't called Dad. *Gage wanting to get back together + me ditching school = Dad hurt.* I paused on the stairs, held my phone awkwardly in my sling-hand, and texted I'M HOME AND FINE, TIRED, autocorrect fixing my spelling.

My homework was to read the memoir's first two chapters. I sat at the table and started the book. Angelou spoke deep-voiced and slow, enunciating each syllable like the voice of destiny.

8

When Dad got home, I still wore those headphones but had red sauce and water for pasta bubbling on the stove. I turned off the book, longing to shout *I saw Mom today!* Through the steam, sadness hung on his face. My pulse turned loud. I knew that guilty sensation for living on without her. He forced a smile.

"This is a nice surprise."

"Sorry," I managed. "About school."

"Please tell me before you leave, Sov."

I started to shrug, but made myself nod. We were slogging through new ground. Solving for *y*.

Dad studied me. I pushed my lies way back in my eyes. This I was practiced at.

"You haven't worn those in years." He chin-pointed at my headphones as he drew his wallet and keys from his pockets and set them in their usual spot, where the breakfast bar met the wall.

"Big John reminded me."

Dad laughed lightly. "Nostalgic bugger. Either they've gotten smaller or you've gotten bigger."

I pulled the silent headphones to rest around my neck. Their gentle pressure had brought back the everything-is-okay sense that had surrounded my life back then. A detail from the vision today came to me: that Sovern had been slightly taller than Mom. When she'd died, Mom and I had been the same height. I leaned into the counter, my whole body weak, because *me being taller than her = no way it was memory*. I looked at Dad. Should I tell him?

"Sov?"

I straightened and stirred the pasta.

"Something's bothering you."

I shrugged.

Dad set the table. I ladled the pasta and sauce into bowls, pulled the salad I'd made from the fridge, and set it all on the table.

Dad sat down. He said, "Drinks," and started to rise, but I lunged up and into the kitchen. My phone in my jeans pocket buzzed with a text. Gage: MISSED YOU IN CALI. I read it again: MISSED YOU IN CALC. I set my phone on the counter and took a long sip of air to divert my nicotine craving.

"Water's fine," Dad said.

I filled a new glass, topped off the one I'd been using, and set the two glasses at our places. Dad started eating. I started eating. Salad crunched in Dad's teeth. My fork scraped against the bowl's bottom as I twirled pasta onto it. The fridge squeaked, marking every cruel second. Eons seemed to stretch between us.

"What have you been listening to?" he finally said.

"English."

"A novel?"

"Memoir."

"About what?"

I could do this: speak. "An African-American girl. Her parents divorce. She's sent to Arkansas. Raised by her grandma." So many words.

"What's it called?"

"*I Know Why*"—I had to pause—"*the Caged Bird Sings.*"

"I read that in school. Pretty brutal. At the end..." He looked at me sharply, and then away.

"What?" I said.

"Caged bird. You've always called this place a prison." Dad shoved a forkful of pasta into his mouth and looked around the room. "They're looking for someone to live in the cabin again."

"What?"

"They want a presence up there. Full-time. They're preparing to do some construction over the summer, already starting to bring up gear, so they want someone there as soon as possible."

I surged forward in my chair, nodding.

"I thought you'd say that. Sov, it won't be like it was before."

I shrugged.

"It's not just your mom. You're older now. You won't be able to escape home from school if you're tired. You'll have to learn to drive a snowmobile—"

"Bonus."

"And a truck in summer."

I turned hot. I'd avoided driving since Mom died. "Bike."

Mom's bronze medal from Mountain Bike Nationals still hung on the garage wall. She'd raced in the first Mountain Bike World Championships. Time was, she had me on a bike constantly.

Dad smiled a little. "You'll have to get up a half-hour earlier for the commute. Going out with friends won't be—"

"What friends?"

Dad shrugged. "Gage?"

My gaze dropped in shame. I pictured nights loitering with Gage in the shadowy arch supports below the Gem Bridge, Crystal Creek flowing below, cheery tourists flowing above. Our legs had dangled over the edge of the concrete pillars as our hands gripped liquor—stolen from the cabinet at Gage's—and our mouths exhaled white smoke against the dark. The line where our arms met was a fever, the adrenaline of maybe getting caught a drug.

I stared down, blinking with realization: All that time, I'd been trying to hurt Dad, sure, but what I'd really been after was his attention. Now, I had it, and I couldn't even meet his eye.

I tasted today's kiss. "Gage and I are done," I said to the table.

I felt more than saw Dad's smile and his nod. "That's a relief."

I forced my gaze to meet his, grimacing, not sure how to react to having done something right.

9

On Friday, Gage watched me slide into my desk. I'd purposely arrived in Calc just before the tardy bell.

"Hey, sexy," he said. "Playing hard to get?"

Rolling eyes = my emotions' inverse.

"Open your books to page 530," Kenowitz said.

I faced front. On my back, Gage drew a heart with his finger. He'd done the same thing the day before, making my skin tingle both times.

"Aren't we skipping a chapter?" said Shelley Millhouse, future valedictorian. Home-schooled till middle school, Shelley used to play with me at the cabin while her mom skied, then later at the Condo. Her house was this cool ski chalet turned bed-and-breakfast, right on Crystal Creek. How strange her life must have been, with strangers sleeping down the hall and eating breakfast in her dining room, but the Millhouses welcomed everyone. Till sixth grade, when Shelley and I ended up in class together, and she witnessed how reading labeled me officially dumb.

"I find it works better," Kenowitz said, "if we learn parametric, vector, and polar functions before infinite series. Infinite series can get confusing."

"Great," George Polinsky said. George had been confused by life in general since kindergarten. It used to bug me, but over the last year, I could relate.

"I'm always available after school. You know that, people. Okay. What's a parametric curve? Imagine the motion of a projectile." Kenowitz penned a curve on the SMART Board's graph screen. I'd looked at the chapter last fall, wondering at the equation for my own life's descent. When I collided with that Shangri-La tree, my descent had paused. That vision of Mom and me two days ago had seemed like the descent starting again, yet tonight Dad and I would move our stuff up to the cabin, and that was definitely ascending.

Gage traced another heart on my back. Two crescents meeting top and bottom. I considered *its* parametric equation.

"So what we end up with are some interesting and cool-looking graphs," Kenowitz concluded. "Look at Section 10.1 on page 531."

I glanced at page 531 and then doodled a line for my future. A wobbly, Mom-less one that made me swallow guilt as I forced it to curve slightly up. I considered its equation, but my mind drifted to imagining Dad, me, and our ski-patrol family at the cabin eating dinner, coyote howls for music. I imagined standing on its deck in my pajamas, gazing at night's infinity, the invisible sea of peaks rolling below.

I pictured the recreation-path vision. This time, I focused on myself as I'd stood, hand pressed to that tree, summer all around. My body remembered that cello-string vibration, and I realized it was the same resonance as when I'd collided with that Shangri-La tree. I straightened in my desk, remembering the porcupines in both trees. Both trees had been spruce.

I gaped at my palm. If I tilted my hand horizontal, the line along the meat of my thumb matched the one I'd just doodled. I suddenly needed to press that palm's line against yesterday's spruce.

Kenowitz's demonstration of parametric equations and how to graph them was drawing to a close. The bell rang.

I shot from my desk, gathered my pencil and graphing calculator, and bolted. At my locker, I shoved my homework into my backpack, knowing it was wrong to ditch again, but no way could I concentrate, let alone sit in a desk. I texted Dad: TIRED. HEADING HOME.

I slung my backpack over my shoulder and made for the door next to the cafeteria, where it was easiest to slip away without being seen. Just before I reached those doors, Gage called, "Sovern?"

I turned.

"Need some company?"

The unsure set of his shoulders stopped me. I gripped my backpack's one strap over my shoulder with both hands.

He shrugged. "I miss you. I miss you bad."

I wanted to rush to him. Instead, I forced out, "That girl you knew—she wasn't really me."

The Sovern from the vision rose in my memory, and I blinked her back.

"Maybe that wasn't me, either," Gage said.

My mouth sagged open.

"Maybe we were both just pissed at the world. Maybe we were the best thing that could have happened to each other," he said.

"Best thing? You broke up with me on the anniversary of my mom's death!"

"I know. I was desperate, see? You were destroying yourself, and I couldn't handle it." He rubbed the back of his head the way he did when I knew he was thinking for real. "I'm sorry."

I'd never heard Gage talk this way. Never heard him apologize. To anyone.

He shoved his hands in his front pockets. "Later."

I watched him round the hall's corner and felt like he'd stuffed my heart in one of those pockets. I bolted out the door.

I tugged up my hood. They'd plowed the path, so walking was easy, and the storm had vacated, leaving crystalline sky. On a deep inhalation, my nostrils stuck together. The spruce came into view, and I stopped, shielded my eyes from the afternoon sun, and searched for a brown-gray lump but found none.

The storm had erased my tracks. I stepped to the spruce and studied its bark. I reached out, pulse in my fingertips. Good, I thought. Gage hadn't taken my heart after all. I laid my palm against the trunk.

Nothing.

From up the path, two jogging women approached, so I stepped aside. Their voices hung in the frigid air. They smiled at me, but I was a delinquent to them, no doubt. One cocked her head and looked up. The other woman looked up too, saying, "Oh!" She pointed at a different spruce than the one I'd just touched as they drifted to the path's far side.

From where I stood, I couldn't see anything, so I walked to where the woman had pointed from, shielded my eyes against the sun, and peered up. A porcupine huddled in that spruce's branches. I considered its base, rooted on Crystal Creek's frozen bank. I'd been at the wrong tree.

The women disappeared around the path's bend as I strode to the correct tree and, innards fluttering, pressed my palm against it. That cello sound shimmered through me and out of each quill hole in my cheek.

Sun shafts. Green's scent.
A rushing river's shout.

Mom and I strolled along the path, farther down now, their backs to me. I circled around the trunk, right to the river's edge, so I could see them. Their heads were tilted close. That warm breeze flowed from vision-me to Mom's dress and set the late spring wildflowers swaying. Vision-me wore a dress too. A dress?

"MIT! See what believing 'I can' will do? Don't ever let anyone tell you something's impossible," Mom said, and her arm wrapping my shoulder squeezed me closer. She kissed vision-me's forehead. My hand almost came to my own forehead, but I forced it still against that trunk.

Dad appeared around the path's corner on my other side, catching up to them. He was smiling, proud, content. His gait was swift but relaxed. The breeze ruffled his hair. "Hey, you two!"

Mom and vision-me turned. Mom held out her hand to him, and he took it. They kissed.

"Mom?" I called.

She saw me then and studied me, head to toe. She paled and shivered.

"Tay?" Dad said.

Her brow furrowed, and her free hand came to it. "Do you—?"

"Mom?" vision-me said.

Mom's gaze tore from me to her.

"I'm here!" I called.

They all looked. Mom's hand fell to her stomach. Vision-me squinted, assessing. Dad stepped toward me, his mouth set.

"Briggs!" Mom grabbed his arm.

Moments ago, they'd been so happy. What had I done? I pulled my palm from the spruce.

Knife cold. Winter light.
Crystal Creek muted by ice.

Woozy, I hunched over, hands on my knees. I stared at my palm in wonder. I looked up at that porcupine and shouted, "How?"

I hugged myself to feel my solidness. I'd seen two different visions now. Two different Moms. Two different Soverns. Was I insane? My mind ricocheted through options. Maybe I was hallucinating from nicotine withdrawal. Maybe I was hallucinating from grief. Or maybe... there had to be a logical explanation. Patterns surrounded me every minute of every day. In a thousand different aspects of life. Patterns explained by math. Math applied to how the world worked was physics.

Suddenly, I knew who might have an answer.

10

I made it back to school just as sixth period ended. Dr. Bell stood outside the main office saying bye to the stream of students flowing out the doors. I moved toward Kenowitz's room against a current of weird looks and judgments. He was there, talking baseball with Handler. The guy lived for the Rockies and the Red Sox and was a walking baseball statistic. George Polinsky waited.

"Sovern?" Kenowitz said as I marched toward him.

I eyed George. His Calculus text was open to page 530. Handler studied me.

"Physics. You taught it?" I said to Kenowitz.

"It's been a while."

"What kind of physics deals with reality?" I blurted.

"Reality?" Kenowitz cocked his head.

"Like what's here and now. What we see." I glanced at Handler. "Maybe what we don't."

"Quantum physics?" Kenowitz said.

"That's the one that deals with dimensions and stuff?"

He and Handler looked at one another, no doubt shocked by my flood of words.

"Is it?" I said.

"Yes," Kenowitz said. "I just taught standard physics, though. You could ask Ms. Willins. I believe she does a unit on quantum physics."

I shook my head. I couldn't stand harpy-faced Willins, the physics teacher. "What do you know about it?"

Kenowitz shifted his weight. "Well, not a lot. I do know that when things get that tiny, they get *weird*." He glanced at Handler. "That's the only way they can describe many of the findings, because they're unexplainable."

"Do other worlds exist?"

"Universes, you mean?" Kenowitz eyed me warily and then glanced at Handler again. "They're certainly possible," he said carefully. "Mathematically probable. Current theory holds there are nine to eleven dimensions, and there may be a multiverse of infinite universes. It's mind-boggling stuff. Why do you ask?"

"Those universes. Past? Present? Future?"

"I'm not sure. I don't think anyone is. It's all theoretical."

I tried to slow down my words, but failed. "Where could I learn about this?"

"YouTube has many videos. The work of Stephen Hawking makes quantum stuff easy to understand." He looked at Handler. "Audio versions of his books exist, I believe."

My dyslexia: legend.

"Will you write his name?"

"Sure." Kenowitz printed *STEPHEN HAWKING* on a scrap of paper and handed it to me.

"Thanks." I headed for the door.

"Sovern." Handler practically walked on my heels. "I was in here to check on your attendance. Seems you missed fifth and sixth periods."

I lifted my arm in its sling, got a shot of rib pain, and winced theatrically. "Tired. Dad knows."

He eyed me. "Other dimensions?"

Obviously I looked like I'd sailed off the crazy cliff, hurtling headlong for Mom. Maybe I had. I shrugged. His lavender shirt said *Hawk Ranch Golf Club* below a logo of a soaring bird.

"Don't tell Dad," I said. "He'll worry I'm just trying to find a way to hang on to Mom."

"Are you?"

My eyes were knives.

"I won't tell him." Handler smiled slyly. "*If* you'll be in my office at the start of fifth period each day."

Fifth was when I usually ditched.

He nodded. "Whatever it takes."

I watched lifties load the freight car with our belongings onto the gondola cable. The car rode out of the lifthouse and started its ascent up the mountain. I carried my suitcase into a normal passenger car. Dad carried his in and sat beside me. Our glass-walled car moved slowly around the giant bullwheel, caught the fast-moving cable, and accelerated out into the night.

Crystal Creek passed below us, half swirling ice and half inky, slow-moving water. Slope-side mansions lined the ski run. Empty or not, they glowed with warm light. I forced my gaze away from Gage's mansion too late and glimpsed him, ankles and arms crossed as he leaned against the frame of his floor-to-ceiling bedroom window. It still felt like he'd stuffed my heart in his pocket, and I salivated for nicotine. I could barely discern his face, but his profile tugged at something inside me. Across the expanse of carpet behind him stretched his bed, and the whole back of my body remembered the softness of its comforter.

I blushed, glad for the gondola car's darkness, and I thanked the little voice that had kept me from giving up my virginity. Was Gage thinking of me? As distance shrank him, I marveled at how situations could invert just like that. I looked to where my sled had sailed off Pride. Dad looked there too.

Town turned miniature and glowy. Car lights streaked past on the interstate. We got high enough that I could see the spot on the path where I'd had the visions. They'd seemed so real. Even now. Mom had been *breathing*, and she was able to turn pale. Her skin, if I could have touched her, would have been warm. Her wrist would have had a firm pulse. And the vision-me? *I* wouldn't be caught dead in a dress. How or why were they all even there on the path? The tinier Crystal Village grew, the weirder I felt.

Dad's hand rested on his knee, and I covered it with

mine. He smiled, but worry laced his face. I thought of my promise to Handler and swallowed.

We reached the gondola's top at Emerald West, and the lift stopped as workers shunted off our freight car and replaced it with a passenger car. The lift started again, cable inching around the big bullwheel before heading back down. When the doors for our car opened, we stepped out to find Tara waiting with a passenger snowcat. A sled-trailer was connected to it, and she'd backed it right to the lift-house doors. The gondola had been the most efficient way to ferry our stuff this far, but Tara's cat would haul it and us the last mile or so up to City Center.

Two lifties maneuvered our freight car into the trailer. They shut the gate, a snug fit, and Tara pulled forward. Tourists milled around us, headed to dinner, tubing, or the view. Dad thanked the lifties.

We climbed into the snowcat's cushy backseat. These passenger cats were meant for hauling high-dollar guests to high-dollar restaurants, so they were all about comfort. Tara climbed into the driver's seat and shut the door. The heater blew loud, muffling the new-age music.

"Heading to the high life, eh?" Tara rarely wore a hat over her pageboy blond hair. Canadian, she ended lots of her sentences with *eh?* She'd raced mountain bikes with Mom years back, and that's how they'd become friends. I figured I'd end up just like Tara, driving a snowcat into dark's solitary quiet.

"Glad to see you, Sovern," she said.

I looked down.

"It'll be good to be back up here," Dad said.

"Maybe I can take Sov for a ride some night?" she said.

Dad just grunted.

"Why not?" I said.

Tara looked at us in the rearview mirror. "They give you a gun?"

Dad stiffened. "Don't want one."

The cat tilted up Sunset Ridge's initial incline to City Center. The trailer behind us clunked as our freight settled. I'd planned to peer out the windows, reveling in this starry view of my favorite world.

"What about Sov?"

"What about her?" Dad said.

I looked closer at Tara's reflection. In the light from the cat's dash, a dark smudge hung below her right eye, and a stitched cut marked her forehead. Was this why she wasn't on her usual route into Crystal Mountain's farthest reaches? Why she was driving this passenger cat, ferrying tourists to and from dinner?

"Hey!" I said. "I'm right here!"

Tara's and Dad's eyes met in the mirror, and his flashed warning. The snowcat leveled a little into the steady climb up the rest of the ridge. Three deer bounded across the lit circumference of its headlights.

"There's some folks damaging stuff on the mountain right now," she said.

Dad blew out his breath and glared out the window.

"Stuff?" I said.

"Breaking out windows on lodges. Stealing food mostly. Weirdly," Tara said.

Stealing food *was* weird, because whoever stole it would have to pack it off the mountain. I remembered Kenowitz saying "weird," and my mind started searching for a pattern.

"What happened to your eye?" I said.

"I saw broken windows at Sapphire East and went to investigate, eh? Climbed out of my cat and never even saw what hit me. I was wearing a hat, for once. Good thing, or I wouldn't be sitting here now."

"Bear?" I said.

"It'd have to be one smart, non-hibernating bear," she said. "With fingerprints."

"They'll catch the guy in a few days," Dad said.

"Seems the prints don't have a match. Maybe a bear after all, eh?" Tara raised her eyebrows at me in the mirror.

I peered out the window, beyond the initial pines into the dark beyond, scanning for danger. Couldn't things have been easy, just once?

City Center's lodge—a simple coffee house and bathrooms—appeared on the left. Ski patrol's headquarters filled the bottom level. Tara steered away from the lodge and the two chairlifts that rose to this spot from front-side and Gold Bowl. She navigated around the cupped hand of pines, and the cabin appeared, lights on, smoke rising from the chimney like a fairy tale.

Wash, Big John, Tucker, Sarge, and Crispy strode out on the deck, ready to move in our stuff. Wash, grinning, raised his arms, and I thought *Me + Dad + my ski-patrol family + the cabin = happily ever after.*

Tara parked the snowcat and left it idling. The guys bounded off the deck to the snowcat's trailer. Dad and I climbed out, and when I got to the back, they already had the trailer's gate down and were unlatching the crate, preparing to carry furniture.

I stood back a little and took it all in. *Them + me = 8.* Infinity upright.

Crispy grinned at me over his shoulder. Both he and Sarge were shorter than I was, but powerfully built. Sarge, seeing him, grinned at me too, and then they sandwiched me in a hug. It was awkward, me being taller and all, and Crispy smelled like burning sugar, but I laughed.

A smile glowed on Dad's face. "Welcome home, Sov."

11

I slept in one of the twin beds in the cabin's bedroom. One for me. One for Dad. A nightstand stood in-between, a window above it. A window was over Dad's bed too, filled now with soft, early-morning light. He ran his hand down my hair and whispered, "See you at lunch."

I smiled through grogginess and knew Wash would leave with him. Weekends on Crystal Mountain were hectic.

Later, beaming sun woke me to Saturday in heaven. I walked onto the deck in flannel pajama pants and a T-shirt, and I raised my one liftable arm like Wash had last night. Despite the sun, February's cold at 11,000 feet gnawed hard. I forced myself to spin once, then shuffled in and shut the door. The thermometer out the kitchen window read 5°F. The clock on the nightstand between our beds read 9:48 am.

I boiled water and stirred a cup of instant cocoa, little

marshmallows swirling. Crispy had left a plate of lemon bars. I put one on a napkin and settled onto the green velvet couch. I took a bite, looked at the bar's black underside, and set it back on the napkin. I lifted the cocoa, let the steam rise into my face, and scanned around the cabin in the morning's fresh light.

The matching leather chairs were crammed like guards on either side of the fireplace. The white curtains Mom had hung over the windows before I was born were still there, time-clashing with the Condo's furniture. The table and chairs seemed tangled between past and present. The space against the far wall where my crib had been—the sides removed to make it a bed as I'd gotten bigger—was a loud empty space. The cabin felt warped. Surely Dad noticed this.

I closed my eyes, and there was that path vision. *Mom paled + Mom shivered = Mom saw me.* They all had.

I rubbed my forehead, willing it calm. No luck. I set my cocoa on the coffee table and got the wooden box Dad had made for my sixth birthday from under my bed. I'd forgotten about it till I'd packed the stuff shoved into the back of my closet at the Condo. Dad had crafted love into it, hoping to curb my devastation at leaving the cabin.

I drew out my first shoes, long as my palm. My favorite smooth white rock from camping near Marble, Colorado. A conch shell from Puerto Rico, its center the color of twilight. A photo of my three-year-old first glide on skis. Another photo of Christmas-me in Wash's lap, holding up my leg in footie pajamas. He wore a Santa hat, the ornamented tree on his left. I studied the corner where that tree had stood, imagined myself and Wash while Mom lifted the camera to her eye: *Say, Presents!*

I pulled out a little leather bag I'd bought from a gray-haired Navajo woman when we visited Monument Valley on a fifth grade school trip. An "amulet bag," the woman had called it. I'd just liked its orange, blue, black, and white diamond pattern. I'd worn it for about a month but never found the right thing to fill it and finally stored it in this box, forgotten for years. I ran my thumb over the intricate beads and realized an equation for its beadwork.

I went to my suitcase and dug out the urine-sample jar holding the quills from my cheek. At the couch, I opened the jar and carefully gathered all eighteen. They just fit into the amulet bag. I folded the flap, sealed it carefully, and slid the beaded strap over my head. A tingling rose in my chest and rolled through my limbs, shimmering last out my cheek. I collapsed back against the couch.

Another thing different about the cabin was Internet. Wireless coverage from City Center's lodge stretched here. I logged on and typed into Google's search bar.

It responded: *Did you mean multiverse?*

I thanked the world for computers. They made my dyslexic life so much easier. I clicked on the sentence, and then on the Wikipedia site. I read the passage three times before I got the words right.

The multiverse (or meta-universe) is the hypothetical set of infinite or finite possible universes (including the Universe we consistently experience) that together comprise everything that exists: the entirety of space, time, matter, and energy as well as the physical laws and constants that describe them.

I moved to the window by the dining table and gazed out: space, time, matter, and energy. *Physical laws and constants = math.* Nicotine would help me think, but living in the clouds made cigarettes hard to come by. A good thing, since I was quitting.

After I got my head around that Wikipedia passage, I found a BBC video on YouTube titled *Parallel Universes.* It discussed our world as having not three dimensions, but eleven. In this eleventh dimension, all normal rules of common sense were abandoned. This eleventh dimension was infinitely long, yet so narrow we couldn't perceive it. A lady scientist had proved with *math equations* that at this eleventh dimension's other end could be a parallel universe, except loaded with gravity. What did that mean exactly? I bookmarked the URL.

As I studied on, I bookmarked another URL. And another. And another. I can get into what I'm doing and lose track of time. This quantum world took shape in my mind, and math evolved from random equations in Kenowitz's class to the actual alphabet of the physical world. These scientists and mathematicians were trying with numbers and experiments to lift God's robe and peek underneath. Their courage sped my pulse and fluttered my innards because I had a bone to pick with God.

Someone pressed buttons on the door's keypad. Dad stepped in. I shut my laptop and spun on my chair.

"You look busy," he said.

I forced myself to say, "Math."

He sat on a bench near the door, pried off his ski boots, and hung his uniform coat on a hook. I hadn't seen that coat's white "+" sign since my sled ride, and I rubbed my cheek at the sensation of quills swaying.

"Cold day," he said.

I turned to watch him in the kitchen.

"Soup?" he said.

"Sure."

He opened a carton of soup and poured it into a pot.

"Dad? When we ... " I couldn't say *crashed*. "When you lost me, in the sled, what kind of tree was that? That fell, I mean."

He turned, still not used to my talking, no doubt. His eyes pulled into themselves, and he shook his head. "Let me see ... this crazy wind kicked up just before it fell—"

"Like a snow whirlwind?"

"I guess so."

I remembered the splintering crack, the blizzard from Dad's edges, and his grunt. My voice sounded thin as I said, "Was it a spruce?"

"Does it matter?"

I nodded.

"It happened so fast." He studied me.

I rested my forehead in my palms.

"You know," Dad said, "it was fuller than a pine. And it smelled like a spruce."

I slid the amulet bag under my T-shirt and felt it settle against my chest, right above my thudding heart. I rose on wobbly legs and pulled spoons from the kitchen's only drawer.

"I've heard of trees blowing down in summer near mountain bikers, but never something like that in winter. Thing is, it wasn't a windy day."

I thought of the snow whirlwind that had rocked me onto my heels, ejecting me toward that Shangri-La spruce. It hadn't been windy till that moment either.

"I investigated that tree my first day back," Dad said. "The crew had already removed the part on Pride early the next morning, of course, but with the vandalism that's been going on, I needed to see the stump. To be sure it wasn't premeditated. There weren't any footprints, or axe or saw marks, or any signs of foul play. The stump looked healthy too. A tree in the prime of its life."

I tried not to show that my pulse had accelerated.

"You know," he said. "I'm glad it fell."

I paused from setting spoons on napkins to look at his broken wrist and the stiff way he stood. He couldn't write, couldn't even drive a snowmobile. Just now, he'd limped over from patrol's headquarters on City Center's far side instead of taking the snowmobile like he used to.

"We're so stubborn, Sov. I'm not sure anything else would have shoved us out of our funk."

I snorted.

Dad saw my blush and kindly turned away.

It was true, though. Nothing but that tree would have changed us, and somehow it had been right there, at the right moment. Both trees that day.

Bookmark:
Newton's Law of Gravity
Isaac Newton

———————

All objects attract each other with gravitational force.
The masses of both objects determine this force,
and it is inversely proportional to the square
of the distance between their centers.

12

After Dad returned to work, I went to the library's website and found Stephen Hawking's recorded books. There were several, but I chose *The Universe in a Nutshell* and downloaded it onto my phone. I tugged on my long underwear and snow pants and pulled on my snow boots, slow with just one hand. I hated hats, but chose a blue-patterned one Mom had given Dad from a box by the door. Over that went the headphones. I had a long walk ahead, down Sunset Ridge, then left before Emerald West and out to Last Chance.

I stepped off the deck onto the groomed swath left by Tara's snowcat last night. I strapped on my snowshoes with my one hand, no easy feat with my sling arm zipped inside my parka. I pressed play for Hawking's book. This hour-long trek would take ten minutes on my snowboard, but the doc had said no snowboarding. *Breaking rules = hurting Dad.* I was on a mission not to hurt Dad.

The air had warmed to 25°F, and the afternoon sun warmed my face as I descended Sunset Ridge. Skiers and boarders winged past. A hawk circled overhead, its circumference widening with each rotation. The British narrator filled my ears. Before me lay Phantom Peak, surrounded by the spines of mountain after mountain, miniature worlds in each of their valleys. From my memory Mom's voice said, M is for *mountain*.

I focused on those mountains to anchor me because I couldn't believe what I was hearing. The narrator was explaining that quantum scientists had figured out the world might be made of microscopic harmonic strings, each having their own vibrations. Each of these strings was connected to a membrane surrounding our universe. There were potentially infinite universes out there, surrounded by these soap-bubble membranes. *M-theory*. Math had proved it. M was for *math* or *membrane* or *M-theory*. I focused on the peaks.

Someone slowed beside me: Sarge, his squat body in a big snowplow. "Hey, Sov. Good to have you back in the neighborhood!"

I paused the book, pulled down the headphones, and nodded. My ski-patrol family had grown used to my silence, so Sarge dove right into filling the empty space. "Settled in?"

I shrugged.

"I'm headed to a meeting at Emerald West. Out for a stroll?"

I nodded.

"I was thinking last night, you've grown an inch since Thanksgiving."

That made me smile. He'd been teasing me about my height ever since seventh grade, when mine had surpassed his.

He saluted, his way of saying goodbye or hello or whatever. He pulled his heels parallel and sped off. Sarge was the fastest skier I'd ever seen.

I put the headphones back on. The scent of hamburgers and French fries rode the air as I neared Emerald West. I turned left, traversing Platinum Bowl on the road leading into it. Another road branched off it to the Platinum Club, a fancy reservation-only restaurant I'd never eaten at. I thought how bored Tara must be, hauling those diners down there instead of heading out on her nightly adventures. Now that I was living up here, I'd probably see Tara more.

The road into the bowl spilled out on a steep run called Hungry Bob, which also led to the restaurant. I dug in my showshoe's claws, my feet angled sideways, as I hoofed my way up across the run. In the trees again, the footing was easier, but the snow deep. I made for Platinum Bowl's groomed ridge.

Maybe when Tara was healed and back to her usual route, I'd ask to go with her one night, not just for her company, but to see my future. I pictured her black eye, and a shiver ran through me. Then I scolded myself. This was *my* mountain. *My* home. M was for *my*. Nothing was going to hurt me up here. Down below, life was brutal, but up here, all was good.

I cut across an intermediate run called Sluice Box and crested the ridge adjacent the lifthouse. I paused where six days ago, tears soaking my goggles, I'd hit rock bottom. I heard myself shout, *I hate tests!* I swayed with remembered fury and craved a cigarette. I pressed my gloved palm against my parka till I felt the amulet bag touch my skin. No doubt I looked ridiculous, wearing those headphones, my one sleeve swaying in the breeze, and my other hand pressed to my heart in a left-handed "Pledge of Allegiance" to the view.

Retracing my route from that day, I walked out the narrow catwalk along the ridge. I kept picturing Big John on that snowmobile, with me strapped down in the sled. As he'd heard what I'd done, he'd slumped, Wash's comforting hand on his shoulder. I rubbed my hat, trying to smooth the furrows of guilt on my brow.

Then the narrator talked about time.

It had shape, he said, and he wondered if space-time could be warped. And if you warped it enough, was it possible to travel back in time?

That halted me. Literally. I looked out on Phantom Peak, where the sun was starting to cast the shadow resembling a face. I considered the narrator's words. Could this explain my visions? Could M be for *Mom*, *me*, and *meet*? Maybe my future really could lie in my past.

Bookmark:
Space-Time
Albert Einstein

———————

Space—length, width, and depth—and time are
interwoven into a four-dimensional fabric. A planet
is like a large ball pressing down on this taut fabric.
Dropped in, a marble will spiral around the larger
ball. This simulates a planet's gravitational
pull on objects in space.

13

Last Chance appeared. Navigating traffic, I retraced my route from the day of the accident. I bisected where that ski class had stood with their instructor, followed the yellow-black boundary ropes, and ducked under where I'd last crossed them. In Shangri-La, I estimated that day's path.

A fresh snowboard track curved through the snow. Gage? I shoved him from my mind. Sinking up to my knees in the deep snow despite snowshoes, I estimated the spot where that whirlwind had ejected me into the forest.

My loud breaths hugged me. That moment's terror surged through me. My fingers tingled. I veered right, held up my arms to push aside branches that matched the scratches on my cheeks, and beheld the spruce I'd hit. Majestic, full, blue-gray. It was a lunker. Two of me would just be able to join hands around its girth. It was slim compared to a sequoia or redwood, but as spruce trees went, this one was a king.

Beneath the tree's shelter, only a thin layer of new snow covered the depression Dad, Wash, and Tucker had made as they'd maneuvered me out. A new trail cut straight from it toward Last Chance. Had Dad come back here? Or maybe risk management needed to investigate the site? The trail was narrow, as if the person had worn regular shoes. Why wouldn't someone use skis, or a board, or snowshoes, or a snowmobile?

I faced the spruce's trunk, gray scaled with reddish brown underneath. I mentally traced its bruise perimeter along my ribs and arm. I looked up but saw no porcupine. I bit the fingertips of my glove with my teeth, pulled my hand out, and stuffed that glove in my parka's pocket. I traced my palm's lines with my eyes and thought, Why not?

I pressed my hand against the bark. The quills in the amulet bag vibrated against my chest, and that cello-string sound shimmered out my cheek, easily twice as strong as before, stealing my breath.

Yellow sun. Hot earth's scent.
Spruce needles beneath my snowshoes.

I crinkled my nose at the punky smell of layered sweat. Fine black strings lifted on the breeze and swept across my face. Hair? I glanced over my shoulder and tried not to panic. I pretzeled my left arm till, right shoulder pressing the trunk, I faced the other direction.

A body leaned against the spruce. Close. The bare arms were muscled like a guy's. His back was turned to me, and a bow rose over his shoulder and hung diagonally down next to a quiver of arrows, their fletching almost grazing my chin.

His hair lifted on the breeze, tickling my cheeks. I turned my face to the side, leaning out and grimacing as strands caught in my lips. I noticed the tip of his ear, peeking out of his hair, just as his hand rose to his head. For some reason, in that pivotal moment, I kept my palm against that spruce.

Then he lurched forward, spinning, his cocked bow aimed on me. A jay squawked to flight. Our loud breaths collided. Before me was the Ute I'd seen at the cabin when I was five. He wore the same sleeveless deerskin shirt, pants, and moccasins. For a moment I couldn't move, but then I lifted my chin, hand stuck against that spruce, and mustered courage.

His squinted eyes moved along my left arm to my palm. He lowered his bow yet kept the arrow drawn.

An amulet bag, like mine but with a different design, rested against his chest. Another bigger bag rode his hip like a fringed purse. He wasn't much taller than me, but he had those piercing dark eyes I remembered from my nightmares. Hooped earrings hung from both his ears. In movies, Native Americans were big-screen gorgeous, but not this guy. At first I thought it was his hair being longer than mine, his earrings being bigger than any I'd ever wear, or the purse at his hip— these womanly things. Yet the way he stood, muscles tensed, bow trained on me, was one-hundred percent male. And real.

He took in my snowshoes, hat, snow pants, and parka with its empty sleeve. Frost still coated my hair. He frowned at my headphones, but I had no free hand to pull them off.

His eyes seemed to question me, then click through answers. I thought I might crumble under the intensity of his gaze. Even though I could just lift my hand and disappear, I glanced instead at the trail to Last Chance.

He watched me do this, snorted, and one side of his mouth quirked up. He said a foreign word.

With no clue what to do, I just stood there like an idiot. Finally I said, "Sovern," and tapped my chest with my sling hand before realizing it was zipped inside my jacket.

He squinted at that moving nub. It must have looked like a heart gone psycho.

"Sov-ern," he said.

I nodded.

He pointed at his chest and said, "Súmáí." It sounded like *Sue-my.*

"Súmáí," I repeated.

He grinned. I grinned. Talk about relief.

He slid his arrow into its quiver without looking, slung his bow over his shoulder, and stood, watching me like a hawk. His image yanked so hard on the place where I'd kept fear when I was little that I caught my breath. He stepped right into my personal space. I leaned back, but he touched my still-cold parka and rubbed my frozen hair between his finger and thumb. He studied the wetness on his fingers. He held up both hands, fingers pointing down, and moved them as if tracing a woman's shape. I turned hot all over, but he did it again, and I realized he was mimicking a skier's track.

I nodded like a fool with relief. My mouth filled with

questions. *How were you there when I was little? What year is this? Is Mom here?*

He inched out his hand till he reached my parka. It took him a second to figure out the zipper, but then he unzipped it slowly and found the sling underneath. He studied my gray T-shirt, and I thanked God I'd put on a bra. He spotted the beaded strap of the amulet bag around my neck. He reached toward it, but I flinched back. My pulse ruled my ears.

He watched me, brows pressed close. He opened his own amulet bag and tilted it until I could see quills within. Despite his sweat scent and greasy hair, I lifted my chin, and his fingers, warm against my skin, sent heat spiking to my toes. His fingernails' smoothness intersected my collarbone. He drew my amulet bag from beneath my T-shirt.

He opened the flap, looked inside, and sipped air. He pinched a quill from my bag. He pinched a quill from his. He held them side-by-side, and they matched—black on one end, white on the other, that code in between. His gaze traveled up the spruce. The porcupine peered down at us. Súmáí and I looked at each other in a world of two words, yet we understood each other completely.

"Sovern!"

Súmáí leapt back—bow drawn faster than seemed possible—and scanned around.

"Sovern!"

Gage.

Our two quills were still pinched between Súmáí's thumb and forefinger as he aimed his ready bow.

"Sovern! What the hell?"

Hands yanked me back. My palm separated from the spruce as Súmáí rushed forward.

Blue light. Cold white.
Crisp air against my lungs.

I slapped at Gage's arms. "Get off!"

"Chill! Fine! What the hell, Sovern? Could you even hear me through those things?"

I pulled off the headphones and blinked down at my unzipped parka and open amulet bag. Up in the spruce, the porcupine glared down.

"Are you all right?" Gage said.

I longed to step back to the trunk and press my palm against it, but no way with Gage watching. I closed my bag and shoved it into my T-shirt, still feeling Súmáí's fingertips against my collarbone.

"What are you doing here, Gage?" I zipped up my parka.

"What do you think? Boarding. I saw your tracks to this tree and followed them. You looked so ... *weird*."

Gage's olive skin was pale and his eyes were pinpoints.

"Are *you* all right?" I said.

Gage took off his helmet and scratched the back of his head with his gloved hand. I considered the equation for his appearance because, for me, *Gage = attraction*.

"I missed you. All right? I was out here because I miss you."

I rubbed my face and made this sound like a gear shearing off a bolt.

"Hey!" he said.

I turned to him, imprinting a star with my snowshoes. "Gage." I sighed. "I can't go back to who I was with you. I just can't. For Dad. For you. For me. The last year, that wasn't really me."

"How dumb do you think I am, Sovern? The whole time we were together, you think I didn't know that?" He pressed his lips and looked out through the forest, swaying a little, and I fought an urge to steady him.

"Sometimes," he said, "your anger would let up, and there'd be this other look on your face. Softer, kinder, and so desperate—like a part of you—the good part—was trapped." He looked down, embarrassed, but then back up, meeting my gaze. "I didn't want to, but I fell in love with that part."

My mouth fell open.

"I broke up with you because it seemed like you were trying to destroy that part, and it scared me, Sovern."

Was I really hearing this? Now? My name still hung in the air in Súmáí's voice. My name in Gage's voice weaved through it. I sipped a breath and listened to my pulse. I walked to him. Off his board, he'd sunk thigh deep in snow, while I floated two feet higher.

"You loved me?"

"Love." He nodded sheepishly.

I squatted down and kissed him. He tasted like tooth-paste, not cigarettes.

Bookmark:
Relativity
Albert Einstein

There is no absolute time that exists for everyone
in the universe. There is also no distance in space
that everyone can agree on. Space and time are
only relative to the person experiencing them.

14

Dad, Wash, and I lounged around the cabin after dinner. They watched a British Premier League soccer game, Wash shouting and thrusting his arms at the TV while Dad chuckled at him. Wash, being Irish, was a soccer fanatic and played league soccer all summer. On the coffee table lay the plate of Crispy's lemon bars, half gone.

At first I'd been dead-set against bringing a TV up here. We hadn't had one when we lived here before, and I was trying to quit my movie addiction. Over the last year, Dad had glanced at me probably a thousand times: a furious lump on that couch, reeking of cigarettes and cast in the TV's eerie glow. No wonder he'd retreated upstairs. Here at the cabin, I'd wanted to start fresh, but with Wash and Dad being sports fans, the TV seemed just right. Especially because soccer had no commercials.

At the table, I opened my laptop and typed in the name Kenowitz had printed.

Did you mean Stephen Hawking?

I clicked on the prompt, anxious to see this guy who was rocking my world.

His image pushed me back in my chair. Obviously paralyzed, Hawking slouched in a wheelchair that resembled a cockpit. The caption called him one of the most brilliant theoretical physicists since Einstein. He wore round glasses, his lower lip jutted out showing bottom teeth, and his head lolled toward one shoulder.

I clicked on the link to his website, magnified the text, and read his bio a bunch of times till I was sure I'd gotten it right.

In 1963, the year Dad was born, Hawking contracted motor neuron disease. Doctors said he had two years to live. But he went on, lived more fully because of it, even though the disease hijacked his body. He became the Lucasian Professor at Cambridge College, England. Isaac freaking Newton was a past Lucasian Professor. In 1985, Hawking got pneumonia, and because he was paralyzed, doctors had to do a tracheotomy. My hand came to my throat as I read that, imagining the sensation of having a hole cut in my windpipe so I could breathe. After that surgery, Hawking couldn't even *talk* anymore. He communicated using his eyebrows to indicate *yes* or *no* to letters. I thought about how if he had dyslexia he'd get his right and left eyebrows confused, but then shame rose in me.

A guy sent Hawking a computer that had lists of words, so he could choose one with eye movements. He wrote lectures and books at the rate of fifteen words per minute. That meant it took him four seconds—an eternity in brain time—to get down a word. That was maybe slower than me. Currently, he was Cambridge's Director of Research at the Center for Theoretical Cosmology. This guy who couldn't even lift his own head, let alone speak, was changing our universe's definition. *He* was peeking up God's robe.

I studied my hands on the table. I fluttered my fingers, and pain sizzled my upper arm. Yet this injury would heal. My ribs would heal. My heart might never heal, but I'd live on. *My* only problem was the tangling alphabet. I rested my forehead on my hands, and as Wash bellowed, "Shite!" at the TV, I swore I'd be less of a whiner.

A text arrived. Gage: LIED THAT KISS. I read it again: LIKED THAT KISS.

I glanced at Dad. Gage would be nothing compared to what I'd done today. Yet what *had* I done today? Had that boogieman from my childhood actually been there in front of me, or was I losing my mind? Brain fritzing, I powered down my computer and stood at the back of the couch, obviously headed toward bed. Dad and Wash didn't even notice.

I considered Súmáí and Gage and the vision-Mom and me and Hawking. How could we all exist? Were Gage and I any more real than vision-Mom or Súmáí? Or even Hawking? My mind searched for a pattern. I couldn't stop thinking about how the narrator reading his book had said time could bend. I studied Dad and Wash, consumed by a soccer game that happened yesterday on the other side of the globe. Right now, that game was more real to them than me standing here. Maybe resting my palm against that spruce was like choosing a channel on the TV? Trees and porcupines as remote controls to other universes?

I stared at Crispy's lemon bars on the coffee table and remembered that group hug from him and Sarge last night. I closed my eyes until that anchoring moment was more real than anything else around me.

I woke to hushed, urgent voices in the main room.

"On the deck," Wash whispered. "I'm sure of it."

"We need to check the pumps," Dad said.

The *pumps* were the snowcat gas station, camouflaged in the pines on City Center's far side.

I rushed from bed toward the sound of rustling coats and scuffing boots.

"Hey, Sov." Wash wriggled his eyebrows.

Dad was serious. "We heard a noise."

Tara's voice rose in my memory: *They give you a gun?* "Do you have guns?" I said.

Dad held up a weird-looking, six-inch gun-thing.

"Tasers." Wash grinned like a maniac.

I rolled my eyes.

"Sov, these are vandals, not murderers. I save lives, not end them. Don't worry. It's probably nothing," Dad said.

Wash mimicked a spy peering around the corner and dashed out the door.

Dad paused, hand on the knob. "Stay inside," he said with a piercing look and left.

The pocket of frigid air they'd let in drifted across me, and I shivered. Out the window, shadow swallowed them. I shuffled to the bedroom, crawled across my bed, leaned against the log wall, and gathered the covers around me.

In the window above Dad's bed, a face appeared. I hate to admit it, but I screamed. I looked closer. It was Súmáí.

He grinned and held up our two quills. He looked left, and I heard the cabin's door rattle and burst open. Súmáí pointed at me, then at his chest, and disappeared.

"Sov?" Dad called.

"I'm fine!" I called back. "Sorry about that."

Dad entered the bedroom. He studied me.

"Find anything?" I said.

"Tracks around the porch. Wash is still out there. You're okay?"

I nodded.

I listened for the door to close behind Dad, then rushed to the bedroom window and peered out. I remembered Súmáí's speed with his bow and Tara's black eye. *Súmáí + Dad and Wash = someone gets hurt, maybe killed.*

I grabbed my parka, rushed onto the deck, and paced back and forth to show my concern for Dad and Wash. *See me, Súmáí,* I prayed, over and over till it became a four-beat rhythm in my head, yet all the while, I wondered if I'd imagined him.

Finally Dad and Wash came trudging back.

"Dammit, Sov! I told you to stay inside!" Dad said.

I scanned the dark and thought I glimpsed movement in the bordering pines. I realized then that Súmáí had been wearing a dark green liftie's parka.

Bookmark:
Clock

_____

Any device that measures time.

15

Of course, I stared at sleep the rest of the night. All I knew about Utes played across the ceiling until I finally got up and went out to the kitchen table to sit and stare into the dark and listen to Wash snore.

Growing up in Crystal Village, I knew Utes inhabited this valley before the whites. Mom had a children's book about them that she read to me. I don't know where I first heard the legend about Utes setting the valley aflame when whites forced them onto reservations. Most locals knew it. Lots of folks said it wasn't true, though. I'd also heard that whites actually set the fire to incite further rage against and flush out any hiding Utes. There was no way to ever know the truth.

In English, Lindholm had taught us how, for thousands of years, many Utes had summered here in the central Rocky Mountains and wintered in southern Colorado's lower elevations. That was before Colorado was a state, just territory. Before Mexico had been forced to give up that territory in the Treaty of Guadalupe Hidalgo. While the outside world had battled, the Utes had gone on with their traditional life, living in wickiups and interacting with Spanish traders. Lindholm taught us they'd warred with a tribe from the eastern plains called the Arapaho. That they'd been forced to reservations in Colorado's western red desert, or Utah's wasteland. That there'd been a drought in that fire year, and lightning's spark may have been what set things aflame. One thing was certain: across Crystal Mountain's back bowls, limbless charred trunks were sprinkled like inverted black icicles.

Nowadays, Utes visited Crystal Village to bless a new lodge or perform a snow dance on a lean year. I hoped they charged a fortune for their services.

From what I'd learned about quantum physics, I figured Súmáí could be from the past, present, or future. But how could he be *here*, prowling around? Away from that spruce and moving freely in *my* universe? Granted, I was new to quantum physics, but I hadn't heard Hawking's narrator speak of anything that would make me think I could actually *enter* other universes.

I remembered the comment about time travel. Maybe Súmáí did come from my universe, but from the time before the fire. Or maybe he came from an alternate reality, where whites had never stolen this valley. Where Europeans had never even conquered America. That set me pondering whether time moved vertically or horizontally or maybe both, and how that would plot on a graph. Stop! I thought. Probability would indicate he was a figment of my crazed mind.

Dad ambled out of the bedroom. He walked to Wash's chain-saw snoring and nudged him.

"Huh? What?" Wash said.

"Wake up."

I couldn't see Wash over the couch's back, but he made a blubbery noise that forced a smile on my face. Dad smiled too as he walked to the kitchen.

"What has you up so early?" Dad said.

I shrugged.

Wash rested his cheek on the couch's back and raised his eyebrows. He sighed. "I *love* the sound of your voice, Sov."

Dad ran water into a teakettle. He lit the burner and set it on the stove. He rubbed his hand back and forth over his cropped hair, and I crinkled my nose at his crew cut. It reminded me of porcupines, though, and before I knew it I'd said, "How many have there been?"

Wash gave a victory thrust of his fist at my words.

"How many what?" Dad said.

I made a face at Wash. "Vandalism attacks."

Dad stiffened and crossed his arms. "Five."

"When did they begin?" I said.

"Two months ago."

"So before my accident." I tried to force myself calm. Of course, Súmáí had been coming here for years. I'd seen him when I was five. The vandalism was recent, though, so maybe that wasn't him.

Dad turned and started pouring coffee into the press. "Yes."

"That tree. On Pride," I had to pause before speaking more. "Do you think it was vandalism?"

He turned and studied me. "Might be. It makes no sense, that healthy tree falling like it did."

"Shite!" Wash's words were sleepy. "What a sight. I almost peed myself."

"Was anything vandalized last night?" I asked.

"I don't think so," Dad said.

"We scared them off with our badass tasers!" Wash said.

"Okay, so they were here last night, and there was the attack on Tara at Sapphire East. When else have they been here?"

The teakettle emitted popping sounds as it warmed. Something in Dad seemed to give. He leaned back against the counter. "A lift shack at City Center was broken into."

"And?"

"They took a liftie uniform," Wash said.

My pulse turned loud in my ears.

"And medicine from our stock," Dad added.

"Ski patrol?" I said.

"I feel so violated," Wash said. As Dad's second in command, he ordered supplies for all three ski-patrol stations. "I catch 'em, I'm tasin' 'em!"

I held up three fingers, seeking more.

"The Platinum Club—" Dad said.

"Stole a bunch of slippers and most of the produce," Wash said. "Those poor folks next day had to walk around in stocking feet with no salads. Hardship." He shook his head, and one side of his lip curled up while his brow pressed down.

I laughed despite myself. I held up four fingers.

"The last one was Sapphire East. Took food again— produce, all the butter, all the salt, and every last bagel."

Five vandal incidents, I calculated. Last night nothing had been stolen, so far as we knew. But on the other trips they'd taken food, clothes, or medicine.

"Maybe a band of homeless vegetarians has moved into Crystal Village," Wash said.

Dad snorted, lifted the whistling teakettle from its burner, and poured steaming water into the coffee press. He still held his torso like glass.

"If they hadn't clobbered Tara, I might have to respect them," Wash said.

I pictured Súmáí's muscled arm, the hand that held our quills curving into a fist that struck. I shuddered.

Dad eyed me, poured two cups of coffee, delivered one to Wash on the couch, and took a sip of his own. Wash slurped as Dad walked to the thermostat and turned up the heat.

"What are you doing today?" he said.

"A snowshoe." I hadn't told Dad I'd gone to the Shangri-La spruce, just that I'd headed out Sunset Ridge. Today, I had to confirm if Súmáí was real.

"Where?" he said.

"Same as yesterday," I said.

"Stay where people can see you. Okay?" Dad said.

I rolled my eyes.

"Huh-uh." Wash pointed at his eyes with two fingers, pointed at me with them, and then pointed at his eyes again.

Bookmark:
Time Dilation

———————

A moving clock runs
slower than a stationary one.

16

I snowshoed on a mission, the headphones filling my ears with Hawking's book. This time the going was easier; I followed my tracks from yesterday and headed out the narrow road to Last Chance ten minutes faster. Tucker skied past me, hauling a sled. He waved and gave me a puzzled look, no doubt wondering what I was doing out there on foot. I was destined to be seen by Dad's employees and friends as long as I was within the borders of Crystal Mountain Resort.

I crossed the boundary ropes, glancing over my shoulder and holding my breath until I was hidden by trees. I looked across the open stretch of Shangri-La. No new snowboard tracks. *No snowboard tracks = no Gage.* I thought of him yesterday, admitting he loved me as he stood thigh-deep in snow, and my legs turned watery. I thought of Dad when I'd lain in that sled at the base of Pride, tears streaming down his face.

What was I doing? Heading toward Súmáí? A figment of my insanity, my childhood image of the boogieman? If not that, then a potentially lethal Ute? I halted, tugged down the headphones, and nudged up my sunglasses to rub my eyes.

Short lines of contrails scuffed the sky. I watched a plane inch across the blue. The narrator had just been explaining Einstein's relativity, and I considered how that plane was moving incredibly fast, but for the passengers peering out its oval windows, the world was still. I was just a spec passing below them. For them, time moved slower. A proven fact. Someone circling Earth forever would be younger at the end of fifty years.

Time and reality. In Dad's reality, I was lounging at the cabin or snowshoeing along a groomed run. In my reality, I might see vision-Mom today. These theories I was listening to—this math—reached to explain the world. And if equations ruled the world, if probability existed, fate was a myth. Maybe God too.

I rubbed my furrowed brow through my hat as my mind circled back to Súmáí. He held answers. I had to reach his two-word world and make him explain it to me. There had to be a way back to Mom.

I neared the spruce and stopped, noticing something I hadn't seen before: the tree bent from the roots, reminding me of the angle of my Upward Dog belly-to-the-floor. Time was, Mom would make me join her for yoga. We'd crack up at how unlimber I was. I could hardly straighten my legs, and I'd keel over during standing poses like Warrior or Tree. But my Upward Dog was primo.

That spruce, after its initial bend, reached toward the sky like it longed to fly. I heard Mom's laugh in my memory, and then I heard her say, *blue spruce*.

The full memory came to me: Mom reading a picture book naming all Colorado's state things. Flower: columbine. Bird: lark bunting. Fish: green cutthroat trout. Tree: blue spruce. She'd made me read the names, and I could not make myself see the Ls or Rs. "Bue spruce," I kept saying. "Lak butting." "Geen cutthoat." *L + R + me = combat.* "Again," Mom said, till I got them right. Now, at almost nineteen, I usually heard their sounds, but I still struggled to get them in the right places on paper.

As I neared the spruce, gold blotches appeared on its red-gray bark. When I stood close, they became places where sap had bled and dried. At eye-level, glossy dribbles marked a newer spot. They seemed like gilded tears. I considered this spruce's age, the decades, maybe centuries, it had witnessed.

I peered up through its branches, pressing my amulet bag to my chest, but discerned no porcupine. Funny how porcupines always seemed like wise old men. With what had happened, they seemed gatekeepers of a bridge invisible to humans.

I looked around. Might humans be the only blind ones? Did the rest of the world exist in multiple realities at once? Or did they move between them? Did the lark bunting and columbine understand multiple existence? Did they understand the spruce's ability to guide me on leaps to other universes? I considered whether all things but humans understood this, even rocks, and I felt so gypped. I shook my head: I was going insane. I *needed* Súmáí to be real.

I stepped to the spruce, and, avoiding the gold spots, pressed my palm to it.

Toasty breeze. Sun overhead.
A hummingbird's thrum.

Mom spoke. I caught my breath. Mom? Here? I pretzeled myself in my arm and found us sitting on a blanket, about twenty yards out in Shangri-La's meadow. I was maybe three years old. Late fall asters and yellow grass surrounded us. That little-me rose on my hands and knees to touch the page of a book Mom held open in her lap. I wore little kid jeans and a T-shirt, and my puffy butt revealed that I still wore pull-up diapers. I'd been murder to potty-train. "B, b, b, b," I said.

"B is for *bighorn sheep*, Colorado's state animal."

"Big horns," little-me said, getting the R just right.

"Yes, their horns curl, don't they?" Mom said.

"Curl," I said.

"And B is for *bumblebee*."

I plopped onto my butt. "There." My voice was so small as I pointed.

"Yes! There's a bumblebee, right there. You're so smart, Sov," Mom said. "What else starts with B?"

"Brown," little-me said, pointing at a brown butterfly.

I had always said *bown*.

"Bread," little-me said.

"Very good!" Mom said.

I had always said *bed*.

"Bear," little-me said.

"Yes," Mom said. "We saw a bear yesterday, didn't we?"

"Babies," little-me said.

"Yes, a momma bear with babies. Remember, always stay away from bears, especially momma bears."

"Bambi was a baby."

"What a smart girl! See what you can do? You said four Bs. Did you hear them?"

I pressed my palm hard against the spruce's rough bark to feel I was really there. I faintly recalled this day, but this little-me had no trouble with R or L. I felt jealous all the way to my fingertips.

"Mom!" I called.

She looked up, and little-me scrabbled into her lap, right on top of the book. *Butt.* Mom wrapped her arms over little-me and scanned around.

"Over here, Mom!"

Her gaze found me, and she leaned forward, making little-me lean too.

"Who's there?" Her voice held fear. I wobbled. She seemed to recognize Dad's old hat, and I realized the Christmas where she'd given it to him would have just passed in my world. She gawked at my face.

"It's me. Sov."

"Sov?"

"I'm eighteen now."

Her head tilted and she paled.

"Momma?" little-me said.

Mom looked from the me in her lap to the tree-me. Her mouth sagged open. "Sovern?"

"I miss you!" I said.

"Miss me?"

I hadn't considered this. I couldn't tell her she'd died.

Mom leaned on one arm, gathered her legs, and stood, little-me on her hip. First steps hesitant, she walked toward me, careful across the slanted ground, the lumps of grass, the flowers and the dirt bulges from voles, till she stood about six feet away. I drank in her brown eyes.

She tallied the curves of my face, my body's stature beneath my snow pants and parka. "You're so tall." She smiled.

"Momma?" Little-me looked like she might be sick.

Mom stepped forward. "What happened to your arm?"

As I opened my mouth to answer, a hand press over mine against that trunk.

Chill wind. White against my face.
Snow cradling my body.

I punched with my one arm, not seeing what I was hitting, just striking out. "Go away, Gage!" My fist connected with the dark green of a liftie jacket. I saw the side-turned face, the hands forcing my shoulders down. I dropped my arm, breathing a train's rhythm. Súmáí locked my gaze.

"Sovern," he said and shook his head no. The ends of his hair brushed my face.

I bucked my body and released a sound of pure fury.

"Sovern!" he said. His eyes said, *Calm down.* His grip

hurt my wrists. Churned snow chilled my neck, upper lip, and cheek. He may not have been much taller than me, but he was way more muscular and so strong. I turned my head to the side. I'd been talking to Mom! She'd been right there!

Súmáí climbed off and offered his hand to help me up, but I slapped it away. I struggled out of our crater, and he chuckled. I brushed snow off my chest and legs.

"Screw you!" I said.

At the tone of my words, his face turned stern. He held up two fingers on his right hand, like Wash had. I thought of Wash's two fingers pointing from his eyes to me and blinked back how much I knew this moment would disappoint him. Súmáí pointed from me to the spruce with his left hand, those fingers on his right still up, and he shook his head fiercely. He did it one more time, and then he ran that palm across the open meadow. He touched the first fingers of both hands together in front of his face and shot them apart, moving his arms up and out. An explosion?

I squinted despite my sunglasses. I pointed to my chest, to the spruce, and then copied his sign for explosion. I raised an eyebrow.

He shook his head. He held up two fingers, pointed from me to where little-me had been in the meadow, and mimed that explosion again.

I understood. *Me + me = bang.* I groaned and brought my hand to my fluttering innards.

His face softened to a compassion I would never have expected, and my sight turned misty. I stepped back, feeling drained, and realized he was loose in my world and apparently very real. I assessed him in that liftie uniform.

My head was fritzing. Angry with everything, I said, "Crystal Mountain doesn't allow male employees to have long hair or earrings. And they have to shower."

I snowshoed to where Mom and little-me had sat on the blanket. I stepped right where I imagined Mom had been, plopped into the snow, and wriggled my butt till I pressed out her lap. Súmáí followed in my tracks, postholing with every step. He stood beside me, looking out at the valley, the river, the interstate snaking along it, the frontage road, the houses, and the shops.

"I wish we could talk." I kept my eyes on the panorama. "I have so many questions."

I could feel him study me with a familiarity that was unnerving. After a while, he sat down too.

I eyed his moccasins. Another giveaway that he wasn't really a liftie. His feet must have been freezing.

We sat for a while, and I felt Súmáí study Dad's hat. He wasn't wearing a hat. Maybe he was envying it. He looked at my profile next, and though I tried to force it down, red inched up my neck. I flinched at the slight tug as he took my hair in his fingers and rubbed it, the frost falling away.

He unzipped his parka, releasing his sweat scent, and I forced myself not to cover my nose as I saw his leather shirt within. He lifted his amulet bag and drew out two quills. Ours, no doubt. He pointed from me to him, and then up toward the branches of the spruce. He pressed his fingertips lightly against his cheek as if he were making dots. How could he know this about me? Did he witness my accident? Then, in the sun's clarifying light, I saw tiny holes patterned *his* cheek.

My breath caught. I pushed my sunglasses to the top of my head and studied his face closer. My sling palm came to my own holes. Cautiously, I brought my fingertips to his cheek. His skin was warmed by the sun, and so smooth compared to the spruce's bark. His flesh felt absolutely real as he nodded and held up two fingers again. Then he crossed them and stole my breath.

Súmáí's gaze shot over my shoulder, and he straightened at the same instant I heard schussing. My hand fell from his cheek as Gage snowboarded past us, his mouth a zero.

"Dammit!" I watched him snake turns down our powder stash.

As he arced back toward the area's boundary and the lift, Súmáí echoed, "Dam-mit."

My head snapped to him.

"Dammit?" He pointed toward where Gage had been.

I laughed and bit my lip. "Dammit," I said, giving Gage a new name, and expanding our world to three words.

Bookmark:
Time Dilation

————

The faster a clock moves through space,
the slower it moves through time. If a clock
could travel at the speed of light, its time
would stop. A beam of light is timeless.

17

Súmáí ascended Sunset Ridge beside me. He was leery about walking along the run's edge, not so much from the skiers and boarders, I sensed, but from needing to lurk in shadow. I didn't have the energy for slogging through the forest, though, so I'd tucked his hair into his coat, made him take off his earrings, and loaned him Dad's hat. Now, in his uniform, he looked like any one of the army of lifties who worked on Crystal Mountain. I breathed hard, but for Súmáí the ascent seemed easy.

He eyed every person sailing down Sunset Ridge, especially the tiny strips of their faces between their goggles and coat collars. He'd seen my white skin, but had he seen it on other people? Was he surprised by how much of it he saw now? A guy with dreadlocks snowboarded past, and Súmáí stopped and watched him glide into the distance.

City Center's lodge appeared ahead. Bringing Súmáí into the Emerald West or City Center lodges had a high probability for disaster. I decided to take him to the cabin instead. It was the only warm private place I could think of, and Dad never came home till after five, especially on weekends.

I glanced at Súmáí moving effortlessly beside me, and wondered what the hell I was doing, bringing home the boogieman from my childhood. Yet back in Shangri-La, when he'd pulled me from Mom, his face had held such compassion, and quill holes marked his cheeks. Most of all, he was *walking around* in *my* world. If he could walk around here, maybe I could move freely in one of Mom's universes. I needed answers.

We veered into the forest, and he seemed to relax. My stomach grumbled. All we had in the cabin were Crispy's lemon bars, and those might scare Súmáí off, so I decided to stop off at the coffee shop in the lodge for a snack. When we were across from it, I gestured for him to wait. I'm not sure why I trusted him to stay there, but I did. I unstrapped my snowshoes and carried them under my arm. The coffee shop served sandwiches and soups, but since it was after 3:00, they'd been put away, and workers were sterilizing the stainless steel counters. One of the perks of Dad's job was a monthly food allowance for his family; I settled for two hot chocolates, a bag of potato chips, and a blond brownie— my favorite foods on the mountain.

As I left the lodge, I glanced around for a ski-patrol coat but against all odds saw none. Súmáí waited in the trees. He took the snowshoes from under my arm, to make walking with the drinks easier for me, and I led him till we were screened by the cupped hand of pines. Little brown geysers sloshed out the mouth holes of the hot chocolates' lids from my gangly steps. I walked to the cabin door, set down the cups, and pressed in the key code.

I opened the door, and when I looked back, it was just like when I was five years old again, because there on the edge of the forest was that scary Ute … yet in liftie clothes from my world, from *my* mountain. He became scary in a whole new way.

Jittery, I gestured with my head for him to join me. A minute later, he prowled through the door. I closed it. I set down the food, went to the bedroom, and made sure the window opened easily in case Súmáí needed to fit through in a pinch. I showed him the escape route, and he flashed a smile. It was more about protecting Dad, though.

"Hungry?" I said.

I peeled off my snow boots and jacket, hung them by the door, and gestured for Súmáí to do the same. He frowned and shook his head.

"Hungry?" I said again. I moved the hot chocolates in front of two chairs.

Súmáí prowled around the cabin. He studied the coats, the couch, the TV, the kitchen. He peered into the bedroom again, poised like someone might attack him. He studied me at the table. I took a sip of hot chocolate and pointed to the other white paper cup, then to him.

He assessed the chair, pulled it back like mine, and sat on its edge. He ran his fingers over the table's grain. The tulips in the table's center caught his attention. He reached out, ran his finger up one's petal, and smelled it, wearing an amazed expression. In that hat, the earrings gone, his tucked-in hair seeming shoulder length, he appeared more ordinary, and I became aware of the symmetry of his face.

I lifted the cup, demonstrating how to drink from the hole. Súmáí lifted his, smelled it, and took a sip. His face shifted with surprise. Good? Bad? I couldn't tell. His brows pressed close, and he sipped again. His brows lifted. He sipped once more and grimaced. He set the cup down.

I laughed and he shot me a dirty look. He yanked off the hat and set it on the table. He wasn't good-looking, not like Gage.

I unwrapped the brownie, spread its cellophane flat, and broke it into pieces. I popped brownie into my mouth. It was sweet and chewy, with chocolate chips and walnuts. Súmáí picked up a piece and smelled it. He held it away from his face and studied it. He carefully placed it in his mouth. His eyebrows rose again, but not quite so much. He spit it out in his hand.

I lunged to the counter, tore off a paper towel, and set it before him. He grew transfixed by its little pastel cabin pattern. I gestured for him to dump what was in his hand on it. He seemed to doubt whether he should do that, staring at the repeat of little cabins on the paper towel's edge, but finally did. I wadded up the paper towel and dumped it in the trash.

I opened the bag of potato chips, just regular ones. I drew one out and crunched it. I offered him a chip. He didn't take it, rather studied it pinched between my fingers. He finally took it and held it up in the sunlight. He smelled it and bit half off. He sucked on it and a slow smile spread on his face.

I ran a glass of water at the tap and set it before him. As he traced its side, something in my chest tugged. He lifted the glass, smelled the water, and took a sip. He grinned. He held the glass up to the light, studying it, and a little rainbow arced on the table.

Súmáí downed the water, and the motion of his Adam's apple drove home, more than anything else, that he was alive and real and sitting in *my* cabin. My skin prickled.

He strode to the sink. I joined him, numb all over, and turned the cold knob. He held his hand underneath the tap and laughed. He cupped his palms, filled them, and took a long drink. He straightened, shaking his head in wonder. I turned off the knob.

"Water," I said.

"Wat-er," he said.

He reached out and turned the knob on and off. I nudged him, turned the hot knob, and put my hand under the tap. He put his hand under it and yanked it back. He looked at me like I'd played a trick on him. I mixed the hot and cold so they wouldn't burn and put both my hands underneath. He stuck one finger in and then both of his hands. I turned the water off, dried my hands on the dish towel, and handed it to him. As he dried his hands, he looked around the room with sorrowful eyes. Eyes like mine after I'd lost Mom. To give him space, I sat at the table and pressed my fingertips hard into my lips to make things feel real. I needed a way to find out what he knew.

Súmáí came to stand behind his chair. He said something. No clue what, but from his expression, from the look he gave me, it must have been so sad. He moved to the door.

"You're leaving?" I was right behind him. "Wait!"

He paused, but I had no clue how to make him stay. He reached toward the doorknob. Desperate, I retrieved the hat from the table and held it out. He eyed it for a full minute. He took it and traced his fingers over its wool. He pulled it on his head.

We stood there like that, not moving, yet so close.

"*Towéiyak*," he finally said. It seemed like *thank you*. From his amulet bag, he drew a quill and held it out.

I took it. "*Towéiyak*?" I said.

Súmáí nodded.

He zipped his coat. Some of his hair had come loose from the collar, and I tucked it back inside. We stood there again, still so close. He touched my quill cheek. I couldn't make my eyes handle this intimacy, and I looked down.

He opened the door and scanned the cabin's surroundings before walking away without looking back. I watched him disappear into the forest before I realized I was standing there in the cold with the door wide open.

I stepped inside and shut the door. I studied the quill he'd given me; its pattern was exactly like my quills. I stood there a long time, my stunned mind groping for something sane to hold on to.

Someone pressed on the door's keypad. It swung open, and Dad stepped in. Like a little kid, I hid that quill behind my back. Dad stopped, startled by my standing so close to the door.

"What's up, Sovern?" He looked exhausted. His face was so drawn it seemed chiseled from stone. He resembled the shadow on Phantom Peak, and that just about broke my heart. Súmáí's touch on my cheek was still fresh. I was *such* a liar—if Dad knew what had just passed in this room, he'd stumble to a chair, collapse into it, and cry like the day of my accident. I remembered his hand over the nub of my own beneath that tarp. How could I do this to him?

As I stood there, looking at Dad, Súmáí hardly seemed real. Maybe that quill pinched between my fingers was actually my own. I slid it into my back pocket. No matter what was real, I was descending into a grid of lies.

"I'm glad to see you, Dad." My voice cracked.

That made him smile, and though it wasn't a lie, I felt like the biggest scum alive.

Bookmark:
Quantum Mechanics
Max Planck

————

Energy does not flow in a steady continuum, but is delivered in discrete amounts. Planck named these quanta. They explain why a burning item will seem to move between distinctly different colors.

18

Early Monday morning, I sat on a snowmobile behind Wash, my one good arm clinging to his waist as he drove down Sunset Ridge toward the gondola. It had snowed on top of last night's grooming, a quick storm leaving a layer of snow so dry it felt like fine sand spraying against our parkas as we zoomed along. A steady stream of horizontal tears leaked across my temples. The tips of my ears were stinging from the cold. I pulled up my hood and pressed my head against Wash's back to hold it in place. I wriggled my toes in my Converse but couldn't feel them.

Last January, when I'd gotten my second-semester schedule, I'd moaned at not having a first-hour class because it meant I had a longer day, and I'd wanted to escape to the mountain in the afternoons. Now I considered the ironies of life, since it gave me more time to get to school.

Wash pulled up to the Emerald West lodge. "Learn somethin' good," he said.

"I'll try." I sighed.

"You all right? You look beat."

"I'm fine," I said.

But I wasn't. I'd stared at the bedroom ceiling all night, searching it for advice as those spruce trees had beckoned to my skin, my bones, even my innards. Yet I knew Dad would hate this, that it would lead to lies. I'd stared at my palm too, studying my lifeline in the dark and sensing that pressing my palm to those trees would make my life's line curve down. I'd finally dozed off near morning, but woke, still torn, till I saw Dad, refreshed and chuckling at one of Wash's jokes as he stood in the light streaming through the kitchen window.

I had to stop. I had to be good. I had to make my life's line curve up.

I waved to Wash and started toward the lifthouse, but in a moment of inspiration, I wheeled into the lodge. Taking decent lunch to school would be the first step. In the restaurant, I snagged a pre-made roast beef sandwich, a brownie, and a water. I stowed them in my backpack and made for the door, just as Big John lumbered out of the men's bathroom tugging on his gloves, Sarge close behind.

"Sovern, good morning!" As a kid, I'd loved Big John's booming voice.

Sarge saluted me, grinning. "Ditto that."

Standing there, side by side, they resembled a giant and a dwarf.

"We're raising the pads," Big John said.

The kid-me had loved it when they'd had to raise the red pads. The pads protected skiers from dying if they were dumb enough to run into the lift towers. Raising the pads meant the snow's blanket had grown even thicker. I'd liked best when storms pummeled Crystal Mountain and the guys couldn't keep up, because it proved that, no matter how we might try to fool ourselves, the weather was in control.

Now I hated that. Mom's death had reversed it.

Make that line curve up, I thought and forced a crooked smile. "Thanks for telling me," I said.

I strode out the doors, their concerned gazes burning my back. The lift attendant waved to me. His green uniform reminded me of Súmáí. After two skiers disembarked from a gondola car, I climbed in. I let my backpack fall to my forearm and onto the bench. The car moved around the bullwheel, doors closing, and then accelerated away from the lodge.

I snapped shut the rectangular windows at the car's top, sat, and leaned back against the glass. I unzipped my parka and let warmth seep into me before the final leg of my commute to school. In all, it would take forty minutes. Not bad. Double my walk from the Condo, but now I could get lunch each day. I forced aside the thought of that spruce along the recreation path.

The gondola car descended a knoll, and Crystal Village came into view. After a weekend away, it seemed foreign. I took in the narrow grid of shops, condos, and outlying homes. I looked toward the white ribbons of the golf course. In winter, its fairways became groomed Nordic tracks.

Mom used to drag Dad and me out there to skate-ski.

Skate-skiing made me breathe so hard I thought I'd barf, but I did it for Mom. She was really good and would win races. She said I was good too, but I didn't believe her. I kept up, though, while Dad trailed behind. I remembered how yesterday I'd breathed like a train as I'd hiked toward the cabin with Súmáí. The old me wouldn't have been huffing like that. All my smoking and movie-watching had taken its toll. I set that thought in my growing wall of resolve.

I ran my fingers over the beads on my amulet bag. Inside it, Súmáí's quill mingled with mine. Yesterday in the cabin, his face had held a loss equal to mine. Was it from seeing my world in the cabin, a life I considered heaven? When visiting other universes, I couldn't take my hand from the spruce and stay there. How was Súmáí able to move freely in my world? Stop! I thought.

At the base of the mountain, I exited the gondola car and strode out of the lifthouse against a current of skiers and boarders, past a heated fountain shooting timed arcs of water. I strode down Ruby Street, past art galleries, hotels, fur shops, jewelry stores, gear shops, clothing stores, a coffee shop, and a candy shop till I came to the famous Gem Bridge with its heated glass roof that bathed people in facets of rainbow light as they crossed Crystal Creek. Across the bridge, I waited for a town shuttle stuffed with tourists to roll by. I crossed out of town and onto the recreation path that led to Crystal High.

About five minutes later, that spruce came into view. Like my Shangri-La spruce, it had girth and that Upward Dog bend at the base before reaching toward the sky. What was the probability of their similarity? I blocked the sun with my hand, and my head reeled at the chances of there also being a brown-gray lump in its upper branches, but that porcupine was there. I stepped toward the tree, itching to press my palm to it. I remembered Súmáí holding up two fingers and shaking his head: *explosion*. His warning. I remembered Wash's two fingers gesturing toward his eyes. His caring.

I studied Crystal Creek's swirled ice, listened to its muffled sound of rushing water, and remembered feeding the clothes I'd stolen into its flow. A chickadee hopped across the ice and pecked at a speck of darkness. I remembered Gage standing with his arms crossed, watching me as I fed those things into the water. I'd been self-destructing and he couldn't handle it. Two days ago in Shangri-La, he'd said "love" and I'd kissed him. Yesterday, I'd let him be renamed Dammit. Could I be any meaner? Any less predictable?

Gage, Dad, Wash, the rest of my ski-patrol family—they were real people, here, now, with feelings. They cared for me. Mom, Súmáí, and the spruce trees were illogical. Insane. Yet I couldn't bring myself to admit they weren't real. I pushed my eyebrows as high as they would go with my fingertips.

I pictured Dad and enlarged his image across all of my mind, blotting out everything else. I inhaled the creek's muffled sound. I had to stay on track with him. With my whole ski-patrol family. I had to keep that lifeline rising. I would go to school, I wouldn't ditch, and I would actually try like I used to.

I rolled back my shoulders and willed this resolve to take root. Today, as a first step, I'd speak in Lindholm's class.

A thousand pounds seemed to press down on me at the thought of talking in front of everyone.

"I can," I said. A promise to Dad, to my ski-patrol family, and to myself.

I arrived at Crystal High from its back side and rounded it on a connector path. As I walked through the doors, I shoved back my hood, eyes adjusting to the florescent light. The immigrant girls huddled on the big steps in the school's entry, loosing high-tinted Spanish and laughing. I crinkled my nose at the repellent scent of the janitor's cleanser. Honestly, officials somewhere must have searched long and hard to find the worst-smelling stuff. Nobody would use it at home.

In the Student Union, Handler stood at a table of Student Council geeks. Shelley Millhouse glanced away from me like I was dirt. Handler nodded to me, and my heart tripped because I'd completely forgotten my promise to meet him before fifth hour. The day seemed to stretch endlessly ahead of me. Maybe I should just tell him the truth, I thought. But what would I say? Anything honest sounded insane. Anything honest would end with a phone call to Dad.

As I walked into Literature of Culture, I came face-to-face with Shelley, bathroom pass in her hand. Up close, her complexion was like velvet. She didn't say anything, and neither did I, but I flung her a screw-you smile.

Lindholm strode to the front of the classroom. She wore a blue-striped dress that hugged her slim figure. She wore a dress almost every day. I liked that predictable thing about her. When was the last time I'd worn a dress? Third grade, maybe? I could have worn one to the winter formal, but Gage and I had snubbed it. I'd scowled and insisted dancing was for dorks. Truth was, my body didn't cup enough happiness to sway that way.

Lindholm started discussing *I Know Why the Caged Bird Sings*, so I set the voice recorder on my desk, turned it on, and ignored the stares. The memoir was narrow, and we were already halfway through. I took a deep breath and sat taller, determined to be a better person, but my face burned at the thought of talking in front of all these people after so much time in silence.

Our discussion was about how church and racial segregation ruled Angelou's life. I thought of how I'd only ever been to church once. For Mom's memorial service.

"So what exactly is Uncle Willy's problem?" Lindholm said. She pointed to someone behind me.

"He's crippled," said Paul Cummings.

The class chuckled at the obviousness of his answer.

"Why is that a problem?" Lindholm asked.

Shelley returned her pass to the trough on the SMART Board and slunk to her seat. I thought of Dad, of Big John's smile, and of Sarge's salute. I remembered Wash, pointing at his eyes and at me. I remembered Tara's eyes in the snow-cat mirror. I pictured the cookies from Crispy on our coffee table and the steady stream of baked love he sent us. I remembered the muffled sound of Crystal Creek beneath ice. For all of them, I raised my hand.

Lindholm suppressed a grin. "Sovern?"

"It's a problem because a man in that place and time was measured by physical labor. By how much cotton he could pick. How he could provide. For his family," I said.

Everyone turned to look at me. No kidding.

"Excellent!" Lindholm said. "And does he have a family, Sovern?"

"No. Well, yes. Through his sister. And Maya and Bailey."

"So why does he stand tall behind the store's counter, then, when the city couple are passing through?"

I looked down at my hands. "He wants someone to see him as a normal person."

"Well done, Sovern," Lindholm said.

I glared at Shelley, and she looked away. Something in her face made me realize that perfect Shelley Millhouse, who should have been in AP Lit or AP Language, was in this class for English losers.

When class was over, I shuffled toward the door, but Lindholm said, "Sovern?" I walked to her desk as the room emptied.

"You're recording class discussion?" she said.

I nodded.

"And you're listening to this book?"

"Uh-huh."

"I'm glad. Your insights are first-rate, and it's good to have you be part of discussion."

I laughed at that, and then bit my lip to stop.

Lindholm eyed me. "You weren't in my class as a freshman."

"No."

"You had Ms. Summers?"

I nodded.

"Remember *The Odyssey?*"

I'd never forget *The Odyssey*. Because I'd listened to it, the ancient language of Odysseus's journey home had jumped to life and I'd heard the whole tale, while the rest of the class had struggled through an abridged version. Like always, Mom had made me read along where I could.

"Do you remember that it was a poem? An epic poem?"

"Uh-huh."

"Do you know why it was a poem?"

"Rhapsodes."

"Very good. That's how they retained culture, and the rhyme made it easier for the rhapsodes to recite it. No one knows why their written language was lost during that time. One of life's mysteries." She shook her head. "Civilization just never knows what might lie around the corner."

I analyzed her. Did she know I'd been traveling through the trees?

"But really, only in recent times have stories been written down. For millennia, stories existed as oral traditions, and rhyme helped them be remembered. In the timeline of humanity, writing is a new phenomenon."

I snorted. She was talking about my dyslexia.

"Sovern?"

Lindholm was just trying to be nice, so I said, "Got it: stories with no writing." I thought of Súmáí. Lindholm had taught us that the Utes had neither reading nor writing.

She shook her head. "We all *need* stories, Sovern. Stories are *bigger* than writing. If we lost the written word, stories would continue on."

I didn't know how to handle this kindness. All I could do was force out, "Thanks."

Bookmark:
Schrödinger's Cat
Erwin Schrödinger

Imagine a cat is sealed in a box. While it's there, the cat exists in an unknowable state. Since it cannot be observed, we can't know whether the cat is alive or dead. It exists in both states until we look into the box.

19

I stowed my lunch from the lodge in my parka's pocket and walked out on the recreation path, but not so far as the spruce. I brushed snow off a bench, sat, and chewed my sandwich and brownie. Some crows squawked around, demanding my attention, hoping I'd feed them, no doubt. I was so tired, and I dreaded seeing Gage in the next class after what had happened yesterday.

I returned to school at the last possible minute, strode into Calculus, and slid into my desk just as the electronic bell stopped ringing.

"Open your books to page 583." Kenowitz took visual attendance from his desk at the room's front and entered it into his laptop. Handler would check on me, no doubt.

"Dating a liftie?" Gage's words hit like spit against my back, and I hunched forward.

"No," I said over my shoulder.

"Right," Gage said.

I knew his expression that stuck to that word—his mouth cocked slightly open with calculation—was usually reserved for his dad. I turned pale and ran my fingers over my brow, pencil balanced between the first two.

"Sovern," Kenowitz said. "Please switch seats with Craig. Crack open that window beside the desk and give yourself some air."

Heat rushed up my neck as everyone watched me gather my books, and Craig passed me, scowling, but Kenowitz switched on the SMART Board, cut the lights, and started talking. I set down my book and folder and cracked the window.

Kenowitz presented a problem where a lion and a ranger were in a nature preserve. He wrote the coordinates of their routes and their speed and started demonstrating how to figure out if their paths would collide. *Collide.* I glanced out the window. This classroom was on the school's far side, closest to the recreation path, so I could see the connector path I walked on. I strained to hear the muted rush of Crystal Creek—hearing its sound would strengthen my resolve to be good—and then motion caught my eye.

In the trees' fringe, a little ways off the path, stood Súmáí. His feet were planted wide as he studied Crystal High. He looked so real. I felt my pulse in my ears, sensed Gage staring, and forced my sight away from the window. I glanced back and Súmáí was gone.

"Incorporating Sovern's method," yanked me back to the classroom. Kenowitz was using my method for parametric equations. Though I'd already finished the problem in my head, I concentrated on him slogging through it to stay in reality.

And then it occurred to me that Gage had *seen* Súmáí in Shangri-La.

Class ended and Gage bolted, but I just sat, staring out the window, willing Súmáí to appear again. If he was real, then Mom in those other worlds was real too. I heard the creek through the open window and remembered my promise. I rested my forehead on the desk and shut my eyes. Finally I shuffled toward the door, but Kenowitz met me.

"It looks as if Gage is a distraction for you?"

I shrugged.

"Why don't you keep that new seat."

I nodded.

"How goes the research into quantum physics?"

"Okay."

I could tell he wanted to hear more, so I forced out, "Hawking is brilliant."

"You found him then?"

"His *Nutshell* book."

"And?"

"*Weird.*"

"I find it hard to reconcile quantum theory with daily life." Kenowitz's eyes behind his gold wire glasses lost focus, and he stared at the bulletin board next to the door.

"It explains *everything*," I said.

He frowned and nodded. "Sovern, are you challenged enough by this class? We could set up an accelerated—"

"It's fine."

"Okay. But I encourage you to keep challenging yourself. Don't figure it all out in five minutes and dismiss it. Keep thinking of innovative ways to solve these problems. See if you can teach me something new again."

I could teach him things that would blow his mind. If I didn't go crazy first. Even so, a weird giddiness lightened my steps as I moved down the hall. Two compliments in one day. *Lindholm's kindness + Kenowitz's kindness = maybe my luck was changing.*

Just before I emerged into the Student Union, someone grabbed my arm.

"Gage?" I rolled my eyes. His hand released its grip. He seemed pale again, and his eyes had pulled to pinpoints.

"Look, Sovern, I'm sorry. It's just … seeing you with that guy … "

I remembered that toothpaste-flavored kiss I'd given him on Saturday and blushed at how Súmáí and I must have appeared the very next day, gazing at one another with my fingers on his cheek. I stepped back. "Love," he'd said, but even if I wanted to, I couldn't love him back because *me + anyone I loved = disaster.*

Handler's voice came from nowhere: "See you in a minute?"

Gage and I flinched. I didn't respond, but Handler said, "Excellent." He looked at Gage. "Still abstaining from college applications?"

"I told you: I'm not leaving Crystal Village." Gage stood braced, mouth cocked slightly open.

"How are you feeling?" Handler asked him.

"Fine." Gage said it like, *Go away.*

"You sure?" Handler said.

"I'm sure."

Handler smiled at both of us, then strolled to the counseling office.

Gage and I looked at each other, intensity gone.

"I wasn't spying on you," he said. "It's just ... Shangri-La? Our stash?"

I felt drawn to him then—wanted to hug him—but my promise pressed close, and I swayed. "I'm really confused right now."

"About what?" Now that he'd spoken the word "love" I could see it in his gaze.

No way could I tell him all the things clogging my mind, yet I owed him something. "About who I am." I realized it was the truest thing I could have said.

Gage chuckled. "Welcome to the club."

I pressed my lips because tears blurred my sight.

"I know who you are, Sovern," he said.

"Right. How can *you* know when *I* don't?"

"I always have." Gage tapped his chest, which should have been dorky. Instead, it loosed a tear down my cheek. He stepped close, wiped that tear with his thumb, and rubbed it between his fingers. "I'll take this as a good sign."

I watched till he disappeared into the lower hall. I blew out a long stream of breath, like when I used to smoke, and I headed to Handler's office.

Bookmark:
Anthropic Principle
Brandon Carter

———————

Data about the universe is affected and biased by our instruments' limitations and by the necessity that somebody be there to collect the data in the first place. No universe exists until it is observed.

20

Handler closed his door but for an inch. Two chairs faced his desk. I slumped into the chair closest to the window. I gazed through the glass onto a courtyard with no doors. I'd looked into this courtyard a bunch, Mom in the other chair, and it always made me wonder about the imbecile who'd designed this building.

"So you and Gage have broken up?" Handler said.

"Uh-huh." A magpie landed on an aspen's narrow branch and set it swaying.

"How long ago?"

"Eight days."

"Things look tense."

I shrugged.

"Gage is having…" Handler squinted.

"What? Having what?"

He pressed his lips and shook his head. His turquoise golf shirt had a logo of two palm trees. "Ms. Lindholm tells me you gave valuable input in the class discussion today."

I nodded. Was there really something going on with Gage, or had Handler done that on purpose to get my attention? I always scrambled to keep my footing with the guy.

"You're listening to recorded books again?"

I nodded absently, still considering how wan Gage had looked in the hall. How he'd looked equally bad in Shangri-La on Saturday. How fast could a person get cancer from smoking?

"Somewhere out there your mom is smiling."

I smirked. Yes, she was.

"What?" he said.

I shook my head.

His eyes turned hypnotic. I could tell he was headed somewhere I did not want to go.

"We moved," I said, to derail him. "To a cabin at the top of Crystal Mountain."

His brows lifted.

"For Dad's work. We lived there before, till I had to come down here to start school." I said "school" in my usual way, like it tasted rotten.

Silence yawned between us. I looked at my hands, then at a photo on the desk's corner of Handler with two guys. His sons, no doubt. They stood on a putting green, a black-and-white checkered flag behind them, the younger boy brandishing a golf ball. They all were grinning, arms slung around each other. It made me wish I had a photo like this of my ski-patrol family. Maybe someday soon I'd take a picture of us. I closed my eyes and thought, Be good. You can.

"Everything's different," I said. I tapped my lips with my fingertips. "The dishes. The pots and pans. They're organized all wrong. The pillows on the couch. Wrong. The flowers on the table. Wrong. I can't seem to get anything right."

"In the cabin? Like your mom had it, you mean?"

I nodded.

"You are your own person, Sovern."

"I know."

"Your mother's gone, Sovern." He said it so kind, it hurt.

"I *know*."

"She's gone." He said it so kind, again.

I willed myself not to respond. "Never!" I shouted.

The silence between us weighed a thousand pounds. My adrenaline craving surged in my limbs clear to my fingertips. I flexed them to ease the craving because I'd sworn off Gage, and I couldn't snowboard. This day had been a zigzag of emotion—Lindholm and Kenowitz's kindnesses, me feeling like maybe I could keep my promise, Gage confirming Súmáí was real, seeing Súmáí out the window, Gage making me cry. And now *this*?

I pressed into my chair. I ran my fingers over my furrowed brow. That's what I got for trying. For talking. I anchored my gaze on the courtyard, grabbed a chunk of my hair, and wrapped it—a barrier— across my mouth to block the scream rising in my throat. *Me + words = failure.*

No way was Mom gone. She was right there in the spruce

trees, just a palm away. My resolve to be good evaporated, and I calmed, dropped my hair, and looked Handler full in the face.

His head tilted. "You all right?"

"Finished?"

"If you like."

"I like."

He opened the desk's wide top drawer and pulled out a pad of late passes. Keeping track of me down to the minute. He filled one out for Art, even though he must have worked something out with Bennett.

I snatched it and he ushered me to the door.

"See you tomorrow?"

I grunted.

Handler stood there, watching, as I forced each straight step—one, two, three, four, five, six—along the counseling office's short hall.

———————

Somehow I survived to the end of the day. I bolted out school's doors, headed for the spruce. Handler was an idiot. What had he been trying to accomplish anyway? He had to know I wasn't about to give up Mom. Ever.

I strode so fast I passed a jogger, her ponytail swinging like a pendulum. A biker rode by going the other direction, his fat winter tires emitting a high zinging against the pavement that sounded like a machine getting ready to explode. I laughed: it sounded how I felt. I remembered Súmáí pointing with two fingers toward where Mom and little-me had been, then to me, and then gesturing an explosion. I remembered Wash pointing to his eyes then back at me, and my promise.

I stopped and shoved my fingers into my hair, tasting my need for adrenaline. My promise to be good, Gage's broken heart, Handler's manipulation, Súmáí, the vandalism, Tara's black eye, the vision-Mom, my freaking dyslexia, the anniversary of Mom's death, and my rebellious mouth that kept speaking when I needed to stay silent—I couldn't sort them into order, couldn't find control. The woman I'd passed jogged by, and then I bent double, hand pressed to my innards. No doubt about it: I was going insane.

Ski boots clumped a rhythm. The Millhouses' bed-and-breakfast was farther down this path, and no doubt that's where these people were headed, even though it was a long walk from the lifts. Their approaching steps were steady, and men's loud, confident voices overlapped them. I straightened, pulling my hood forward to mask my face just before they rounded the corner.

"I told Hardy, but he didn't believe me," one guy said.

The other guy shook his head. "That'll cost him."

A third guy laughed and said, "Yes, about a grand."

The three walked abreast, taking up the path's width, each carrying his skis on his shoulder and his poles in the other hand. Their steps seemed an inexorable rhythm, and though they saw me, they showed no sign of stepping aside.

As I slunk to the path's edge, I realized I'd been slinking for a year. Fate had taken Mom and ruined my relationship with Dad, and I'd just slunk aside and let it. This weird thing happened then. Maybe *cold + that zigzag day = hallucination*. All I know is those guys transformed to wearing robes and became fate—so confident and cocky—and I loathed them with everything I had. I marched back onto the path, forcing them to swerve or collide with me, and I shouted, "I hate you!"

It was like a movie. The rhythm of their steps turned to chaos as they stared at me in horror. Two guys bumped into each other, one of them clocking the other in the helmet with his skis as he tripped off the path's edge. On the other side, the third guy gave me a wide berth. They walked along the path's sides for a bit, glancing over their shoulders—obviously afraid of me—before stepping back to the middle. Just before they disappeared from sight, I yelled, "I decide my own life!"

I reached the spruce. Up close, this trunk had sap spots too. Dried tears. I traced my fingers over one, seeing Gage as he'd rubbed my tear between his fingers. I blinked back the image and smirked at my hand. Just a palm away. I pressed that palm against bark.

Drunk bee bumping my parka.
Mountain biker zooming past.
Airborne pollen softening
everything's edges.

My nose tickled and I sneezed.

Steps approached. "Sov? Why aren't you at school?" Mom strode toward me.

My mouth fell open, but no words came. I melted with relief. Handler was wrong: Mom lived.

"Sov? Why are you wearing that parka?"

I stared at my Converse.

"Sov, honey. What's wrong?"

The care lacing her voice made tears charge my sight. Behind her head fluttered a brown butterfly with white-outlined wings.

"Did you and Gage break up?"

I straightened. "Gage?"

"Are you two having trouble?"

"What?"

"Push back that hood." Mom stepped forward, reached out, and my hood fell. She noticed my missing arm and unzipped my parka so the collar relaxed down, and she squinted at my sling. "What happened? Why wasn't I called?"

She noticed my red T-shirt, my dirty jeans, my Converse, and her nose crinkled. "You didn't leave home in those clothes. Sovern, what's going on?" She reached out to wipe my cheek, but I stepped back.

"Mom?" It was all I could muster.

She glanced at her watch. "Our meeting with Mr. Handler is in ten minutes."

"I need you." I started bawling.

She tilted her head. After a minute, she reached out to hug me. I wanted that hug so bad. "Step away from that tree, silly."

"I can't."

"Can't?"

"I'm not from here. I'm another Sov."

"What?" Worry built in her face.

"Could you just hug me? Just a hug?"

She seemed to actually see me then, how altered I must have been from the Sovern she lived with. She touched my cheek, and a wave shimmered out of it. Mom stepped back like she'd been shoved. Her eyes widened, then narrowed, and she stepped forward and wrapped her arms around me.

A stronger wave moved through us, and spruce needles rained down, but she held tight. I wished I had an arm to wrap around her too, instead of it being there between us. The love and comfort emitted by her embrace was exactly as I remembered it. My tears soaked her shoulder, but she didn't move till I stopped crying. I finally pulled back and dared her scrutiny.

"I think you owe me some answers," Mom said. "We're missing a meeting. You know how I feel about that kind of thing."

She still didn't get it. I studied her face, plain by anyone else's standards, yet so beautiful to me. I looked at her eyebrow's crescent scar and realized that another me was sitting in Handler's office, staring into that doorless courtyard and wondering where this Mom was. Mom was never late, and that other me would be worried. I was stealing Mom from myself. Like fate had stolen her from me. It made my head spin.

"I'm not your Sov."

"Of course you're mine."

I shook my head hard, but my lower lip trembled. I felt my palm against that trunk, bringing me to a Mom I could never have. How long could I keep her? "Go! Sorry!"

Mom nodded. "Okay." She held out her arm. "Come on."

Handler was right, after all. "I'm not your Sov! Be happy, Mom. I love you." I pulled my hand from the spruce.

Snow's crunch underfoot.
Cold's bite. Blue light.

A sense of transparency forced me to my knees. I gulped yet couldn't drink enough air. I wobbled to my feet but fell back down. I curled into a ball to hold myself together, to keep from disintegrating into a billion molecules that drifted away on the frosty air.

Bookmark:
Heisenberg's Uncertainty Principle
Werner Heisenberg

In the very measuring of an object, we affect it. The same is true for observing an object's position. This creates uncertainty when determining data.

21

"Sovern?" A chick's voice.

I reached toward full consciousness but I couldn't move. Couldn't talk.

"Sovern! Are you all right?"

I knew that voice. I'd heard it today. Yet I still couldn't place it.

"Sovern, I'm going to call for an ambulance."

Great: Shelley Millhouse. Could this day get any worse?

With every ounce of will I had, I sat up, swaying, my hands reaching out. No doubt I looked drunk.

"I'm calling now." I heard Shelley slide her phone from her pocket.

I forced out, "No!" My eyelids were bricks. They inched open, searching for light, but it was dark out. Had that much time passed? I discerned Shelley crouching next to me, phone in hand.

"You look terrible," she said. "We should call an ambulance."

"No!" I rolled onto my hands and knees. The world swayed, and I rocked back to kneeling. I glanced at her. Judgment covered her face.

"I'm not drunk. Or stoned." Despite trying not to, I slurred my words. "I'm not!"

She stood and looked down at me with horrified pity. "Okay, Sovern, you're not drunk or stoned."

I squinted at my knees till I could make out the weave in my jeans. My legs were very cold, I realized. My feet were pins and needles. My hands ice. I was shaking. I probably *could* use an ambulance, but *ambulance + me = how would I explain this to Dad?*

I took a deep breath and coughed on the icy air. I tried to stand. Shelley's arm came around my waist. With her help, I staggered to my feet, but I was bigger than her, and she worked hard to steady me. We swayed, and without thinking, I pressed my hand against that spruce.

Recreation path gone. Wildflowers.
A brown butterfly with white outlined wings.

Shelley gasped, and I yanked back my hand. I winced as she stumbled against my right side and flinched, mouth open.

"What was that?" she said.

"You saw it?"

Conflicting thoughts played across her face. I should

have let her think she was crazy. I definitely owed her, after how she'd ended our friendship.

"I told you I'm not drunk," I said.

She studied me. The dark translated her brown coat and hair to black.

"Fine," I said. "You're crazy." I turned and started toward the gondola, but I had to rest my hands on my knees to steady myself.

Shelley gripped my arm. "You need to get someplace warm."

"Can you help me to the gondola?" A quarter mile—I could endure her that far. She'd become such a goody-two-shoes—I couldn't stand her—yet she'd seen that vision. This crappy day's second confirmation that I wasn't insane.

"I live at City Center," I added. "Please, I'm trying to go home."

"You live on the mountain again?" Her face was contorted by how hard she was thinking.

"Obviously," I said.

She moved to my right side. She eyed me, and then touched me, testing. When nothing happened, she draped my arm across her shoulders. She glanced at the spruce.

We shuffled along the path. I was four inches taller than her, so my arm wasn't uncomfortable, but she still struggled to keep me upright and moving. After a hundred yards or so, I started to feel my feet touch the frosty asphalt. Sensation crept up my legs, and I began carrying my own weight.

Another five minutes, and I said, "I think I can walk

now." Shelley let go but escorted me like a bodyguard across Gem Bridge and up Ruby Street.

The gondola appeared, all lights against the night, ready to haul folks to dinner at the top. No skiers were around. The clock tower read 5:30, and I felt a millimeter of relief. At least it wasn't midnight. Dad would be home by now, but he hadn't been there long—I could come up with an excuse for being this kind of late. I straightened, willing myself strong enough to act like nothing had happened. We walked across the groomed snow to the gondola's maze.

"Thanks." I said it snotty.

Shelley gnawed her lip, definitely trying to make sense of the last twenty minutes.

I blew out a breath. "Actually, thanks."

"*You* made that happen," she said. Not a question.

"Don't tell anyone." Our eyes locked. "Please."

Dad's voice startled us. "Well, hello, Shelley. I haven't seen you in ages." He approached, holding a clipboard pressed against his chest.

Shelley croaked, "Yes."

He studied our odd expressions, but we didn't offer any explanation. "How are your folks?" he said.

"Good." Shelley Millhouse, reduced to one word answers.

Dad assessed us. "Going up?" he finally said to me.

I nodded, and he strolled to the lifthouse. Shelley and I watched him.

"See you," I said.

"See you," Shelley said. Her hands, deep in her pockets, pushed out the front of her coat.

At the lifthouse door, I glanced back, and she still stood there, watching. I nodded to her, and she nodded back. I followed Dad into a gondola car, my mind scrabbling for what to say. I slouched down, and Crystal Village rushed small below us as the car began its ascent.

"I had a meeting that ran late." Dad looked at me, expecting a reciprocal explanation, but I couldn't make myself lie, and I certainly couldn't tell him the truth. I slouched back against the glass wall, worn out.

"You haven't hung out with Shelley in years," he said carefully.

I snorted. "We just met on the path. I'm not good enough for perfect Shelley Millhouse."

I spotted her, still standing there, watching our car ascend. I looked at Dad—Mr. Practical. Mr. Safety—and felt like such a schmuck again. I tugged on his arm. He was still holding the clipboard, so he set it on the bench. My hand was warm in his. In his grip, I could feel him struggling against his need to demand an answer for why I was late. I squeezed his hand and looked down. In the gondola's murky light, my fair skin seemed to glow in his grip. I looked closer: my hand actually did emit a faint amber glow.

Dad eyed our hands. He scanned up at the gondola car's ceiling, around the windows, and back down at my hand. Searching, no doubt, for what might be making it glow.

"It's my skin!" I let go of his hand and held out my own, which gently illuminated the dark around it. I looked at my reflection in the glass, and my glowing face gaped back.

Silence was off the agenda now. I had to tell him. "I hugged Mom today."

He turned on the bench to look at me fully, his expression a stew of horror, pain, worry, and regret. He touched my cheek in wonder. "Sovern?"

"You've heard of quantum physics, yes?"

He frowned. "A little."

"Well, I'm living proof. I visited Mom in another universe today. I've visited her four times, but today we touched. And now..." I held up my hand, turned it.

Dad stiffened. "Sovern, listen to me. Your mother is dead—"

"No!" I said. He sounded just like Handler. "She lives! In multiple universes. In future ones, three of the times. Once when I was little."

"Universes?"

"Uh-huh. I'm not sure what they are really, or what you'd call them. I just know that the Soverns there aren't quite me, so they're not my future, or my past. The little-me, she didn't have dyslexia. The future ones, well, they had their acts together."

Dad ran his hand back over his crew cut. "Unzip your parka," he said.

I unzipped it and folded down the collar so he could see the skin at my neck.

He sucked in air. "What have you done to yourself?"

"It started when I crashed into that spruce on Shangri-La. I don't understand why, but that porcupine has something to do with it." Súmáí arrived in my mind, and I nudged him aside. One thing at a time. "Somehow, my accident opened a gateway. Sort of like the remote for our TV."

Dad just sat there, so I went on.

"If I touch the right kind of tree, a spruce with a certain shape—a porcupine has to be in it—I can see into a different universe. If I take my hand from the spruce, I'm back in my own reality."

"A spruce."

"Uh-huh."

"That's why you asked about the tree on Pride?"

"Uh-huh. I think these spruce might exist in multiple universes at once. Maybe all trees do, and the spruce are just gateways. Maybe everything—animals, rocks, plants—exists in multiple universes. Everything but us."

Dad sat straight, totally alert. I guessed it was partly from me speaking so many words. "Humans, you mean?"

"Uh-huh."

He squinted at the points of light from houses on the opposing mountainside. "How did she look?"

"Ah, Dad—she was Mom. She was so Mom. Her hug was so Mom."

He winced but stayed quiet. When we neared the Emerald West lodge, he said, "Let's ride around again."

Tourists did it all the time. We entered the lifthouse's harsh lights, and I looked at my hand. No glow in here. Dad plucked a spruce needle from my hair, and then slouched back against the car's glass wall and waved to the liftie when he peeked in. Nobody downloaded into our car, thank God, and we rounded the bullwheel. We whooshed out, the car rocking fore and aft as we descended back toward Crystal Village.

Dad said, "Sov, I don't know what to do. I don't know how to help you."

"Help?" He didn't believe me. I glared at him across the murk, lit by my body's glow. "Dad, look at me!" I gestured at myself.

"Sovern—"

"I'm not making this up!"

"Sov—"

"It's real!"

He shook his head like he hadn't heard me. "It's a good sign that you were with Shelley, but—"

"*That's* a good sign?" Why did the whole world think Shelley Millhouse was perfect? Except, just now, she'd kept silent for me, despite—

I suddenly knew how I could prove to Dad this was real. "I can take you to Mom!"

Dad focused on those points of light on the opposing mountain like they were a destination he'd never attain. He was quiet so long I said, "Dad?"

"At least you're talking." He shook his head. "Okay, Sov. Take me to her." From his tone, I could tell he was humoring me.

Bookmark:
The Copenhagen Interpretation
Niels Bohr

———

A quantum particle exists in all of its possible states at once. Only when observed is a quantum particle forced into one probability: the state that we observe. Since it may be forced into a different observable state each time, this explains why a quantum particle seems to behave erratically.

22

Dad stowed his clipboard with the lifties at the base, and we headed out of the gondola and through Crystal Village. I shivered, still not warm. Deep-down weariness made the world syrupy. Going back into the cold night like this and leading Dad to the spruce might be the dumbest thing I'd ever done, which was saying a ton.

"Could I hold your arm?" I said.

"Sure."

Dad glanced at me about every ten steps.

"I'm fine," I said.

When we reached the recreation path's spruce, I thought I could make out a porcupine-sized lump. Car lights on the interstate and frontage road a quarter mile away softened the darkness and showed him as a tense, resigned shadow. His doubt formed a cloud around us.

"Okay." I wriggled my arm out of its sling.

"Sov!"

"I'll put it back when we're done." My arm swished through my parka's sleeve, the brace tight against fabric, and I took Dad's calloused hand. "Whatever you do, don't let go."

I looked away from his pity and heard Crystal Creek's frozen gurgle. I glanced at the stars, said a silent prayer, and pressed my palm to bark.

Green grass shoots. Daylight
making me blink. A skiff of cloud.

Dad's grip on my hand tightened. His head swiveled around, and then he looked at me with wide eyes. "How—?"

Steps approached on the path, from the direction of school. I recognized their cadence and squeezed Dad's hand just as Mom appeared. She was dressed in the same skirt and blouse, but a ball of tissues bulged in her hand. The way she rounded the curve, staring at the spruce, I knew this was the Mom from earlier today. No doubt she was returning from the meeting with Handler and me. Had I brought us back to her—to this universe—by thinking of her? I realized that each time I'd seen her, the vision linked up with whatever I'd been thinking about when I touched the tree.

Now she halted and her hand came to her throat. "Briggs?"

"Taylor," Dad whispered.

"Briggs!" Mom rushed to him.

I squeezed Dad's hand to remind him not to let go. They hugged, and Dad's breath caught as a wave shimmered through me. Spruce needles drizzled down. Mom rested her head against his chest, her mouth open in a sob. There, so close, was that crescent scar.

Dad pressed his cheek to her hair. He breathed hard and strands of blond pulled into his lips.

"You're alive!" Mom said.

Dad weaved his cast hand's fingertips through her hair and pressed them against the back of her neck. Mom gasped, then smiled. Her hand rose to the back of his neck, lower down, near the base's bump. Their most intimate gesture, which always made me look away. Dad leaned down, Mom reached up, and they kissed. This time, I couldn't look away. I might need to remember this moment forever.

As I watched, I realized Dad's suffering was ten times mine. Love like theirs happened rarely, and, even here across universes, was a force beyond reckoning. *Dad + Mom = me. Me = their love.* If their love was erased, what became of me?

The shimmering increased to sparks that robbed my breath. The spruce vibrated, so I pressed my palm harder against it. Mom stepped back, and her hand against Dad's chest still held tissues. Soggy tissues. She smiled at me, and I tried to smile back, but I was suddenly so tired and I felt consciousness slipping away.

"Sov?" she said.

"Taylor!" Dad's voice was a coyote howl.

Snow mashing my cheek. Stars blinking through the spruce's branches.
Dad's warmth collapsing across my legs.

Our clasped hands let go.

––––––––––

I woke on my feet, a strong arm around my waist.

"Dad?"

"Sov." Dad's voice was not next to me.

"Shelley?" I said and blinked. I blinked till I recognized Súmáí, straining to keep Dad and me on our feet.

"I think I can help now." Dad appeared on my right, his face and neck emitting a faint glow. Around my waist, his arm overlapped Súmáí's.

They propelled me forward, my Converse skidding along the frosty recreation path. After a bit, I started moving my feet with them and got my weight over my legs again. I wanted so badly to take in Súmáí—he was *real* and I was *not* insane—but I was drunk with fatigue. We crossed the bridge and ascended Ruby Street in a hazy déjà vu. The gondola came into view, and Súmáí stopped.

Dad looked at him and then at me. "Sov, do you think you can walk?"

I let go of their arms and stood on my own. I managed three wobbly steps. "If I hold your arm."

Dad stepped forward and held out his arm. Súmáí stayed back. Dad turned, puzzled, and I realized he thought Súmáí was just a liftie who'd happened upon us.

"Thanks," I said.

Súmáí nodded to Dad.

I could see Dad weighing things, knew he wished this liftie would say nothing about finding us, but he couldn't even ask because it would look bad. Poor Dad: wish granted.

I held up my hand to wave. Súmáí held up his hand, and despite everything, our gaze turned familiar. Dad saw this, and then locked onto Súmáí's hat. I turned and clutched Dad's arm, and we promenaded toward the gondola. I had to force every step away from Súmáí. I willed myself not to look back. Dad and I entered a car and collapsed on its bench. At the last instant, a liftie stuck in his head.

"Your clipboard, Briggs."

I could tell it took all of Dad's energy to sit up and take it. Across the top sheet, *vandalism* was scrawled in his left-handed writing.

"Thanks," he managed.

The doors closed. Despite my grogginess, I felt torn in two, half of me wanting to pry those doors open and sprint to Súmáí, the other half wanting to be with Dad. He slouched back and dropped the clipboard onto the bench. After a minute, he drew his phone from his jacket's pocket and dialed.

"Wash. You at the cabin? Good. We need a ride home from the gondola. Pronto."

As we rose past Gage's house, I looked for him through his bedroom window, but he wasn't there. Today's Mom had asked about him.

I pictured her and Dad's kiss and saw the soggy tissues in her hand. I felt Súmáí's arm around my waist and saw Dad recognize his hat. The gondola car bounced over pulleys at the top of a tower. Everything seemed to swirl on the same breath. My world reeled, and, for the third time that day, I lost consciousness.

Bookmark:
Wave Function

When plotted on a graph, all the possible
states of an object take the form of a
wave. This is called wave function.

23

The sun striped across me, and crows squawked a ruckus out the cabin's bedroom window. I rubbed sleep from my face and held up my hands. No glow. Yet if I looked closely, I fancied the sunlight passed through them like watery milk.

Sitting up, weary to the bone, I hovered my hand over the down comforter. Its shadow seemed half as dark as it used to be. I took a chest-filling sip of air. I couldn't remember riding with Wash on the snowmobile. Nothing after passing out in the gondola car.

A mug clunked against the table, and one of its chairs creaked with weight. The alarm clock on the nightstand read 9:30 am. No school for me today, that was for sure. And it was Tuesday, Dad's day off. Had it really only been a week since my accident? An odd symmetry seemed to surround that. Last night, showing Dad the truth had seemed brilliant. I remembered his howl as Mom had been yanked from his arms. Because of me, he'd lost her a second time. I'd hurt him again. I'd been an idiot.

I threw back the covers and shambled to the bedroom door. I leaned against its jamb and watched Dad sip coffee. He set down the mug and studied his cast hand. From where I stood, I could see the fine dark hairs that covered the tops of his fingers, and the cast, grungy from use, was signed by all of ski patrol. Yet I knew he was remembering the pulse of Mom's neck beneath his fingertips.

I slid into the chair next to him and took that hand. His eyes seemed chapped around their rims. "I'm sorry," I said.

He clamped his lips and shook his head.

Silence seemed the best conversation. I listened carefully to that silence and could make out the sounds of the lifts running and overlapping conversations, each with its own purpose. So many lives. So many realities.

"I don't know what that was," Dad said. "Where we were last night. But in that place, *I*, not your mother, was dead."

I remembered Mom saying *You're alive!* and thought of the soggy tissues. She'd been meeting with Handler. Might it have been because the me in that universe wasn't handling Dad's death? That scenario played out in my mind till Dad said, "Seems the Briggs are doomed to suffer."

"Gage told me brigs are sailing ships. Beautiful sailing ships."

Dad snorted.

I leaned down into his line of sight. "Dad. One time, I visited another universe, a different one from where we were yesterday. You and Mom and me, we were all walking down that path. It was summer, and I think I'd just graduated because Mom was talking about MIT. We were all happy, and I was going there."

He searched my face for truth.

"There could be endless universes out there. Maybe even one where you and Mom never had me."

His gaze seemed to tilt, and he sagged back in his chair. "It doesn't matter."

"What?"

"You could explain it all, demonstrate the mathematical reality of what happened last night, prove it beyond doubt—"

"It's *real*."

"But it doesn't matter! Sov—" He realized his loud voice and spoke quieter. "*This* is our life. *This* is what we've been dealt."

"But it doesn't have to stay this way. That was another universe, yes? Maybe one aspect of time. But I also think time is curved and can be bent. If that's true, maybe a person can go back in her *own* time and *change* things."

Dad gripped his cast with his other hand and squeezed it a little. After a minute, he shook his head. "I don't know if I believe in God, but that sounds morally wrong."

I laughed once and spit out, "Morally?" I gathered my composure. "Listen, Mom could be alive, with us, here! I could go back to that moment in the car, keep my mouth shut, and she'd keep her hand on the steering wheel, and—"

"Don't do that to yourself!" I'd never told him before

that I'd killed Mom. Now, he looked furious. "Sov, you cannot blame yourself for her death. It was an accident."

I shook my head. "You weren't there, Dad. I was whining about school, and she put her hand on my leg to comfort me. I'm sorry."

Dad grunted. "God, Sov, is this why you haven't talked?" He shook his head. "It's not your fault!"

"You weren't there!" I yelled.

"Do you remember why you even were on the highway that day?" He was almost whispering. "You were on your way to pick *me* up from a meeting. I'd suggested you girls come get me, and we'd all go out for dinner afterward. Remember?"

I nodded.

"I've spent the last year feeling like *I* caused that crash. I checked the weather that morning. I knew the storm was coming; I should have changed our plans." He shook his head. "It's time to move on, Sov."

We sat in silence for a long time, both of us reluctant to give up guilt.

"Last night, we were unconscious in freezing temperatures," he finally said. "If that liftie hadn't come along, we could have died. Whatever you're doing, it's dangerous. Really dangerous."

I wanted to spout something about Súmáí, but I realized that real as he might be, Súmáí wasn't from *my* life. I might never see him again. And I hadn't told Dad how I'd also been unconscious in the cold all alone, only to be woken by Shelley.

"Sovern, I can't control you—you've certainly proven

that over the last year—but I'm begging you: please, don't go wherever that is anymore. If I lost you too…"

I remembered how, during my rescue, he'd stared at Phantom Peak like it was a lifeline. Poor Dad. He was the most important person in my world. Why did I keep screwing up?

"Promise you won't go back," he repeated.

I looked at my translucent hands.

"Sovern, please!"

"I promise."

Dad blew out his breath, walked to the counter, and poured himself another cup of coffee.

"When'd you get up?" I asked.

He returned to the table. "I never really went to bed."

We both flinched as his phone rang. His ringtone was "Strawberry Fields," one of his and Mom's favorite songs. They'd been crazy for the Beatles. I'd loaded it on his phone the week before Mom died. It vibrated too, shuddering against the table's hardness like Mom's trapped spirit trying to bust out.

"Hello. Yes, Perry." Perry was Handler's first name. Dad looked at me as he spoke. "I know she's absent. She's here with me. We both have a bug. Thanks for calling."

Dad set his phone back on the table, all thoughtful. He sat down, placed his forearms on either side of it, and leaned toward me, intent.

"Now, tell me why that guy last night—that guy who happened to show up on the recreation path, at night, just when we needed him—was wearing my hat."

I shrugged.

"I checked. That hat's gone from the basket."

I reached out, ran my finger up a red tulip's petal. If Dad thought visiting Mom was morally wrong, Súmáí would put him over the top. Especially since I suspected Súmáí was the vandal.

"I never get these right," I said.

"What?"

"The flowers never look how Mom had them."

Dad sighed and shook his head. "Don't do that to yourself, Sov."

"His name's Súmáí."

"Unusual name," Dad said.

I shrugged.

"And he's a liftie?"

"Uh-huh." I'd been prepared to spill the truth, but Dad was giving me an out. It wasn't really a lie—somewhere in time, Súmáí *did* work on the mountain, doing whatever it was that employed the Utes back then. Erecting wickiups? Hunting? Gathering nuts and berries? Was he from the past of this universe, or the past of another? Maybe even the present of another.

"Are you dating him?"

"It's not like that."

Dad's face relaxed. "Then how did he get my hat?"

"I met him on one of my snowshoe hikes. I was wearing it, and he needed a hat. That's all."

"And last night?"

I shrugged. "Right place, right time?"

Dad searched my face for truth. I could see when he decided to drop it. "You're not wearing your sling."

"My arm's fine."

"Wear it," he said.

"Dad!"

"Wear it!"

I shot the heat from my eyes at the table and ran my thumbnail down a curve of woodgrain. I shoved back, chair screaking, and stalked toward the bedroom.

"Sovern," he said as I reached the door. "I only want what's best for you."

I turned around, surprised. Usually he just abandoned me to my rage.

"The accident, school, Gage, the whole last year, now this ... even these flowers. You're destroying yourself trying to keep her alive. You didn't kill her, and you have to accept that she's gone."

My hand pressed my stomach.

"*This* is our universe, Sov. *This* is what life has given us. Our test."

"Screw tests!"

Dad shook his head. "It doesn't work that way."

"Just because you see the world through antique eyes doesn't mean I have to! The world is so different from what you've believed. Don't *you* see? Did you know that right now, right here"—I threw out my arm—"nine, maybe eleven dimensions surround us? Not three. Eleven! We just can't perceive them, and just because we can't perceive a thing doesn't mean it doesn't exist!"

"Doesn't it?" He scanned the wood floor at his side like it held truth and shook his head.

"Dad, I can tap other universes! Maybe other times. Why me? Why now?"

"You're far sharper than me about these things. No doubt about it. But things are the way they are for a reason. Just because you *can* do a thing, doesn't mean you *should*. It's not right."

Was he really saying "can" like that, after I'd repeated it yesterday, trying to hold on to my promise to be good? Another failed test. It felt like life was yanking the rug out from under my feet. But a grain of truth in what he'd said hit me like a punch. I barked a growl of frustration and threw my hands in the air. It stole my energy, and I slumped against the doorjamb. Dad was with me in a second, helping me to bed, but I could tell he felt puny too.

Bookmark:
Many Worlds Theory
Hugh Everett III

———————

Observation does not stop quantum matter
from behaving in multiple forms, rather it makes
quantum matter split into copies of itself to
account for all its possibilities. These
possibilities proceed independently.

24

Dad finally conked out, so I hung in the main room, grumpy from his stubbornness, but also because I'd failed and hurt him again. I needed to conquer two days of homework, the last thing I wanted to do. I pulled out my phone and found *I Know Why the Caged Bird Sings.*

Outside, snow fell in wet clots that the wind chucked at everything. I prayed Súmáí wasn't in it. First week of March, our biggest snow month. Our doctor visit was a week from Saturday. I hoped I'd be able to snowboard soon.

Rhythmic snores forced their way under the closed bedroom door. Dad had never slept in the middle of the day like this, not even after Mom died. Mostly he came to bed after me and got up first. He loosed a honker snore, then there was a pause, and I pictured him rolling over. I must have been sleeping pretty heavily not to be woken by that at night. I remembered Wash's snores from when I was little, when we'd both slept in the cabin's main room. After Wash, a person could sleep through a bomb blast.

Hungry, I went to the cupboard and mentally thanked Wash. He'd obviously been to City Market the day before. It was almost noon, so I felt okay about choosing a bag of potato chips. I pinched it open and reclined on the couch. I set the bag in the cranny between my hip and the couch's green velvet and slid on my headphones.

Angelou's voice filled my head, and I ate. And ate. The book turned really sad. She had to leave Stamps, Arkansas, for a new life with her parents. Her new life, the life she'd dreamed of for years, was awful. Awful, like getting raped by her mother's boyfriend. Angelou finally told someone, and the boyfriend was murdered, probably by family and friends. Sure that she'd caused his death, Angelou quit talking.

Had Lindholm chosen this book for *my* benefit? Did she know *I'd* quit talking because my whining had caused that crunched Honda? I cringed, remembering myself the day I hit the Shangri-La tree, yelling at the interstate. Loosing that wail after the porcupine shot its quills in me. Tucker, Wash, and Dad flinching as I let go a third wail, at fate. That last one over Pride's edge. Yesterday, I'd even yelled at Handler. Last night, my words had brought Dad to that tree. Why couldn't I just shut up? Protect the world from me with silence?

I glanced at the bedroom door. On 2/22, something in me had *needed* to scream. To hurl my rage on the air. I studied my hands, heard Dad's snore, and pressed my lips tight.

I reached into the chip bag but found I'd polished off

the whole thing. I returned to the cupboard and snagged a bag of tortilla chips. I pinched it open and set it next to my hip just like the first. I ate. And ate. I bit the chips in pieces, sucking on them till the salt was gone, then chewing the mush. Corn chips devoured, I headed to the cupboard and came back with a box of wheat crackers, coaching myself to speak only when necessary.

A knock sounded at the door. I stood, forgetting about the crackers and spilling them. Wash opened the door, and I held my fingers to my lips.

"Hey," he whispered. "How long's he been out?" He was carrying a sheet cake topped with foil, no doubt from Crispy.

I herded crackers back into their box, brushed crumbs off the cushion, and wondered how much Dad had told him about what had happened. "Couple hours." Those words couldn't hurt anyone.

Wash shook his head. "What happened last night? You two were toast."

"Lunch?"

"Hell yes!" Wash whispered. He set the cake on the table.

I got out fixings for peanut butter and honey sandwiches. His favorite.

"Get those potato chips I bought."

"Gone."

"Get the corn chips then."

"Gone."

"And you were chowing crackers when I got here? Hungry or what?"

I shrugged. He eyed me, turned his head slightly, and listened to Dad's snore. "He's never done this."

I stared at the four slices of bread I'd laid out. I ladled the knife into the peanut butter and spread it. Wash grabbed the honey, but it was cold and thick. He walked to the microwave, popped the lid, and set the bear-shaped container in for thirty seconds.

"Big John, Tucker, all the guys send their regards." He returned and coated every millimeter of the bread golden. "They miss your smiling face."

I grunted, flashed him a *whatever* smile, and slapped the peanut butter slices on top.

Wash took his sandwich. Honey dribbled down the sides and onto his hand. He tore into it, which is how Wash ate everything. He usually consumed two, maybe three sandwiches, so I left the things out. I took a bite and chewed. Honey ran down my hand too, and I sucked it off. Next thing I knew, I'd brought the salt shaker from the counter and was coating my sandwich. I took a bite, and it tasted so right.

Wash watched me, lips pursed. "I could just get you a salt lick. Mount it on a stick so you could carry it around like a lollipop."

My mouth fell open.

"Manners," Wash whispered.

Salt.

"Sov, what the hell's going on around here? Last night you two were rag dolls. I had to sit you in front and your Dad behind, then strap you both to me so you wouldn't fall off the snowmobile."

It felt weird, hearing things that I'd done without even knowing it.

"Now Briggs is in there sawing logs," Wash continued. "Middle of the day! And you're out here, not at school. Inhaling salt like ... like ... "

"A porcupine," I whispered.

"Yes!"

Wash watched as my mind raced over that discovery. "Sov ... you, Briggs, the guys, and Tara ... you're my only family."

I considered silence, and how it could hurt people too. Yesterday, I'd resolved to be good. I factored in the danger of the spruce trees. Why couldn't I settle into a steady rising equation?

I sighed. "I know." I looked at my left hand, resting on the table in a slab of sunlight, and as I laid that hand on Wash's arm, it cast a thick shadow. "You're all my family too," I said, and I felt that promise to be good surge back to me.

Bookmark:
Quantum Immortality

In quantum theory, a person dying is only
one of two possibilities. In another "branch"
of that person's "universal tree," he survives.

25

As I strode into school the next morning, warmth burned my cold cheeks. Dr. Bell stood facing the big steps, the immigrant girls listening. Some mornings, they'd be bawling, and word would spread that the authorities had rounded up and deported their parents. At least their parents are alive, I thought, but then I felt guilty. I still had Dad and Wash and my ski-patrol family. And now I lived in the cabin. I pushed back my hood and smelled the janitor's barfy cleaner lingering on the air.

In the first hall, lockers slamming seemed like a sort of drumroll. I dreaded facing Shelley Millhouse in English. She'd had a whole day to reflect on what had happened at the spruce, and that couldn't be good. She'd probably stare at me the whole period.

She didn't stare, though. Instead, she turned sideways

in her front-row desk and never even looked at me, and I studied the false-calm way her elbow rested across the back of her seat. What could she possibly be thinking? Neither of us contributed to class discussion—I barely heard it, actually—and I was glad for the voice recorder on my desk. To stop myself from staring at Shelley, I studied my palm.

Class ended, and Shelley bolted. I blew out my breath and gathered my folder, pencil, and copy of *I Know Why the Caged Bird Sings*. I was close to last out of the room, thinking how weak I'd been after my last two travels through the spruce. On my earlier visits, I'd been mentally shaken but physically okay. Touching Mom must have been what made me so weak. Dad had been weak too, and he'd kissed Mom.

I remembered Súmáí miming an explosion. Though I'd understood what he'd meant at the time, it finally sank in: I *could not* touch those vision-selves. If touching Mom had made me that weak, touching another me would probably mean death. Maybe the death of more than just me.

I rolled my eyes and then my shoulders. It doesn't matter anyway, I thought. I promised. I can.

"Hey." Shelley was leaning against a section of locker-less wall.

"Hey," I said.

"You all right?" she asked. "You were absent yesterday."

"I'm fine."

At the hall's far end, someone shouted above the slamming lockers, and we both looked that direction. Shelley glanced at people passing and whispered, "What *was* that, Sovern?"

"It's complicated—"

"Try me," she said.

"I don't—"

"I'm not as dumb as you think," she said. "I may not be a genius like you, but I'm not stupid."

"Genius?" I laughed.

Shelley grimaced. "What happened?"

"Forget it."

"I *lied* for you," she said.

"You didn't say a word."

Shelley grimaced again. She was right, no doubt, and if she hadn't come along and found me, things could have been really bad.

I took a long drag of air. "I think maybe it was another universe."

I had to hand it to Shelley. She just swallowed once, nodded, and said, "I thought so."

"Honestly?"

"It's the only logical solution. Clark is studying physics at CU." Clark was her brother. "He's so into all this stuff. He's always talking about it."

"You can't tell anyone," I said.

"So you were…what…*drained* from visiting another universe?"

I pressed my lips and shrugged.

"What are you doing, Sovern?"

"I'm not *doing* anything."

One of Shelley's eyebrows shot up.

"It just happened. Really. Don't tell anyone."

She squinted at me and held out a white scrap of paper.

I took it. "What's this?"

"My number. I want to help."

"Help?"

"Yes. With whatever. You're doing research or something, right?"

I shook my head.

"Well, you should. You could change the world."

"*Change the world?*"

Shelley stomped her foot. "For a freaking genius, you are so dumb sometimes! God! Think beyond yourself, Sovern."

Think beyond myself? I'd been doing nothing else for the last twenty-four hours. "I do things alone," I said.

I stepped past her and headed to my locker without looking back. Yet all through lunch, Shelley's words and her expression repeated in my brain. Especially *You could change the world.*

My head was raw by the time I approached Calculus. But during class, Gage only glanced at me once. I started studying him, for a change, from my seat by the window as he stared ahead and took notes. Gage, taking notes? When class ended, he gathered his stuff and dashed.

I ambled down the hall, watching my Converse and considering assumptions we make about other people. *You could change the world.* I switched out my books at my locker and headed to Handler's office. *You could change the world.* He looked up from his desk. *You could change the world.*

"Hello, Sovern."

I imagined him saying *Hello, Sovern* to me in other universes. Each Sovern different somehow. Of course, Handler'd be different too.

He shut his door but for an inch. I studied the entryless courtyard. *You could change the world.* He sat behind his desk, orange golf shirt a blur against my vision. "Is your father feeling better?" he said.

"Uh-huh." Yesterday, *Dad + salt = he returned to work this morning.* The rims of his eyes still looked chapped, though. "He knows about me researching quantum physics. I told him." *This is the life we've been given. Our test.*

Handler nodded.

"So our agreement's off. I don't *have* to be here." I'd planned to end the meeting after saying that, but the unexpected ways Shelley and Gage were acting now made me sit a moment longer. Mostly, I needed relief from Shelley's voice repeating, *You could change the world.* I ran my fingers over my lips and imagined sealing them.

"You left here pretty upset two days ago," Handler said. "Do you want to talk about it?"

Two days? Was that all it was? It seemed like a month.

"Sovern, what I was trying to express was that you can still love your mother after her death."

The room heated up a hundred degrees, and my hand came to my stomach. I fluttered my fingers to ease the adrenaline craving surging through me. If I admitted Mom was really gone, it would change everything. Loving a ... *dead person* was a different sort of love. I'd glimpsed it once, right before I started dating Gage, and it had scared me way more than my accident with the Shangri-La spruce or sailing off Pride. It had made my innards churn and made me crave acts like ditching, riding at speed's dangerous edge, or nicotine kisses. Anything that would blot out the hollow void of loving a dead thing.

I looked into Handler's penetrating gaze and sneered. "Never." I moved to the door, not waiting for a pass to Art. "Like I said, Dad knows now, so we're done."

After school, I headed to City Market and bought six bags of chips and a cylinder of sea salt. I loped out the doors to find Gage's BMW idling at the curb. Its passenger window descended and Gabe leaned over. "Hey," he said. "Need a ride?"

I looked toward the recreation path. "I'll walk."

"It's cold."

"I'm tough."

He laughed. "Don't I know it."

Our eyes met, and though mine still emitted fury from my meeting with Handler, his lacked anger and rebellion.

"Are you stalking me?" I said.

"Listen, you don't answer texts and you're hard as hell to find. There's something I want to say. Can I give you a ride?"

"I'm walking," I said.

"You're carrying two bags of groceries."

"They're light."

He snorted. "You are one stubborn chick. Over there."

He chin-pointed toward the back side of the lot, where the spur from the recreation path entered. Window zooming up, he pulled away.

I stepped out of the flow of the shopping traffic, considering bolting. Across the lot, Gage climbed from his car and pressed his fob. The BMW's lights flashed and it beeped.

He walked toward me. "Can I take a bag?"

I shook my head.

"Give me a bag. I'll feel stupid letting a one-armed chick carry two bags."

Sighing, I gave him one, which he took in his outside hand so we could walk closer. We listened to the soft snare drum of swaying plastic bags, and a bubble of awkwardness surrounded us.

"Are you pissed at me?" he said. "I can't blame you. I've been an asshole." He paused to let this sink in. "I tried to apologize, but really, I should just have listened. You bring out the asshole in me, Sovern."

I glanced at him. He seemed pale again, and his gait was slow.

"I didn't know I was supposed to answer those texts," I said.

Gage grinned at the clouds, shook his head, and said, "You're the coolest chick I know."

"You don't look right, Gage. Are you sick?"

"Just tired. Sovern, listen. I can't explain it—I've tried, believe me—but it feels like I'm supposed to be with you. In whatever way it works out."

I bit my lip as my anger drained away. In that one vision,

Mom had seemed genuinely sad that Gage and I might have broken up. Did that mean we were destined to be together?

We approached the spruce on the recreation path, and I kept walking but studied the trampled snow at its base. I recognized Súmáí's moccasin print on the path's edge. From two days ago? Or might he be lurking in the forest right now? I scanned around.

After we crossed the Gem Bridge, our steps sounding hollow on the wood, Gage said, "Sovern?"

I stopped. Gage stopped. I forced myself to face him square. He looked haggard, but the play of symmetry between his lips, nose, and brown eyes below that knit cap must have fit into some equation for beauty, because it had always been irresistible to me.

"I'd bore you," I said.

"Sovern. We snowboarded together constantly. We liked the same music. We laughed at the same things. You're brilliant. Even if you don't talk much, even if you don't get social stuff like texting, just being with you feels ... well ... right."

My eyes longed to flee, but I kept them on his face. He'd told me he loved me—so brave—and look what I'd done. Maybe I wasn't fully recovered after all, because I swayed. Gage steadied my arm. When I looked up, both of us were uncharted territory. Variables.

I wanted to kiss him, but if I was going to promise Dad about staying away from trees, I was also going to make good on what I'd told him about being done with Gage.

We started toward the gondola, heard its hum, and he said, "Where are you going, anyway?"

"We moved."

"Moved?"

"To City Center," I said.

"Seriously?"

"Uh-huh. It's great."

"When?"

"Five days ago."

Gage gazed up the gondola's cables. He walked slower, scratching the back of his head through his hat, and I sensed he was revising the reality he'd imagined me in over the last five days, moved his images of what I was doing up to City Center. He stopped at the lift's rope maze. "Wish I had my pass."

The liftie checked mine with his hand scanner through my parka's pocket.

I held out my hand, and Gage gave me the grocery sack. "That's a lot of chips."

"Bye."

He leaned forward and kissed me, just above my jaw-bone. He smelled like laundry soap. He shoved his hands in his jeans pockets and walked to the gondola's far side, no doubt heading up the run's edge to his house. He paused and waved. I waved.

I boarded a gondola car and set the bags on the seat. I watched him, miniature below me, headed up the groomed slope to his house.

Sure, he'd always turned me molten. Sure, he'd always been illogically attractive to me, but I'd always assumed I'd really only been using him to get Dad's attention. Yet we did like the same music. We did laugh at the same jokes. Things did feel right, somehow, when I was with him. Might there be a way Dad could accept him? My thoughts leapt to Súmáí, and confusion's weight sagged me. Súmáí wasn't even from my reality.

For relief, I tore my gaze from Gage, the size of my pinkie now. I formed in my mind the Sovern who Dad wanted me to be. The Sovern from before Mom died. Yet Mom-less. A Sovern who didn't rebel. A Sovern who accepted life and moved forward. A Sovern who didn't date Gage. A Sovern who loved a dead mother. A Sovern whose equation curved up.

Bookmark:
Action at a Distance

An object can be moved, changed, or
affected by another object even though they
are separated in space. Causes for this
could be electromagnetism or gravity.

26

Day nine of no palm to spruce—and no cigarettes, no pot, no alcohol, no movies, no Gage outside of school. My goal was to make it to tomorrow and achieve double-digit days of good behavior.

Now, in Calculus, Kenowitz said, "These equations we're starting today involve motion in two dimensions, and suddenly things become more confusing. With motion in one dimension, you are dealing with either vertical motion (y in terms of t) or horizontal motion (x in terms of t). With these next equations, you are combining these ideas. Picture the flight of a soccer ball that has been kicked. It moves vertically and horizontally. Be careful not to confuse the speed of the object with the slope of its path. It has to do with the fact that dy over dx is the slope, but dy over dt is vertical velocity and dx over dt is horizontal velocity. Combining them, dy over dx equals dy over dt over dx over dt. This is different from the speed."

I raised my hand.

"Sovern?" Kenowitz said.

"I know an easier way."

His grin was priceless.

At the SMART Board, I said, "It's simpler to add another dimension like this."

Kenowitz studied what I'd written, nodding for a full minute. "Okay," he said. "Let's try this on the next problem."

As I returned to my seat by the window, pride was pasted on Gage's face.

Of course the shortcut worked on the next problem. And all the rest. Kenowitz switched off the SMART Board. He looked across the room. "People, let's do the homework tonight incorporating Sovern's method."

The bell rang and everyone's attention turned to leaving. I stacked my folder, book, and calculator and kept my eyes from the window, like I had for nine days.

Kenowitz stood by the door. "Sovern?" He waited for everyone to leave. "I've been teaching for twenty-one years, was in college and grad school for six years before that. In all that time, I have never met a math genius—"

I laughed. "*Genius?*"

Kenowitz's face turned stern and he nodded. "A true *genius*. Sovern, I don't want to embarrass you, but it's important that you understand you have a *gift*."

I pressed my lips not to argue.

Gage waited for me in the hall. We walked along, me confused and off balance.

"That new *Star Trek* movie's out Friday. Want to go?" he said.

I was playing Kenowitz's praise over and over in my head. "Huh?"

"*Star Trek*. Want to go Friday night?"

"Oh."

"Don't sound so excited."

"It's just—"

"Just what?" Gage said.

"It's Dad…"

"He doesn't like me."

"I pretty much used you to drive him nuts."

"Used me?" He snorted. "I guess I did the same to my folks."

My steps faltered. *I* couldn't be that bad. But as I scanned over the last year, I saw that any sane parent would have flipped out at their son dating the person I'd been. Mom would be so upset, knowing that.

Seconds ago, I'd been sorting through a compliment. Now, my legs wouldn't support the weight of who I'd been, so I lunged to a stretch of blue wall and propped myself against it.

"Right now, I just need to figure out things with Dad," I said.

Gage shrugged. "How about I talk to him?"

"What?"

"Convince him I'm not so bad. Tell him I'm turning over a new leaf."

I opened my eyes. Had he actually said *leaf*?

"Sovern?"

Everything seemed connected in some equation I had no clue how to form. Double-digits, I told myself. Keep your equation curving up. I shook my head. "I need some space." I bolted down the hall before I could change my mind. It conjured when I'd walked away from Shelley, and that made me feel even worse.

———————

Friday night—day eleven post-spruce—Dad and I burrowed on the couch watching a sci-fi movie. My first movie since the accident. I felt proud of that. Proud, too, that I wasn't at *Star Trek* with Gage.

Dad was in a thoughtful mood. No doubt our time at the spruce was still right there with him. Way to go, Sovern, I thought.

"Popcorn?" I said.

He paused the movie as I went to the kitchen and slid a bag into the microwave. The lit microwave hummed, the bag swelling inside.

"I haven't had a call from Handler in a while." Dad turned to me over the couch's back.

I leaned my hip into the counter.

"Thanks," he said.

Kernels started bulleting the bag.

"I saw Gage today," he said.

"What?"

"At the halfpipe."

The halfpipe had stadium lights and stayed open till ten on Fridays and Saturdays. Gage and I used to free-ride on Crystal Mountain's runs mostly, but some weekends we'd hung at the pipe.

"A kid missed his trick and landed on the table." Landing on the table, the horizontal top edges of the halfpipe, was the worst kind of accident.

"And?"

"He's alive, but his back's in pieces."

"Was Gage with the guy?"

"No. But he approached me afterward and asked if we could talk. It took me a minute to put together who he was, since I've only seen him a couple times."

I grew interested in the wood floor, shamed by how Gage and I had lurked around. "And?"

"And he asked permission to date you. Like asking permission to marry or something."

I swallowed back a fierce anger. "What did he say?"

"Something like, *Mr. Briggs, sir, I know we got off on the wrong foot, but, well, I'm reforming, cleaning up my act. Sovern is about the best thing that's ever happened to me. We've been broken up, but I wonder if you'd mind if we started going out again.*"

The microwave pinged off. I couldn't keep myself from saying, "And?"

"He seemed so sincere that I gave him my blessing."

"Blessing?"

"Well, not in so many words, but I said it was fine." Dad chuckled, and I wished I could glimpse the scene playing out before his eyes. "Not sure how this affects that liftie... Súmáí?"

"Dad, Súmáí's not—" I stopped myself before saying *from this world.*

Dad gave me a look and turned back to the TV.

I pinched open the popcorn, steaming my face. I poured it into a bowl and coated it with extra salt. I carried the bowl and a glass of water to the coffee table. Dad already had a brown bottle of beer. I settled beside him and as he turned it in his hand, I considered that round bottle's symmetry. In two dimensions, that symmetry was infinite. I considered three dimensions and pictured a sphere. A sphere like the soap bubble membranes of universes.

"I liked Gage." Dad nudged me with his shoulder.

I'd just shoved a handful of popcorn into my mouth, and I gave him a lumpy smile. I eyed the glass of water and thought of Súmáí's wonder when I'd given him a glass just like this. Such a simple thing.

"I can tell him no." Dad watched me.

"It's fine." I was equal parts pissed at Gage and flattered.

"Something's not right."

"I just wish I could take back the last year."

Dad scratched his cheek. "So do I." He leaned forward and nudged me again. "Can't wait for our doc appointments tomorrow."

I knew he was just being nice. Saturday mornings were his busiest times, and no doubt this Saturday appointment was about me not missing any more school. "I hope I'll be able to snowboard again. It's supposed to dump tonight."

"I hope I'll get this cast off, so I can drive." We both knew he meant a snowmobile.

Dad sighed, relaxed back, and pressed play. Don't ask me what happened in the rest of the movie; my head churned with confusion about Gage.

Bookmark:
Entanglement

Entanglement results when two particles
meet and develop a link sharing one existence.
Even widely separated in space, measurement of one
influences the other. These particles are expressed by
the same mathematical equation, or wave function.
Because it cannot be explained, this is
also known as spooky action.

27

After our doctor appointments, Dad and I bypassed Crystal Mountain's ten-o'clock rush-hour crowd by using the employee line to get to the gondola. Then we would hop on a snowmobile—Dad had gotten his cast off, so he could drive, and I was free of my sling, though I was supposed to keep wearing the brace.

In the gondola car, we kept waving around our freed limbs, testing them out. Having my arm in my parka's sleeve felt so good, even if it was tight over the brace.

As we crested a row of cliffs, a group of snowboarders stood at the edge, trying to muster the guts to jump.

"Job security for you," I said.

Dad grunted.

We sped into the lifthouse, and Dad and I moved around the knot of skiers and boarders to one of two snowmobiles adjacent the ski-patrol station. We climbed on, and he drove cautiously up the edge of Sunset Ridge. It felt good to have him driving again. Like our life could maybe settle into something resembling normal. He pulled up in front of the cabin, and I climbed off.

"Take it easy!" he said over the loud engine.

"I will if you will!"

I entered the cabin, grinning and shaking my head. *Take it easy*. Neither Dad nor I knew how to do that.

I slid my hand into my jeans' back pocket and found Shelley's phone number. The jeans had been washed, and the scrap of paper was limp with frayed edges. I plopped onto the couch and unfolded it. Her phone number, written in blue ink, was blurred but still readable. *I want to help*, Shelley had said. I tried to remember the details of our split in sixth grade. Kenowitz had called me a true genius— maybe I'd intimidated her?

But worrying about Shelley was the last thing I needed in my life. Gage too. I needed them all to just leave me alone. This was my twelfth day of being good, and I was determined to stay in double digits. I wadded Shelley's number and tossed it on the coffee table.

I went into the bedroom and tugged on long underwear—a top and bottoms—and my snowboard pants. Three weeks without boarding had been a test of my sanity. I paused at the table and tried a butterscotch cookie from a plate Crispy had sent. It was only lightly burned, so I wolfed down four, thinking how he'd be psyched. *Food = love* for Crispy. I heard Gage say "love" and cringed;

love was the last thing I'd sought from him. I blew out my breath. I buckled on my helmet, tugged on my gloves, and grabbed my board from beside the door.

Love.

You could change the world.

"I need some space!" I muttered as I strode off the deck.

Just beyond the sheltering pines that curled around the cabin, a run called Always ribboned into Gold Bowl. Inconvenient from the lifts, it stayed untracked on a powder day. I buckled in, ahh-ing at my board's sensation beneath my feet. I'd weave in and out of the fluff along the run's edge and blot out the voices in my head. I kicked my right foot into the fall line and rocked forward and back, easing my board into gravity.

As I picked up speed, I skimmed to the snow's surface. I pressured my toes, leaned in, and turned left. I weighted my heels, leaned back, and turned right. Relief spread through me. I carved a few more turns in the open before heading toward a glade. I wove around three aspens and out. Wove in again and passed an Upward Dog spruce with yellow spots.

I stopped so fast I fell uphill, arms disappearing in powder. I swam my way to kneeling.

Like with the spruce on Shangri-La, a well with no snow surrounded this trunk, and from it a thin trail led away toward City Center. I peered up and spied a brown-gray lump in its high branches.

I rolled over and looked down Gold Bowl, gulping air. I pictured Dad and closed my eyes to clarify his image. I rose and started gliding away, forcing myself not to look back.

I longed to straightline and reach for speed, but I forced myself to make precise turns.

I popped out onto the road leading to Gold Bowl's base, joining people who'd funneled down from other runs. At the road's end, we clogged into the lift's full maze, a twenty-minute wait. Powder days on Saturdays were the kiss of death because *every idiot from Denver* + *every gung-ho local* + *regular tourists* = *gridlock*. I maneuvered through bodies to the singles line. Normally, I'd grumble the whole time I waited in lines. This time, I hardly noticed.

My head spun with speculation about that spruce. That must have been why Súmáí was at the cabin so much. How many Upward Dog spruces were there? Was there a grid connecting the whole mountain? How about all of Crystal Village? How about Colorado? Or the planet, maybe, if other species of trees could work? Maybe they just needed to be Upward Dog–shaped with tear stains. What happened where forests were clear-cut, like the Amazon? I couldn't get my head around the scope of it all. I glanced at the few hundred bodies surrounding me. If they suspected what I was thinking, I'd be committed to an asylum.

Before I knew it, I'd merged with three skiers and headed into the trough to load the chair. We sat down and took off. The dorks I sat with brought down the safety bar without warning, banging the back of my helmet.

"Sorry," a guy said.

It jolted me from my trance, and I glanced back and saw the lift's line bulging out of the maze. No coming back here today.

"So where are you from?" A woman sat beside me. Her feet rested primly on the safety bar's footrest, her white mittens in prayer position on the bar.

Chatters. Great. "Here," I said.

"That must be wonderful," she said.

I shrugged. A cigarette would help sort my thoughts.

"What do you do?" she said.

"Do?"

"Do you work?" she said,

"I'm in school." Were all humans programmed to ask the same dumb questions?

"High school?" said a guy beside the woman. I could see only his rental skis. According to their sticker, his name was *Ken*.

"Uh-huh." The way I said it was a conversation stopper, and the woman turned away from me to address the guys. I scanned the bowl for more Upward Dog spruce. If one was close to Emerald West, then Súmáí wouldn't have had far to drag the food he'd taken from there. What was he up to anyway?

Ahead and to our chairlift's right, two ski patrol knelt on either side of a guy below an X made from skis stuck in the snow. Like SOS, it was the universal skiing sign for help.

The injured skier sat, one leg out straight and shaking his head. He'd probably torn his knee ligaments, the most common injury on powder days. The chair neared, and the ski patrolmen became Crispy and Wash. Wash saw me out of the corner of his eye, gave a thumbs-up, and said, "See you at dinner."

The hurt guy looked at him.

Wash chin-pointed toward me. "Our kid."

Crispy waved.

The woman, Ken, and the guy at the chair's end eyed me.

I faced the view until they looked away. I squinted, trying to make out tiny waves, little M-theory strings, something revealing in the air that stretched across the bowl. The word "Nobel" grabbed my attention. The woman's white mitten waved like she was embarrassed.

"Honestly, Karen." Ken pronounced her name funny, like he was from the South, but he didn't have an accent. "A particle physicist working with human cells? This is groundbreaking work. Don't give up on it."

"The possibilities created by entanglement are mind-boggling," the guy on the end said.

Karen clapped her mittens together twice gently. "Yes, well, some would say I'm a crackpot, applying spooky action to humans."

Before I knew it, I said, "You're working with spooky action?"

Their helmeted heads turned to me, Ken leaning forward to see me around Karen. She pressed back to view me fully. "Yes. You're familiar with quantum theory?"

I wanted to shout, *Hell yes!* Instead, I said, "Do you think entanglement could stretch across the multiverse?"

Through Karen's yellow-lensed goggles, I saw her assess me. "My research has been with people within our own universe."

I tried to sound nonchalant. "And?"

"And I don't have conclusive proof yet."

"But something makes you keep researching?"

Karen exchanged glances with the two guys. "Yes."

I blew out my breath and sat back.

"You have experience with this?" Ken said, a taunt in his words.

I wanted to slug him, but I said to Karen, "Have you proven whatever you're doing mathematically?"

"We're close."

"Where do you work?" I said.

"MIT."

My body's temperature shot up fifty degrees as I remembered that vision of Mom and me on the recreation path. That me had been headed to MIT. "Is any of your research online? Are any of your papers published?"

"There was one in *Science Daily*."

"When?"

"About a year ago."

"Is it recorded?"

"Recorded?"

"Like, I could listen to it?"

"No." Karen tilted her head. "How about you give me your email and I'll send you the link?"

I turned to her. She was tiny, and her eyes crinkled at the outside corners like rays. "You'd do that?" I said.

"Sure."

I spelled out my email, careful to get the letters right.

"Sovern? That's your name?"

I nodded.

"That's a great name. Mine's Cairn." She spelled it out. "Like the rock markers on a hiking trail." We neared the lift's summit.

"My mom named me," I said.

"My dad," Cairn said.

The lift grew loud as we entered the lifthouse. I'm not sure what made me do it, but I leaned in. "Will you send me your equation?"

As I rose and slid away, Cairn's mouth hung open. She concentrated on navigating from the chair and stopped by using her poles, gangly as a fawn learning to walk. Ken and the other guy had moved about ten feet away, and they stood there impatient to get moving. Cairn gathered her composure and eyed me. "It's very advanced math."

"I'll keep it secret. I just want to see it."

"You're asking to see my life's work."

I let out a huge sigh. "My mom—" I looked away. "What are the chances of me ending up on that chairlift with you, now of all times?" When I looked back, Cairn was scrutinizing me through those goggles.

"Now is important?" she asked.

"Math is…" How could I express that I needed for math to rule the world? That if math ruled the world, maybe fate didn't? "Math is…well…it won't leave me alone. I don't know all the fancy terms advanced people in colleges use, but I…I just understand it. For me, math has no words. It just makes the world make sense. And I have experience with entanglement."

"Experience?"

"Personal experience."

"You've—"

"I'm not crazy!"

She pursed her lips and studied me for what felt like forever. "Okay," she said. "We're stuck, and I guess it couldn't hurt." She glanced over her shoulder, but Ken and the other guy were long gone. "Nice to meet you, Sovern."

Cairn poled away, the backs of her skis fanning into a beginner's wedge as she headed down Sunset Ridge. She'd come up from the bottom of Gold Bowl, all expert terrain, and since she'd survived that, *Cairn = one tough lady + willing to take risks*. And no doubt I was a risk.

Bookmark:
The Arrow of Time
Arthur Eddington

In our world, an arm never un-breaks.
A body never un-ages. Events always move
forward—an "asymmetry"—though the
mathematical laws of physics work equally
well going forward or backward in time.

28

I gave up on snowboarding in the crowds and started toward the cabin. Big John skated across the teeming area, carrying an armful of red bamboo poles, headed, no doubt, to mark hazards.

"Congratulations, Sov!" he called.

I held up my liberated arm and waved, but my head was grappling with the idea of scientists like Cairn existing, researching human applications of quantum theory. *Testing* them. Maybe what I had experienced wouldn't be considered so insane after all.

In the cabin, I hung my parka by the door and settled, snow pants rustling, on the couch. I stared at the wadded scrap of paper with Shelley's number. *You could change the world.* I rested my elbows on my knees and scrubbed my face with my hands. My phone pinged with a text. Gage: TWO FITTED AGAIN? MOVE? I re-read it: TWO FISTED AGAIN? MOVIE?

I was still so pissed that he'd talked to Dad, but it was a sweet thing to do, and Dad had almost seemed to want me to date him. I did enjoy *Star Trek*, and it would distract my mind. Maybe it would keep me from going to that spruce on Always.

K, I texted back. TIME?

SHE RESPONDS! GONDOLA BASE. SEVEN.

K.

I leaned back, and my memory saw Cairn assessing me. Shelley's number on the table seemed to whisper *You could change the world*. I picked it up, walked to the kitchen, and dropped it in the trash can at the end of the counter. But I made it only three steps before I turned back and retrieved it. I went to the bedroom and stowed it in my wooden box.

I paced the bedroom's short length, tugging out my amulet bag to rub its beaded surface. Was Súmáí's quill from the same porcupine? Did that animal travel through universes, or exist in them all at once? I flopped onto my bed and stared at the ceiling for a long time, trying to make sense of it all.

I blew out my breath, shuffled to the kitchen, and grabbed a bag of chips. I thought of Gage insisting on carrying my grocery bag with these chips. He'd been so pale.

I settled at the table, powered up my laptop, and pinched open the bag. I had a few emails from teachers about assignments. One had arrived from Cairn. Already. I opened it.

Hi Sovern,

It was a pleasure to meet you today. Here is the link to the article in Science Daily. Also, attached is the mathematical formulation that's been stumping us.

Though I know you said you don't understand fancy terms, all its parts are explained in the introductory material. I'd love to know what you think! And please remember that this work is confidential.

All best,
Cairn Hart

After five reads to get the words right, I figured out that the *Science Daily* article talked about her risky yet groundbreaking research into spooky action using particles taken from one woman's cell. In Bio, I'd learned that there were countless particles in a cell, but I'd never really considered that fact beyond having to memorize it for a test. Cairn had placed these particles on the east and west coasts of the continent—one at MIT in Boston, and one at Stanford in California. When a particle in Boston was shot with polarized light, the angle and slant of the wave it emitted was measured by a laser. Meanwhile, at the exact same instant, the particle at Stanford set off a wave that was its exact opposite. Cairn hadn't been able to reproduce the results from her experiment, and now she was searching for mathematical proof.

I opened the attachment, and Cairn's equation filled my screen. I'd never seen a problem this advanced, and it took me a long time to read through the introduction before I even got to the equation. There's this place I get with math, where an equation's patterns take over and the numbers become things beyond their names. It's heavenly.

After about an hour, I sensed a glitch in the equation's symmetry. I imagined smoothing the glitch, reasoned out how to express that in numbers, and emailed Cairn back, suggesting an equation derived from hers. I knew it wasn't the solution, and that I could be totally wrong, but what could it hurt? I'd never see her again anyway.

I powered off my computer, Cairn's research whirling in my head. She was a real person who'd actually succeeded in having two particles show connection across space and time. Could my traveling to Mom in different universes stem from spooky action? Could Súmáí showing up in my universe be due to entanglement?

I'd sensed and seen in Cairn's math that her equation's flaw lay in trying to deal only with the present. I was coming to realize that past, present, and future might all exist at once, while also reaching across universes. That it was all a whirling entity. I thought of the equations we'd last done in Calculus that had added another dimension. My equation would incorporate dimension on dimension on dimension.

A true genius. Perhaps I *could* change the world. First though, I needed answers.

Before I realized I was doing it, I'd tugged on my parka. Who'd I been kidding? I'd kept my snow pants on for a reason. I'd always been headed to that new Upward Dog spruce.

———

I didn't retrace my weaving snowboard track. Instead, I snowshoed the most direct route on Always till I needed to veer left.

The spruce towered before me. Afternoon sun lit a brown-gray lump in its upper branches. My pulse, already hammering from snowshoeing, amplified. I moved to the trunk. Sure enough, beneath the new snow, the area leading into its well was tamped down. Súmáí, no doubt. How long had he been doing this? I thought of his warning to me. The way he'd held up his two fingers and gestured an explosion. If spooky action could stretch between two people, maybe *he'd* started all this. Maybe I'd been drawn to that first spruce on the anniversary of Mom's death by something *he'd* done. I thought back to that snow whirlwind ejecting me straight right, as if I'd been on a recoiling rubber band.

I took a wide breath and scanned the powder field, my tracks from earlier the only human sign. I turned downhill and could see part of the chairlift, the confetti bodies trailing out of the maze. Answers. I needed answers.

Peering at the porcupine, I said, "I need to find Súmáí," and prayed I'd end up with the Súmáí I knew. I unzipped my parka, drew out my amulet bag, and gripped it. I pressed my other palm to the spruce.

Loud birds. Splash of Indian paintbrush
Singeing sunlight.

Once I'd adjusted to it being summer, Gold Bowl appeared the same as always. Except, no. There weren't any signs or ropes marking the runs on its distant, treeless boundary. Instead, it was covered with majestic old spruce. The glades and open areas Crystal Mountain was so famous for were a fraction of the size they were in my world. I looked left, where all my life one of the charred, swirling trunks that jabbed up throughout the bowls had stood. A huge living spruce stood there now. I turned toward Gold Bowl's base and gasped.

Tepees. Maybe fifteen.

Sorry, Lindholm, I thought. Tepees, not wickiups.

A creek, icebound and silent in my world, flowed just beyond the chair's maze, and nobody paid it any attention. Here, it determined the tepees' location like a vein.

"Súmáí?"

When I'd pressed my palm to a spruce before, whoever I'd been thinking of had appeared.

"Súmáí!"

Well, I'd wait. I slid my palm down the bark and sat. With two working arms now, I was able to unstrap my snowshoes. I crossed my legs, tugged off my hat, and nudged down my parka till it hung around the forearm of my hand pressed against the spruce.

I'd never had time to really take in the other universes I'd visited. It occurred to me that my visits had been in spring, summer, and fall, but never in snow. Had I done that? Then I noticed the quiet. On Crystal Mountain during the day, a constant hum of lifts, snowmobiles, and people skiing or boarding enveloped it. Here, it sounded like evenings or summers at the cabin. Except even stiller. I peered up, and the clouds seemed the same. After a minute, I realized there was no plane noise falling from the sky. No tire hum rising from asphalt down the valley.

Where was Súmáí? This world seemed like his, but maybe it was another. Believe. I had to believe. I imagined his face from the night he'd helped Dad and me, its worried expression.

Why hadn't Súmáí been back since then? A crow landed in a tree nearby and squawked. I leaned my head against the spruce's trunk. At least the sun was warm.

Snuffling. A mewlish bark. I bolted straight. Had I been dreaming? I looked around, felt my palm against the spruce, and got my bearings. That bark came again on my left. I knew that sound: a bear cub.

I scrambled to my feet and orbited to the spruce's far side, trying to make myself narrow, just as a mother bear appeared through the pines. She grunted and lifted her nose to the air. Bears, I knew, had terrible sight but incredible noses. Sure enough, she caught my scent and sniffed once, twice. My Gore-Tex clothes and my body, filled with brownies and chips, must have smelled foreign. She focused on my spruce. She lowered her head and rocked from foot to foot, mouth slightly open, fangs bared.

Sorry, Dad, I thought, and guilt almost collapsed me to my knees.

The bear circled—ten yards out—to gain a better view. Her cub barked from high in a tree. I reminded myself I could pull my palm away, be gone in an instant, and I calmed enough to consider how this bear was protecting that cub the way Mom had protected me. I pressed both hands to the spruce, continuing to maneuver so it was between us. My boots crunched needles.

The bear stepped closer and stopped, head tilted, listening. A thin crescent scar rose above her left eye. Behind her head flitted a brown butterfly with white-outlined wings. My mouth dropped open.

The bear charged. I yanked my hand from the trunk, facing her, waiting for winter to appear.

The scene switched to slow motion. I'd never noticed gravity in these other worlds, but now my feet became a thousand pounds I could not budge. The bear blurred toward me—a blast of musky scent—and I felt its paws press my shoulders. I slammed onto my back and blurted pain as claws pierced my chest.

"Mom!" I screamed. "It's me!"

Her beady brown eyes reflected my ghostly image. We regarded one another for seconds, an eternity. She snorted, her head snapping down, her weight compressing my chest like resuscitation. She hopped off, hustled to the side, and studied me. Her cub barked from its tree. Still, she studied me.

She bellowed, rose on her hind legs, and charged the spruce, slashing it with her claws. She turned, and I saw her milk-laden teats. She dropped to all fours, snorted again, and sauntered toward her cub. It scampered down the tree and hopped at her face. She glanced over her shoulder three times before they disappeared into the forest.

Dark spots rose in my vision. I couldn't move. Blood from the bear's punctures trickled over my shoulders, down my back, and was sponged by my long underwear. I inhaled against the pain in my chest and smelled my own fear. The sun was scorching. A fly circled my face. *You could change the world.* Right. I couldn't even pass one simple test: my promise to Dad. I was a failure.

I loosed one bleak laugh at that foreign sky.

29

"Sovern?"

It was Súmáí.

"Sovern!"

Gravity seemed to glue every part of me to the ground, and I struggled to lift even my eyelids. His cool fingers rested against my quill-spotted cheek. I raised my arm, clumsy, and he took my hand and held it. He leaned down. Was he going to kiss me? I flinched.

I sat up, wincing. He inventoried me from my face to my boots. He studied my long underwear shirt, and, pressing my chin to my chest, I saw an arcing red smear. I pointed toward the Upward Dog spruce. He sighed like he was deciding something. He strode to it and studied the claw marks oozing with golden sap.

I realized fully that I was sitting in one of Súmáí's universes. Don't panic, I thought. You've found him. Stay and learn. Even so, my breaths came shallow and fast.

Súmáí saw this and knelt before me. He dipped his finger inside my shirt's collar. I sucked air through my teeth at the bloody cloth's tug on my skin. He peeked in and his brows pressed close. He helped me up and guided me toward the spruce. I struggled to stand straight and could feel it would be a while before that happened easily, yet I managed to plant my feet and stop him. I touched his chest, pointed to my eyes, and touched his chest again.

Súmáí shook his head. He pointed to the blood on me and to the spruce.

I pointed to the tepees at Gold Bowl's base, my eyes, and the tepees again.

He looked across the bowl and scratched the back of his head. Finally, he pressed his lips and nodded. He ran his hand over my hair and down its length.

I stiffened and stepped back. Had I given him a cue I'd missed? Was this a universe where we'd been intimate? Was this even the Súmáí I'd met before? He'd touched my cheek, though, in that way we had.

He pointed at my chest, then his, and he crossed his fingers. My pulse amplified at that, and then even more as his arm curled around my back. I tried to relax but couldn't. To mask it, I took his arm by its wrist and kept my fingers there till I felt *his* pulse, willing it to slow mine. He tilted his head and seemed to look beyond me at something sad, like he had in the cabin.

He pointed down the mountain and gestured walking with two fingers. I shrugged, tried my wobbly legs, and found I could manage.

He led me down Gold Bowl, following its natural contour till we emerged where this morning I'd come out on the road and joined with a crowd of skiers. Now we followed a trace trail snaking through a field of tall grass. To make things seem real, I focused on the fuzzy tips brushing the backs of my fingers like whispering numbers.

Every step issued a jolt of pain, and blood glued my long underwear shirt to my back. My cracked ribs felt like they'd cracked again, and my arm throbbed against its brace. The heat lifted the scents of dirt, new growth, and my own blood, making me even woozier.

To keep going, I studied Súmáí. His hair stretched down his back, intersecting his quiver and bow's diagonal line. My gaze followed the line of his back to the belt of his deerskin pants, then followed their tan profile down to his moccasins. The first time we'd met, when we'd surprised each other, I'd been repelled. Now I felt drawn to him clear to my bones. But it was nothing like a crush. I stumbled, and he turned faster than seemed possible.

Because I knew he couldn't understand, I said, "Why am I so drawn to you?"

He seemed to struggle not to touch me. Maybe I *was* with a different Súmáí. If not, I had definitely missed something. Súmáí's actions and my walking around in this world meant the equation for all this had altered. He saw my confusion, half-smiled, and started down again.

From the thousand times I'd snowboarded it, I knew this draw intimately, knew all of the back bowls like I knew a mirror's reflection of my face, so I understood where we were when he stopped short of the tepees and led me around the village's eastern edge. He motioned for me to stay and pressed his finger to his lips. I watched him disappear into the forest, still seeing that gesture for silence. I laughed once, and then I couldn't stop laughing. If anyone could hear me, they'd think I'd gone crazy. Maybe I had.

I scanned around, making sure no animals would charge me, and settled gingerly on a fallen log. I eyed my snow boots and realized I'd left my snowshoes, hat, and parka at the spruce, my phone in its pocket. I glanced at the sun. Each of my visits to Mom seemed to have had a purpose—a pattern I couldn't quite discern. That pattern whispered, unceasing, against my brain. Was I here on *this* day, loose in *this* universe, for a reason?

I rocked to ease the soreness building in my body. That bear was Mom. No doubt. She'd recognized me. Had she brought me here? Or Súmáí? If that was Mom, then maybe that cub was me. If so, I was pretty freaking cute. I ran my fingers back through my hair and then flinched at Súmáí standing beside me.

"Don't do that!" I said.

He grinned and pressed his finger to his lips again.

"You have no idea how ironic that is," I said.

Tucked under his arm were clothing—elk-skin, deer-skin, I couldn't tell the difference—and a rag. I rose like an old lady and he led me away from the tepees, farther east, following the creek. We walked a while, crossing into the Silver Bowl drainage, where a tributary flowed into it. Just above this confluence, one of those house-sized rocks that makes you wonder how it got there rested half in the creek.

Súmáí walked to its upriver side. Here the water swelled, forming a pool. He lifted his bow and quiver over his head, and then his sleeveless shirt and amulet bag. He toed off his moccasins. As he unlaced his pants at the sides of his belt, I tried to seem nonchalant. But only the legs fell away, so that a deerskin rectangle hung from his belt halfway down his thighs, front and back. Lindholm had never talked about *this*.

"Get a grip, Sovern," I muttered. I'd been making out with Gage for months. I blinked back the sensation of his kiss as Súmáí stepped into the water, sheathed knife at his hip. He held the rag.

I pulled off my snow boots, peeled out of my snow pants, yanked off my ski socks, and stomped down my long underwear. I stood there like an absolute dork in my *Tuesday* days-of-the-week panties and that long underwear shirt. I took off my arm brace and started to lift the shirt over my head, but Súmáí said something, so I stopped. He gestured for me to come into the water.

That first step's cold was brutal. Clear, clear water swirled around my feet. Súmáí grinned, stepped toward me, and held out his hand. I forced my gaze from how his body glimmered with water beads and took his hand, clenching my teeth as I waded in. I paused, lifted off my amulet bag, and slung it to the bank. The water was to our chests in four steps. Súmáí lowered himself to his neck, so I did too.

The water seeped into my shirt, and as it met the glue of my blood, softening it, I realized why Súmáí had encouraged me to keep on my shirt. I shivered. He pulled me to him and wrapped his arms around me, loosely. Testing. I failed not to seem nervous. His arms loosened.

My mind zoomed around for footing. What were the rules now? What was too fast when time was undefined? An unknown? I *had* to be here, now, for a reason. Mom's aching claw marks ringed my chest, and Súmáí's arms circled my waist. I forced back thoughts of Dad.

After a bit, Súmáí tested the glue of my shirt's dried blood. He took the hem, and I helped him tug it over my head. He tossed it to the bank. He moved us to waist-deep water.

With the rag, he washed my back and shoulders, working around the straps of my bra. He washed gently at first, then harder, adding fine gravel from the pool's floor. That scrubbing, combined with the freezing water, felt great. The swelling and soreness eased, though each goose bump on my flesh felt sharp. Súmáí turned me to him and washed gently across my chest. I gnawed my lip against the pain.

When it was clean, he sucked in his breath and traced Mom's punctures. They curved from my shoulders to my clavicle, then down, meeting in a dip over my heart where the bear's inner claws had been. I remembered Gage tracing a heart on my back. Gage was better-looking. Why was I so attracted to Súmáí? I could feel that attraction, literally, in my bones. I closed my eyes against memories of Gage, and when I opened them again, Súmáí looked at me with such intensity I hunched forward. From the cold, he must have thought, because he led me out of the pool.

Arms crossed for warmth, I followed, feeling pale and idiotic in my underwear and bra. Súmáí lay flat on his back in the grass, so I lay beside him, a total dork, but the sun seared my skin with welcome heat. His every movement seemed careful not to be intimate. We watched clouds migrate. A hawk spiraled above. I wondered how we must look from up there.

Súmáí rolled onto his side and propped himself on his elbow. He took in my length. I tried not to feel ashamed. I imagined his finger running along my outer curves to the punctures on my chest. Slow down, Sov, I thought.

His head snapped to the side, tense and listening.

He rose catlike, pulled me to my feet, grabbed his bow and quiver, and guided me behind him in one swift movement as he faced the opposite bank. For the second time that day, I worked to make myself narrow.

I reached down, retrieving a perfect skipping rock, and followed the line of Súmáí's gaze, but saw nothing. He raised his bow just as a guy stepped out of the forest. Then another. One was blond, the other dark-haired, both with beards that had overgrown their faces while their hair hung scraggy below sweat-ringed hats. They reeked of cigarettes. The blond sauntered to the pool's edge on the opposite bank.

You see a million sepia photos of people back in the day, and their trousers, suspenders, coats, and brimmed leather hats seem normal, but when there's one right in front of you, it's like a modern person playing dress-up. Or like you've dropped into a movie. I stifled a laugh till I saw the guy's intent face and the harsh line of his mouth. The dark-haired guy stepped to his side and smirked. Both wore gun belts.

"We got ourselves a near-naked Indian." The blond guy said. "How'd you get that white woman?"

The dark-haired guy shot Súmáí a scalding look. In Spanish he said, *"No debe estar aqui."*

I frowned. Why shouldn't Súmáí be here?

He didn't answer, of course. He just kept his arrow aimed on the blond guy's chest.

"Donde robo' la mujer?" the blond guy said.

"He didn't steal me, asshole!" I said in Spanish.

Súmáí tensed.

"Entonces eres una puta," the dark-haired one said.

The probability of getting shot was high, yet I loaded that stone in my finger like Dad had shown me a thousand times. I stepped from behind Súmáí, faced the scumbags full-on, and said, "I'm no whore."

If you're talking fabric, the line separating a bikini from a bra and panties is a fine one, but when you're facing horny scumbags, that line seems a mile wide. I rolled back my sore shoulders. The men startled but composed themselves. Their eyes roamed over me, snagged on the punctures around my neck and then my pink *Tuesday* underwear.

"Damned if she isn't a beauty," the blond guy said, sort of reverent, and then his gaze clicked with calculation.

The dark-haired guy grunted. He spoke in English this time. "Wrong day. Can't read?"

I winged the stone at his sneer and dove toward the

boulder. Soreness had altered my aim, but both guys' arms flinched up and the stone hit the dark-haired guy's ear. He stumbled back, his deafening shot missing high, just as an arrow pierced his chest.

The blond guy shot, but Súmáí was lunging behind the rock, string twanging. The blond guy fell next to his partner. Arrow shafts rose from their chests like props.

I hunched over and my hand came to my mouth. I glanced at Súmáí, but he was staring at the men, seeming to see a thousand omens. He jogged above the pool and hopped across the creek on three stones. Yanking his arrows from the guys' chests, he wiped them clean on their shirts. He drew his knife from his hip and knelt at the dark-haired guy's head.

I spun to my pile of clothes, then remembered the clothes Súmáí had brought and moved to those instead. Of course he's scalping these guys, I told myself. He's a *real* Ute. This is *not* a movie, and those arrows are *not* props. *Scalping was a sign of bravery and manhood,* Ms. Lindholm had said. I gulped air. This was all happening too fast.

My hands shook as I put on my amulet bag and pressed it to my chest. The creek had left me smelling like clean earth. I unfurled the deerskin shirt and tugged it over my head. I expected it to feel stiff, but it was supple. I rolled up its long sleeves and strapped on my arm brace. There were leggings, and the leather rectangles on the belt. I belted on the rectangles, then struggled to tie on the leggings with jittery fingers.

Was this why I was here? To help Súmáí kill two men? I pulled on my snow boots. When I straightened, Súmáí stood beside me.

I flinched. "Don't do that!"

One side of his mouth curled up. Two bloody scalps— one blond, one brown—hung from his hip.

I hooked hair back from my face with my finger, feeling him notice how my hand shook.

"*Hablas español,*" he said.

I grinned despite it all and said, "*Sí.* "

30

I followed Súmáí to where the dead guys had emerged from the forest, and then along their tracks to two horses. Behind their saddles were strapped mining pans and short shovels. I wondered if Súmáí understood these men's greed for gold or silver or whatever else they could sell. I scanned Silver Bowl, I'd never considered the real history behind the names that in my world seemed like a sort of game. In my world, they mined cold white gold here, the light fluffy kind a person could soar through.

Súmáí handed me the reins of one of the horses. It was reddish brown with a white oval on its forehead, and I kept it at arm's length. Other than watching pony rides at the fair, I'd never been near a horse and knew them only from movies. Súmáí laughed gently.

"We will go on foot," he said in Spanish.

He led his horse down the valley toward his village. I mimicked how he held the reins, relieved when the big animal followed me. I focused on each step, each breath, noting the horse's sharp scent as I tried to sense reality. *Mom's attack + Súmáí's affection + these miners = things happening way too fast.* I looked down at my deerskin covered legs and felt myself balancing on sanity's blade.

As we crossed the tributary draining from Silver Bowl, I was glad for the rubber of my snow boots as the horse clopped against the rocks and splashed water behind me. I tried to take it all in stride, but I was already nervous as hell and shaking. As I hopped to the far bank, I noticed I wasn't nearly as stiff as before. That icy creek water had helped. Tomorrow, across my chest, the pain would be awful, but at least my legs were moving better. Tomorrow? I thought. What did tomorrow even mean here?

A man spoke. Súmáí halted. Four Utes frowned down at him from horseback. I lurked near his horse's rear, not the smartest thing, but it seemed the lesser danger. I peeked around and saw Súmáí hold up the scalps. The Utes' eyes darted to me and I ducked back.

"Sovern." Súmáí gestured with his hand.

I stepped out, leading my horse till it stood beside Súmáí's. They nickered at one another. Looking at those Utes, I felt like I was on a movie set again, but no way did I think they were just props. Two were older than Súmáí. Two looked about the same age. All their faces had similar round shapes. The younger ones wore deerskin leggings and plaid flannel shirts. An older one wore a deerskin shirt like mine, and a blue bandana wrapped his head.

The older Ute in front seemed in charge. His braids were wrapped with rawhide. Over one ear, at the start of his braid, a white feather plumed up. A brown feather plumed up from the other. He wore a choker of white beads. His deerskin shirt and leggings were fringed. He spoke scalding words to Súmáí, and Súmáí seethed something equally hot. He regarded me.

"This is Sovern," Súmáí said in Spanish. "She comes from the trees."

The other older Ute straightened with surprise but translated the Spanish into another language. Theirs, no doubt.

From the trees. So Súmáí had told his people about trees and quantum travel to other universes? I wasn't sure whether to nod, curtsey, or offer my hand, so I just eased back my shoulders and tried to muster courage.

The four Utes straightened on their mounts. They inspected me down to my boots, along my arm brace, and back to my light hair and pale skin. So pale. It occurred to me that I was glad I'd smeared on sunscreen before going snowboarding. A rosy sunburn would be hell to explain to Dad. And then, just as I realized I'd have to explain the punctures on my chest, I became aware of the light's angle.

I'd been here for hours. In my universe, Dad would be home soon.

The leader spoke. Súmáí said something in a tone that made me brace. I looked at the defiant set of his shoulders, at the hands that itched to clench into fists. The leader seemed to scold him. Súmáí turned stony.

"He says we will discuss this at camp," he said to me. Then, to the translator, "Take the horses. We will go on foot."

The translator looked at him oddly, but spoke to the younger guys who took the horses, and they all left. Súmáí stood, mouth cocked slightly open as he watched them go, his body tense as a ready bow.

I was suddenly so tired. I needed to get somewhere familiar, someplace boring, even. I had a weird longing for school.

"Súmáí, it's getting late. Dad will be worried. I have to go home."

"Who is *Dad*?"

"My father," I said.

"The man who was sick at the tree?" Súmáí's accented Spanish and the way he used the words sounded exotic.

"Yes. Who did you think he was?"

"You are a good daughter." Relief and tenderness filled Súmáí's face, but I couldn't ignore the scalps at his hip.

"Actually, I'm not." I blew out a breath, thinking how Dad would flip if he knew what I was doing just then. *I* could hardly get my head around it. And *I'd* screwed up *again*. Broken my promise. I hung on to that thought. Failure, at least, was familiar.

"My father expects much of me. I try to be a good son." Súmáí shook his head and lifted his gaze to Phantom Peak, framed by the valley's V. The face cast there by the late-afternoon sun was far more distinct than in my universe. A face with an unsettling, willful expression. So the rumor was true. What really stood out, though, wasn't the face: it was the eyes. Somehow the shadows created two eerie dark points that seemed to scrutinize me.

"Right now, he waits for me to bring you to him," Súmáí finished.

"Your father's the one with the feathers? Is he the chief?"

Súmáí nodded. "The other was my uncle." He glanced at the sun. "You can stay here many days, but you will return on the same day you left, and the sun will not have moved in the sky."

His words were easy to follow, yet I had to sort them from the novelty of hearing his voice. I blinked to force rational thought. "So I could stay a week?"

"Week? I do not know this word."

"How long have you been coming to my world?"

"Two moons."

Moons equaled months, I guessed. "But when I was five, I saw you."

He didn't speak, yet in his eyes lay many things I *needed* to know.

"Did you see my…" I didn't have a Spanish word for *snowboard*. "My crash? When the…" I didn't have a word for *porcupine* or *quills* either. "The animal shot the needles in my cheek?"

"*El puerco espín?* No."

The Spanish word sounded so much like *porcupine*, I decided that must have been its source. "How did you come to my land then?"

He shrugged. "I was hunting. A mother bear chased me up the tree you traveled with today. A porcupine was in the tree. It defended itself, and I fell, but the mother bear did not attack. Instead, she danced a victory dance and left. My leg was hurt, so I used my hand against the tree to stand, and I entered your world. I saw Dammit."

I looked at him, puzzled.

Súmáí made the track of a snowboard with his hands, the way he had that first day we'd met. I remembered sitting in Shangri-La the second day we'd met, after he'd dragged me from Mom and made me furious. Gage had boarded past, his mouth a zero.

"Oh, *Dammit*." I laughed and rubbed my forehead, soreness slowing my motion. "The first time, you saw him snowboarding?" I used the English word.

"Yes. The first time. You were there. Following. You are skilled."

I laughed a little, trying to remember when we'd last boarded down Always. "And then?"

"I saw him speak angry words with his father."

"Where?"

"On the stones leading to his dwelling."

It took me a second to figure out he meant Gage's cobblestone driveway, shaped in a lollipop with a fountain in the middle. That meant there was a spruce tree near Gage's driveway. I could easily picture their argument. I'd only ever heard them argue. Súmáí may not have spoken English, yet he understood their relationship.

"Next, I saw Dammit with you."

"When he found me at the tree?"

"No. Before." He looked away. "You were ... together."

"Oh." I thought of the countless times Gage and I had paused to make out in the shadows, felt the way his smoky kisses had blotted out the pain of Mom. And that's how Súmáí had found me? Through Gage? My mind reeled through possibilities, through probabilities, through symmetries, and through concepts like fate. That elusive pattern whispered against my brain.

"You used to breathe many fire sticks." He crinkled his nose. "I don't like fire sticks."

I decided to change the subject. "How'd you learn to speak Spanish?"

"Traders come this way. They speak Spanish. And many times I traveled with my uncle to Santa Fe to trade. We would stay for a moon. How do you speak Spanish?"

"School." One good thing from that prison, I thought.

"I have seen a white man's school. It was like a cage."

A photo came back to me from Lindholm's class: Ute children at a school in Grand Junction. Girls dressed like whites and boys dressed in military uniforms with their hair hacked short. I bit my lip.

"My father will be angry if you go. You will stay?"

I could relate to angry fathers, so I said, teasing, "At the tree, you wanted me to leave."

He cocked his head and smiled wryly. "You will stay?"

"For now."

31

We entered the village of tepees filling the meadow at the creek's edge. Five children sprinted to us, shouting "Súmáí!" They ushered us in, with a spotted white dog trotting behind. A yellow and a black dog romped up too. I forced myself not to cover my nose at the reek of horse, human sweat, raw meat, and smoke.

To our right, two women hung strips of meat on tiered pole racks. They stopped to watch us pass. A woman and girl rose from scraping a hide staked flat in the dirt. Other women paused from their work over a fire. All of them seemed a foot shorter than me and most wore fringed deerskin dresses, belted at the waist. I felt Súmáí's pants hugging my legs. Necklaces must have been a big deal, because everybody wore one—men, women, children. Most men wore earrings. A bunch of the women and men wore *slippers*. The sheepskin kind from the Platinum Club.

Súmáí's father sat on a flat waist-high boulder at the creek's edge with a striped cotton blanket draped across his legs. The other three guys sat, legs crossed, on the ground at his sides. As we approached, they watched how my feet intersected the dirt, how my arms arced the air, how my chin and neck made a firm right angle. My cheeks flamed.

Just before we'd reached the camp, Súmáí had stopped so quickly I'd almost run into him. "My father can be … " He'd eyed the horizon. He'd blown out his breath and scratched the back of his head. "You are strong," he'd said. Now, from the chief's expression, I understood what Súmáí meant. More Utes emerged from tepees and from the forest at the meadow's edge.

When we stood before his father, Súmáí said something that ended with the word "*español*." The Ute on his father's right, his uncle, nodded to him. Súmáí stood like a challenge.

Súmáí's father spoke, and his uncle translated what he said into Spanish. "I am Chief Úwápaa. You are from the lands of the trees?"

I glanced at Súmáí. "Yes."

"Why have you come?"

I glanced at Súmáí again. He stared straight ahead, but I sensed from the shift in his body that he was waiting to hear my answer too.

"To find Súmáí."

Out the corner of my eye, Súmáí's jaw muscle twitched.

His father's eyes narrowed. "What do you seek from my son?"

Answers, I thought, but before I could speak, Súmáí

said, "I sought her first." The cocked-gun way he stood as he faced his father was weirdly familiar. "I drew her here."

"She is white," his father said.

"In her land, all men live together," Súmáí said.

His words made me picture the immigrant girls on the steps of school and the trailer park down the valley. Thing was, compared to Súmáí's world, we did live together.

"And the Utes?"

"I have found none."

Chief Úwápaa said something scolding to Súmáí, and Súmáí responded with one word. I decided *Súmáí + his father = battle*. The chief's focus swung to me, and I braced.

"I live here, in these mountains," I said, "many years in the future." I didn't mention it might be a whole other universe.

"Father," Súmáí said, "we know not what we seek, only that we are drawn."

My legs turned watery. Yesterday, I'd told myself Súmáí wasn't real. Now here I stood, woozy with … what exactly was it between us? Slow down! I thought. You're here for answers.

Chief Úwápaa grunted.

"The bear spirit has chosen her," Súmáí said, and then he switched to his own language and spoke directly to his father.

Chief Úwápaa's chin lifted, and his brows lowered. Again, I had this weird déjà vu sensation. The chief spoke, but Súmáí's uncle did not translate.

Súmáí turned, scanning his gathered tribe, a movie set come to life before me.

"Come, Father, I will show you." Súmáí took my hand. Around us hissed intakes of breath. As he led me through the ring of murmuring bodies, my gaze fell on a girl about my age braced in head-to-toe fury. Her hair was cut shorter than the other women, and if her eyes had been arrows, I'd have been dead. I fought an urge to yank my hand from Súmáí's, sprint off, and grope the patterns of what was happening.

Súmáí led me to a tepee. Inside, wool blankets stretching over willow boughs lined the perimeter, along with two tall storage baskets. A fire ring marked the center.

"Take off your shirt," he said.

"What?"

"Take off your shirt."

The chief and Súmáí's uncle entered. The other two guys followed, but Súmáí stepped before them.

The chief nodded.

The guys shot me pissed-off looks but backed out of the tepee, an echo of Gage's buddies. I took a calming breath. I unstrapped my brace and peeled off my shirt. For the third time that day, I rolled back my aching shoulders, set my jaw, and lifted my chin.

Chief Úwápaa kept his gaze on my neckline. He stepped close. I willed myself not to move. I tried to hide my wince as he touched the punctures I had yet to see. He traced their arc, following the dip to where the inner claws had been, then up to my other clavicle, and over its scallop to my other shoulder.

Súmáí said something in Ute, and his father squinted at my cheek. He ran his finger over the faint bumps I thought would never disappear. He pressed his lips and looked at Súmáí. Then he assessed me for a long time.

We were the same height. Skin hung in bags below his

lacerating eyes. His cheeks sagged below that, as if tugged down by years of hardship. Great. Another test. I considered an equation for his face's symmetry to distract myself.

When he finally spoke, Súmáí grinned.

Súmáí's uncle translated. "Woman of the Trees, Chief Úwápaa says you are chosen. He names you Bear Necklace."

32

It's hard to explain that naming moment. I mean, I loved the name Mom gave me, but there was something about the way Chief Úwápaa said my new name, the respect in it: *Woman of the Trees*. Honestly? *Bear Necklace*. Really? Plus, no one had ever called me a "woman." Though I'd be nineteen in May, I was still just a Crystal High junior. A screwed-up, rebellious teenager, monitored by the school counselor. Briggs's brat, babysat by her ski-patrol family. Yet how Chief Úwápaa named me, and not even in my own language, made it easy for me to stand with my shoulders back. I *had* come from the trees. I *did* have a necklace of punctures from a bear's claws. Mom's claws.

"Tonight, we dance in your honor," Súmáí said.

"What?"

"We will dance. We have already danced the Bear Dance of the first thunder. This dance will honor the bear's choice."

I was here for answers. Dancing was definitely not on the agenda. "I can't."

He shook his head. "All dance. Do you wish me to dance with another?"

I thought of how Gage and I had laughed at just the thought of us at the winter formal. Sovern Briggs did not dance. Yet when I considered Súmáí with someone else, I blurted, "No."

"Then you dance."

I wanted to slap the smirk off his face.

"The women will prepare you."

"Prepare?"

He led me out of the tepee. Two women waited there. I recognized the furious one.

"This is my mother." His mother nodded once and I nodded back. Súmáí eyed the furious woman. "And this is Túwámúpůch, the widow of my brother."

"Widow?" I said. "Súmáí, I'm so sorry."

He ignored me and eyed that horizon again, but only for a minute. He squinted at Túwámúpůch and spoke in his language—low, steady—a warning.

Túwámúpůch spat words at him, and they glared at one another. I wondered if *Túwámúpůch* meant *pissed off*. He spoke again, and I wished I understood Ute because her glare fell to her feet.

I did not want to deal with this chick, and all this was using up valuable time when I could be seeking answers from Súmáí. "I don't—"

"Go," he said.

Down the valley, Phantom Peak seemed to watch me with those eerie eyes. How had I ended up in this situation? Yet this dance was in my honor. How could I not go?

Two girls of maybe seven walked past carrying colorful cloth dolls, and they giggled and smiled at us. As I followed Súmáí's mom back into his family's tepee—Túwámúpúch trailing through the low flap—I noticed that they both wore sheepskin slippers. Stolen slippers. Dogs barked on the far side of camp. Sounds of movement and excitement came from that direction.

Súmáí's mom lifted the hem of my shirt, gesturing for me to take it off. She sniffed at Súmáí's leggings and pointed at those too. I faced the tepee wall, unclasped my brace, and took off my shirt. I slid off my snow boots and peeled out of the leggings, then the belt with the rectangles. The word "breechcloth" came to me as I turned, wearing only my bra and *Tuesday* panties. Both women gaped at my punctures.

I felt pale as snow and just as likely to melt. I looked down at my chest and found purple bloomed around the punctures I could see. Scabs were forming on the holes, like the centers of flowers. Both women bowed their heads, though Túwámúpúch did not seem happy about it. Súmáí's mom spoke—no clue what she said—but it sounded reverent. Her hair was as short as Túwámúpúch's, and I remembered Lindholm saying that Ute women cut their hair when they mourned.

She moved to a pile of belongings between the blankets spread over willow boughs and returned with a sand-colored deerskin dress. Down its front stretched two rows of porcupine quills stitched between red and blue beads. Fringe hung round its short sleeves and hem. She held it out to me.

"*Gracias,*" I said.

She seemed to know this *thank you* and nodded. "*Towé-iyak,*" she said.

"*Towéiyak?*" I remembered Súmáí as he'd accepted Dad's hat. "*Gracias?*"

She smiled and nodded.

Túwámúpúch fumed.

Súmáí's mom scolded her, and she reluctantly stepped forward, took the dress, and held its hem open to slide it over my head, turning her face aside like I reeked. I stood there, taking in that open dress and that furious girl.

Túwámúpúch said something scalding, and I dipped my head into the dress, dove my hands through the arms, and straightened as she tugged it down to knee-length. She roughly slid a wide belt around my waist. I lifted my arms, and she spoke—low and unkind—as she buckled it.

Keep searching for answers, I reassured myself. I ran my fingers over bear claws stitched along the belt's leather. Today, that bear's crescent scar had been no coincidence. That had been Mom. I recalled her claws piercing my chest and rolled my aching shoulders. My thoughts skipped to Súmáí, almost remembering what he'd reminded me of when he'd stood so rebelliously before his father. He'd said he saw Gage first, that I'd been following Gage. He said he'd seen Gage fight with his dad, some time when I wasn't there.

Túwámúpúch set knee-high moccasins before me, I stepped into them, and she laced the fronts.

Súmáí's mom, bone-comb in hand, took a lock of my light hair and held it on her fingers, eyeing it. She moved behind me, and I heard her sniff before the comb tugged tangles from this morning's snowboarding, the bear encounter, the creek's pool, the scumbag attack, and the breeze as Chief Úwápaa had assessed me.

Was it really only this morning that I'd gone to the doctor with Dad? *Take it easy.* My pulse skipped a beat. No way could I hide my chest's bruises or its future scars. What the hell was I doing? I eyed my arm brace, lying on the ground, and decided to leave it off. As I searched for a place to set it, I saw, resting at the head of one of the beds, Dad's hat that I'd given Súmáí.

The first beat of a drum sounded outside. The first note of a dance to honor *me*, Bear Necklace, Woman of the Trees.

33

Over my shoulder, twilight cast Phantom Peak orangey-purple. Around me, it translated the colors, and as I followed Súmáí's mom, that light made me remember myself strapped down in that ski-patrol sled, bucking over the moguls at the top of Last Chance, easing left onto the road as Big John drove, the quills in my cheek swaying. In my mind's eye, Dad whizzed past on skis, towed by that snowmobile. The sensation was so real that I felt the heat pack across my chest, the goose bumps on my flesh, and my innards churning at Mom's absence.

2/22.

The first star winked on. "Please let me find Mom," I whispered to it. "And please don't let me hurt Dad again." Could a person make two wishes? Mom had never clarified that.

We entered an open area between the tepees where people gathered—sitting on logs, standing, eating, talking—around a big fire. Bodies parted and everyone quieted as Súmáí's mom led me across the space to where Chief Úwápaa stood. Súmáí stood beside him, dark eyes glittering. The chief nodded and I nodded back. He spoke.

Súmáí said, "My father says you are now ready. He says for a white woman you look nice."

I smiled and bit my lip. My shoulders longed to hunch, but stiffness kept them back.

Chief Úwápaa gestured to a log adjacent his. Stiffly, I sat on it, and a woman brought me a metal plate of meat with something wet, ground up roots with berries, maybe.

"*Towéiyak,*" I said.

She nodded.

Súmáí settled next to his father, and his uncle sat on the chief's other side. The two other guys sat next to Súmáí.

There weren't any utensils, so I scanned around and saw that people ate with their fingers. I was too worked up to eat, but people were watching, so I took a bite of the meat.

I'd never tasted game before. It had a pungent flavor, and I wondered what kind of animal I chewed. I hadn't eaten since those cookies of Crispy's before leaving the cabin, so my hunger took over. The wet stuff tasted like a cooking disaster—bitter, with the little bits of berries making me able to choke down the other part. I frowned, trying to figure out what from this valley might be filling my mouth.

My eyes met Súmáí's. He grinned and nodded. I remembered how he'd frowned at the brownie and hot chocolate I'd given him in the cabin. Okay, I thought, we're even.

A woman gathered my plate and cup. The last light diminished in the sky, and the fire illuminated one side of all things around it, casting sinewy shadows. Súmáí's mother appeared at the fire's edge. She must have gone back to change because she wore a fine dress, and a bead was weaved into the front of her hair's part. I noticed she wore a necklace made of teeth—maybe elk. Some looked like mini-tusks and some looked like molars. Her sagging face matched the chief's. Their eyes met and then jumped to me. I tried not to show my fear. Get answers. For Mom, I thought.

Súmáí's mom began speaking, and as Súmáí translated into Spanish, I had to force myself to concentrate on his words. "This night, we honor the Bear Spirit, but also the trees. Long ago, two brothers hunted in spring. They came upon a bear. The bear rubbed itself against a tree, turning and attacking the tree with its claws and growling."

This grabbed my attention. Súmáí glanced at me but continued to translate.

"They watched and watched the bear. Finally, they grew brave. 'What are you doing?' one brother said. The bear said, 'To learn that story, one of you must stay with me a year. The other must return to your village and tell your people what has passed.'

"The next spring, the brother from the village returned to the tree. He came upon two bears. 'Where is my brother?'

he said. 'You do not recognize him?' the bear said. 'He stands next to me.'

"The brother stayed for a while. They talked and sang songs, and then the bear sent him home to his village. 'You must go back and teach your people these songs. Tell them that when you dance for me, the woman must choose the man. Make two lines. The women must face the sunrise. The men, the sunset. You must dance as a standing bear. In this way you honor and celebrate winter's death, spring's birth, and my waking.'"

There was nothing around me but Súmáí's voice, translating. The bear, the spruce, and me: it couldn't be coincidence. The bear in this story understood the trees' power; the bear today did too. Bears had probably always known that certain spruce were gateways. No doubt that tree in the tale was a spruce. And could the two brothers actually be two selves, one visiting the other? As I had done?

Súmáí had first gone to Gage. I looked from Súmáí to the chief and considered the tension between them. A déjà vu of the cocked-gun way Súmáí had stood before his father, his mouth slightly open with calculation, came into sharp focus. Súmáí was shorter, slimmer than Gage and not nearly so attractive to me, but his body's profile was Gage's exactly.

I was standing, but I didn't remember rising. My hand covered my mouth. All activity stopped.

"Sovern?" Súmáí said.

"You're Gage!"

"Gage?"

"*Dammit!*"

255

His face took on sadness, and he nodded slightly.

I searched the stars for something to cling to, but they spiraled away. I'd been seeking answers, but this?

I was screaming before I realized it—a raspy wail—and my fists rose to my chest to ease the soreness from the bear. I screamed again, even harder. All that time, I'd hung with Gage feeling like I could be someone else. Now I saw it had been me being exactly me. No wonder he'd felt like we were supposed to be together. There was no escaping me. Across universes. Across time. What sort of cruel test was this?

"I hate tests!" I yelled. My fists dropped to my sides and I breathed through my teeth. I reeled, that scream from the day of my accident right there, overlapping this moment. Maybe the last few weeks had all been a dream. Maybe I was still strapped to my snowboard, standing beside the lift-house on 2/22.

My teeth cooled as air whistled through them. My chest heaved as it had that day, and then I felt a new pain. Not the black-hole pain of Mom's loss, but a blinding white pain that radiated out of the scabs on my chest.

Before me was not snowscape, but a pool of golden light and Ute faces. My eyes groped them, even the chief. Finally, they landed on Súmáí. From his expression, I could see he understood how I felt.

Chief Úwápaa spoke.

Súmáí smiled sadly. "He says this is strong magic."

No, I thought. It's science and math, and we're just digits in an equation. I buried my face in my hands and sought something anchoring in their smell but found only the scent of meat, roots, and berries. "Too fast," I said. I needed room to slow my mind so I could reason through what was happening. I turned and ran.

I loped along the creek's bank, headed in the direction of the pool, but I had no destination so didn't run long. Besides, I was too sore. I ran through the pines about a half mile, until a stand of aspens appeared that stretched up the mountainside. There was no moon, and beneath their canopy it was ink dark. I wandered in, hands out, then stopped and spread my fingers, touching the darkness, savoring its blank screen. I inhaled the dark, let it fill and calm me. After a bit, a night bird started cooing at regular intervals.

Steps approached through the grass.

"Súmáí?"

"*Sí*," he said.

"That bear today. It was a mother bear, and she—"

"I saw the claw marks," he said.

I listened to the grass give way as he sat, listened to him pull his knees up and clasp his hands around them.

"She also marked that tree the day she chased me," he added.

"It's like the story you told," I said. The scent of the campfire rode the breeze.

"I have thought this too," he said.

"I think that bear was my mother."

Súmáí said nothing.

"How can you be Gage?"

"*Gage*. That is his true name?"

"Yes. Sorry. 'Dammit' is a thing we say in anger."

Súmáí snorted. "He is white."

"He's the enemy, you mean?"

He nodded. "The trees kept bringing me to him. He does many things as I do. Also, there is the father."

"How can this be happening? I've seen other Soverns, other versions of me, but never me in another—"

That Mom-bear's cub was probably me.

"I cannot say how I know he is me," Súmáí said. "I just know."

I hated to admit it, but I also knew Gage was Súmáí. I wished I knew if we were in my universe. Then I'd have to contemplate reincarnation. Yet reincarnation could exist in other universes and maybe across them. I considered time moving vertically and laterally again. Maybe it even moved in parametric vectors or spirals. It was a maze of possibilities that set my head on fire. I needed solid answers. Some knowns for my equation.

"The trees seem to bring me to different…" I paused, realizing Súmáí might not know the word "universe," but he certainly understood the concept. "To different lands for a reason. Why am I here? Today?"

He didn't answer.

"Was it so I'd have another chance with this Mom, in your world?" I said. "She's a bear, Súmáí. How does that help me?"

"Another chance," he repeated, almost a whisper.

He grasped my moccasin just above my ankle, moved

up its leather till he found my bare knee. "I cried out—like you did tonight—when I first understood that Gage was my spirit," he said. "I was angry with the Great Spirit. For many days I planned to kill Gage. To end my life afterward so I could never become white. Then I saw other Gages in other lands—"

"You mean, you saw Gage having other lives?"

He nodded. "I knew I could not kill them all."

I kept touching the darkness—a lifeline to sanity—but his hand was warm on my knee.

"Then the trees brought you." He turned quiet, and we listened to the night birds and the crickets. "Sometimes I worry you are not real," he said. "That my mind makes you from want. That none of this happens."

"Uh-huh."

"Gage has you there." His grip tightened. We listened to one another breathe. "You are real."

I knelt in the grass beside him. "First you don't talk, then you say these ... *things*. It's not fair."

"I am a skilled hunter." I could hear his smile in the dark as his hand moved to the small of my back.

"Too fast," I whispered.

His hand moved away, and where it had been felt cold and hollow.

"Why us? Why now?" I said.

"I do not know."

I felt like I was streaking across time. Across existence. Pain radiated out of my chest, and my mind ached. I needed an anchor, something solid beneath my hands, and despite thinking *Too fast!* I found Súmáí's arms, groped up them to his face and traced it. His fingers found my face and traced it.

"You are real," I said.

He nodded.

My fingertips followed the curve from his neck, over his Adam's apple, to the underside of his jaw. I found his ear, pictured how its tip peeked out of his hair. The second tip of ear I'd fallen for, or maybe the first. How could we be here together?

Yet over the last year, living on without Mom had seemed less real than this.

34

Súmáí's night vision was definitely better than mine. He led me from the aspen grove past an owl's low hoot-hoot, our feet hissing through the grass, and into the diameter of firelight. His people sat or stood around his uncle, who was telling a story in Ute and gesturing with his hands. The uncle's focus darted to us for only a second, but that was enough, and many heads turned. Two women, backs to us, leaned together, and one of them craned over her shoulder. It was Súmáí's mother, and she grimaced.

Well, what did I expect? If the tables were turned, Dad would freak. And then I remembered Gage saying how his family wasn't psyched about me.

Súmáí's uncle finished his story. There was no applause, no praise. Instead, a drumbeat started, slow and steady. People rose and movement filled the open area. I spied an old man, seated with a flat drum suspended between his legs. He hit it with a stick that had one end wrapped in rawhide. Another man sat beside him, and as the drumbeat sped to a hopping rhythm, that man set a notched white stick about a foot long against a log before him and bumped a regular stick up and down it, making a grating sound. They began to chant.

"What's he doing?" I said.

Súmáí followed my eyes. "He's making the sound of the bear scratching the tree."

I tried to remember what that had sounded like, but I couldn't.

"What's that white thing he holds?" I asked.

"A *morache*. Bear growler. Elk jaw bone."

Women were approaching men and flicking the fringe of their colored shawls at them. Partners, they joined the double line and faced each other, women looking east, men west, like in the story Súmáí's mother had told. Túwámúpǔch walked past, glum-faced, and flicked her shawl at a boy of maybe fourteen.

"Túwámúpǔch doesn't like me," I said.

"She hoped we would be husband and wife when her grieving time had ended." Súmáí squeezed my hand. "But now you are my wife."

"*Wife?*" I stepped back and felt the blood rush from my face. "I can't be your wife! I—"

His face held humor as he scanned his village. "They think we have lain together."

"Súmáí, I can't stay here. I have to go back."

He squinted at me in the firelight. "In your world, you are with me. Here, you are with me. Why?"

"I don't know."

He rocked back on his heels with a gaze that said *I do*. I wanted to slap him.

"Don't call me *wife*!" I repeated. "Just don't!"

Súmáí's mother appeared and offered me a sky blue shawl. She spoke. Súmáí translated, working to keep a straight face. "She says, 'Here, *daughter*.'"

I glared at him but took the shawl and spread it over my shoulders. His mother eyed me and nodded. She said something sad-sounding to Súmáí. He snapped something back, and she scolded him. Súmáí stared after her as she walked across the open space to the chief and flicked her shawl at him. The chief rose and they walked to the line.

"Do you fight with everyone?"

Súmáí smirked. "I am a warrior."

The gazes on us were embarrassing. "What did she say?"

"She said the bear, the trees, and the Great Spirit have brought us together."

I gnawed my lip. "That's not all she said."

"Not all. Are you going to ask me to dance?"

Wife. His mother considered us married too. My pulse sped to the drum's rhythm. It was time to go home. Already I'd begun hurting him. "Súmáí, I—"

"I have learned not to fight the will of the trees," he said. "The dance is not difficult. You will see."

The will of the trees. That made me scan his face, and then the night sky. The drum pulsed in my head and my body ached from the bear's charge, yet I said, "Tell me what you know about the trees."

He shook his head. "Now we dance to honor you and the bear."

You and the bear. Me and Mom. I looked around. I did not want to do this, but I didn't want to disappoint Súmáí's people more. And Súmáí least of all. I scowled and flicked my shawl at him.

He grasped the fringe, his eyes a challenge.

We joined the line, and, as if everyone had been waiting at a dinner table, the dancing began. I stood there, watching. But Súmáí was right: the dance was simple. Three steps forward, three back. Over and over. Forward and back, forward and back, forward and back. It was hypnotic. I let the rhythm take me, let it settle my jitters and ease my aching head. I smelled the dust beneath our moccasins, the pines, the grass, the wind. *The will of the trees.* I eyed the stars; we were made of dust from collapsed stars, I'd read. I liked that. Stardust for hair. Stardust for skin. Stardust for blood. Stardust for bones.

After a while, my skin seemed to transform to fur. My fingers seemed to be claws. I felt Mom's animal fury at the things she knew, while I had lain a few feet away, frustrated by what I *didn't* know.

I danced. And danced.

I lost track of time. I started to feel less like a bear and more like one particle of an endless wave, our line a wave of women meeting men, a wave meeting across eternity. I looked up, and Earth seemed miniscule, insignificant against that infinity of lights. I reached out, longing for Súmáí's hand as an anchor across so much space and time. He didn't take my hand, though. He just shook his head, gesturing *not here.*

How much time passed? No clue. My feet started to ache and my shoulders throbbed with the drum. Drowsiness seeped through me, and I sagged.

Súmáí led me away from the fire to his tepee. He went in, and when he came out, he was carrying blankets under his arm. He led me back to that stand of aspens. By sound, I knew he was stomping down the grass and spreading one blanket, then another over that. Next to his head, he lay his bow, its arrows, and his knife. I stared at that bed, considering the wisdom of getting in it with him, but exhaustion won out. I climbed in, thinking my shoulders' ache would keep me from sleeping. I inhaled Súmáí's scent. *Me + love = disaster,* I thought, and that's all I remember.

35

The sun filtering through the aspens woke me. Súmáí's warmth intersected my spine as he lay sleeping on his opposite side. I rolled onto my back, gnawing my lip against searing pain. I studied the rise of his shoulder, which met the rolled-back edge of our blanket. I picked up a thick lock of his hair, my movements so stiff, and draped it across my face. It smelled like dried grass and smoke. I opened my mouth and let strands fall in as I looked up, through hashes of dark and light, at aspen boughs and saw a slide show of yesterday's events: the bear, the pool, the miners.

I'd helped kill two men. Bad men, granted, but killing nonetheless. The day had moved so fast, I hadn't had a chance to fully consider them. Now I felt sick. Yet none of this was . . . what? Real? Sane? How far into the future would I have to go for this to be sane?

We lay in a flat spot. To my left jutted a chest-high boulder. My heart skipped as the physical world came into focus: we were at the bottom of Eternity, one of my favorite runs. Every time I boarded here, I'd swing in from the west and hit this jump. I felt how I'd pop off its lip, flying—one, two, three, four—till gravity dragged me to landing's *whoomf* and my arms rose in victory.

A tear meandered down my temple. That's where I belonged. Where snowboarding off a jump, smoking, doing drugs, ditching school, and dating a dangerous guy constituted life's greatest risks. When Súmáí woke, I'd learn what he knew about the trees, see if it held a clue to getting Mom back, and get out. I closed my mouth tight on his hair.

He stirred and rolled to face me. He rested his head on his arm. I rolled, grimacing, and attempted to bring my arm up like his but was too sore. I searched his face, saw Gage in its symmetry and in how his brows made a little V when they pressed close. He saw the wet at my temple, frowned, and wiped it with his finger.

I braced because I thought he might try to kiss me. Instead, he wiped my tear on his bottom lip, and whatever drew me to him increased by a power of ten.

———————

As we entered the village, Súmáí's people glanced at us, but this time they continued what they were doing—eating breakfast, scraping hides, hanging meat. The breeze carried the scent of horses and dung and smoke. Two women were walking into the willows along the creek's bank, carrying burden baskets like backpacks. Those three-foot-long baskets matched the ones in photos Lindholm had shown us. The Utes, she'd said, made baskets prized and traded for by all tribes. She'd taught us that Utes spent their summers hoarding food for the winter. Most days, men hunted and women collected berries and roots and trapped small game. Constant work. Survival.

We passed Súmáí's uncle's tepee. Out front, Túwámúpǔch held the bottom of a deer leg. She ran a knife down it and peeled back the fur, making me swallow hard. Beside her, a baby was laced in a cradleboard and propped against a stump, just a little face watching. That baby was about the cutest thing I'd ever seen, and at the same time the saddest because I realized it belonged to Túwámúpǔch. As I watched Súmáí smile down at his niece or nephew, I felt the vastness of Túwámúpǔch's sorrow. It might be even greater than mine for Mom. Súmáí's brother must have died about a year ago, based on this baby's age. And I was blocking her from marrying Súmáí, maybe finding happiness again.

"Is that a boy or a girl?" I asked.

"Boy," Súmáí said.

"Was she happy with your brother?"

"Yes."

We glanced back and caught Túwámúpǔch glaring at us.

Outside Súmáí's tepee, his mother bent over a small fire with a metal grill balanced on its rock ring. She set an iron skillet on it. As she lifted an inch-wide white square of paper, my breath caught. Grinning at me, she peeled paper off both sides of the square and dropped a slice of butter in the skillet.

The tiny precise papers and the sliver of butter seemed ridiculous in this world. Predetermined, narrow servings. I saw the grid of the Condo. I smelled the barfy cleanser from school and heard the electronic ring of its bell. My life in the future appeared, narrow passages ruled by thick black boundaries laid out by clocks.

She tossed the little papers onto the fire, and they ignited as she set a pre-halved bagel in the sizzling butter.

I cleared my throat. "Súmáí, really? Those are from the lodges."

He waggled his eyebrows. "I am a great hunter."

I pointed at his mother's feet. "And those slippers?"

He nodded, rubbed the back of his head, and shrugged.

I was half-angry, half-laughing, till I remembered Tara's stitches and black eye. I heard her say, *They give you a gun?* Though my mouth was watering from hunger, I strode around the tepee and looked across Gold Bowl toward the ridge to Silver Bowl, where Sapphire East's luxurious log structure would one day perch. I remembered standing right here amid a crowd of skiers, heard their chit-chat, banter, and laughter set against the chairlift's electric hum.

Súmáí joined me. Yesterday, I'd helped him kill two miners. He'd *scalped* them.

"You hit my friend," I said.

He sighed and held out the toasted bagel. I shook my head. He loosed a frustrated breath. "My people are hungry, Sovern."

"You hit Tara! Knocked her out! Do you remember that? She would have been...riding a big..." I found the closest Spanish word: "*Máquina.*"

"I have seen the loud machines with suns that move at night and flatten the snow. A machine like that would help my people."

I barked a laugh. "She's my friend!"

"It was dark. Her clothes were big. I thought she was a man." Súmáí glared at the bagel. "You do not understand—we are at war with the white enemy."

Are.

"They have stolen our lands." He calmed his voice. "They have brought sickness, killing many Utes. They force us onto reservations. In our ancestral meeting places, they build agencies that give out bad food and thin blankets. They are cunning. Ouray has met with the whites and signed away our lands. My family does not like Ouray. He does not have this right. He is a coward. He will not *fight*!"

I flinched at how hard Súmáí spoke that last word. I remembered his lightning speed as he'd shot the miners. Another photograph from Lindholm's class rose in my memory: Chief Ouray, leader and negotiator for all the Utes; his wife Chipeta; maybe another Ute; and two white guys in old-timey suits. All seated. All posing after signing a treaty in Washington. What year was that?

"Our people have finally fought and slain a cruel white agent. He will not tell lies in the spirit world."

Events ticked through my mind as I tried to recall history's chronology.

"Meeker? You mean Meeker?" Meeker had been an Indian agent in northern Colorado. In my world, there was a town named after him.

Súmáí looked surprised. "He is the one."

Meeker had died with a spear through his mouth, which even the history books said he deserved, but during Súmáí's time, it had sealed the Utes' fate. I now knew exactly where we hung in time. The date, like all numbers, returned to me easily from Lindholm's class over a month ago: 1879. Days where yellow journalists were writing headlines like *The Utes Must Go*. The final days of Súmáí's people in these mountains.

"When did this happen?"

Súmáí shrugged. "Ten moons ago."

"You stayed here through the winter?" Okay, I calculated, 1880 then.

"A warmer place. Down the valley." He gestured west.

"You won't move to the reservation?" I didn't have the heart to tell him that Chief Ouray had actually been a shrewd negotiator, had succeeded where other tribes had not, and he'd brought his people many peaceful years they wouldn't have had otherwise. Now, after the "Meeker Massacre," the years of the Utes' patient peacefulness would be meaningless. Ouray had been able to negotiate nothing but a military escort to a reservation in the plateaus and arroyos of Utah. The Utes had been ordered to gather in Grand Junction for the long march. Banished.

But Súmáí's people hadn't gone. That's what those miners had meant when they'd said, *You aren't supposed to be here.*

"My family does not follow Ouray. The Great Spirit gave our ancestors these mountains. We will not leave."

A dog barked playfully on the tepee's other side, and children's excited voices followed, moving through camp. An adult voice spoke, saying something obviously adult. I thought of the people I'd met—Súmáí's proud father, his uncle, his worrying mother, Túwámúpúch—and the dance in my honor.

Súmáí watched me—fierce, a *warrior*—and I knew he'd never feel bad about attacking Tara. I tried to mask how this scared me, how I knew he was destined to fail. Staying here with him would hurt like losing Mom did. I had to learn what he knew about the trees and get out.

"Súmáí, I—"

He held up his hand like a traffic cop. "Do not tell me what will come. Your land steals my hope." He stared at the bagel's two halves. Cooking in butter had mottled the bread yellow and dark brown.

I felt like such a jerk. I'd been about to tell him I was leaving, yet he thought I'd been trying to save him with knowledge of the future. I bit my lip and accepted half the bagel. While there might be ridiculous pre-sliced butter and boundaries everywhere, things were cushy in my world. I wouldn't even have to pay for the food he held. Suddenly life held too many contradictions.

I looked at the sun, loosed a noise like a frustrated animal, and stormed toward the trail leading up to the Always spruce. Get out! Just get out now! I told myself.

"Sovern!"

I stopped. Súmáí arrived at my side. Though I willed myself not to look at him, my eyes betrayed me. His face held so much pain I caught my breath. "Súmáí?"

He smiled a little. "We return to two words."

I pressed my forehead against his chest, higher than where it met Gage's chest. Súmáí's hand came to my back and moved up between my shoulder blades, and it was comforting. Finally, I stepped back.

"The hunting in your world is good." He smiled sadly at the bagel-half I held.

I grimaced.

"Game *here* is scarce," he said.

I pictured Túwámúpúch's deer leg and realized that by "hunting," he didn't mean just stuff from lodges. "You hunt in my land?"

He nodded.

"That deer leg Túwámúpúch had—"

He nodded.

I had to think about that. "Will more white men come looking for those two from yesterday?"

Súmáí shrugged. "Let them come."

"What happened to their scalps?"

"My mother will sew them to my shirt," he said.

"A shirt? You have a shirt of scalps?"

"I earned my first scalp at fourteen winters. It is how I became a man."

"Fourteen?" At fourteen, I'd been skate skiing and snowboarding and hating the Condo.

"It is a rite of passage for Ute boys to go alone to a special place. They stay three days, seeking a vision from the spirit world. That vision guides them through life." He glanced at me in a weird way.

"What did you see?"

"I cannot speak of it," he said.

"But you scalped someone?"

"A white man came upon me. I was weak from hunger, but I killed him."

"How many winters are you now?" I estimated he was twenty-three or twenty-four.

"Nineteen."

"Nineteen? I thought you were older."

"How many are you?" he said.

"Almost nineteen."

Súmáí's smile was wide. "You are old to become a wife, but I guess you'll do."

I snorted, scanned Gold Bowl—full of live trees—and understood why I'd been crying as I woke. Whether I stayed or left, we were out of time.

36

W here are the men?" I set down the tin cup of willow-
bark tea Súmáí's mom had brewed to ease my soreness.

"Hunting."

Clad again in Súmáí's shirt and breeches, I stretched out
my limbs. After breakfast, I'd refused to wear the ordinary
dress Súmáí's mom had offered, choosing his clothes instead.
When he'd handed me a pair of sheepskin slippers with a play-
ful smile, I'd rolled my eyes but put them on. The dress from
the night before was stored next to Súmáí's bed—mine to
keep—but no way could I bring it back with me. How would
I explain it to Dad?

Súmáí's mom went into the tepee, moving as stiffly as
me. She emerged carrying the two scalps from yesterday and
a shirt of patchwork hair. Long, short, curly, straight, black,

brown, red, blond. Some shiny, some dull. It was eerie. Yesterday, those miners had been alive.

I felt nauseous as I watched her lift a long white needle and thread it. Her fingers' joints were so big her hands seemed cartoonish. I glanced at her cup of willow bark tea and wondered how much she drank to ease her arthritis.

"Are we going hunting then?" I needed to get back to the Always spruce. On the hike there, I would pick Súmáí's brain one more time, and then I'd go home.

"You want to hunt?" Súmáí said and glanced at his mother.

"I'm not hanging out here." I tried to make it sound like I was only avoiding sitting around with the women, which wasn't hard. "Besides, I need to get my parka and hat from by the tree."

He frowned and scratched the back of his head, Gage's habit, and it made the knot in my stomach pull tighter. Why did I have to lie to everyone? Then Súmáí took a deep breath and nodded. He went into the tepee, leaving me and his mother sitting across from each other. She didn't say anything, just worked, but disapproval rode off her in waves. Súmáí emerged with his bow and quiver slung over his shoulder. He spoke to her. She eyed him, then me, and nodded grudgingly.

"*Towéiyak*," I said.

Her frown lessened a little at that.

"We will go on foot," Súmáí said. "If we have success, we will pull our kill. It is downhill."

I wouldn't even let myself consider dragging a dead dear or elk. I dismissed his words, intent on that Always spruce.

As we walked out of camp, straight up the draw on the

future road I'd snowboarded down yesterday morning, every last one of my muscles rebelled. I could tell Súmáí shortened his strides for me.

"You remember," he said.

"Remember?"

"*Towéiyak*. From when you gave me the hat."

"Sort of. Your mother reminded me too."

He threw back his head and laughed. "That is the way of my mother."

My every step was a chore demanding attention. In about fifteen minutes, though, my muscles eased a bit. "Where will you hunt?" I asked.

"Near the tree where we met." He pointed toward Shangri-La. "Sometimes game grazes there."

"Is that why you were there that day?"

He seemed to sort things and nodded.

"That's a long walk. Could you travel there by tree?" I bit my lip because I'd used "you" instead of "we."

He stopped, assessing me. "That is not the way of the trees."

I decided to press my advantage. "But it would save us so much—"

"The trees do not move that way."

"You've tried?"

"Yes."

"What happened?"

"Always I travel to other lands."

I'd gone to Mom on my first two trips, but on the third, I'd found Súmáí. A stranger. No, not a stranger, I corrected myself, remembering my childhood boogieman. What other lands had Súmáí seen? Had he brought me to this land, or had Mom? Why here? Why now? I sipped a breath: a pattern, an equation existed for this. "How did you get to Sapphire East then?"

"Sapphire East?"

"The lodge that will be over there." I pointed.

"We call it Big Ridge. The first time, I rode hidden on the machine." He started walking backward, nodding and grinning, daring me to be offended again by his hurting Tara. A test.

"I hate tests," I spat in English.

"What?" he said in Spanish.

"*Nada*," I said. *Nothing.* "And the food? How did you carry it?"

"There is a tree near Sapphire East." He pronounced the name pretty well. "From there I pulled it down to my village."

"That's a long way."

He shrugged. "I made trips for scouting and trips for hunting. I had men from my village come to the tree with horses to carry back the food. It was difficult because the trees do not bring me to other lands in—" He'd obviously said something he hadn't wanted to.

I stopped walking. "Order? The trees don't bring you in order?"

He didn't stop.

Why would he not just tell me this? I forced my glare from his slim powerful body to the surroundings. Be nice, I coached myself, and started walking again.

I'd assumed Súmáí and I had been seeing one another in a linear order. Till yesterday, I hadn't seen him for a while. Was this because he couldn't get back? He'd been so desperate-seeming, so forward when he'd found me lying there after the Mom-bear attack. Had he encountered other Soverns, in other worlds? Had he met the ones I'd seen? Did he know a future Sovern from my own world, beyond the me that was following him now? Had they fallen in love, and now I was here like a frustrating echo? That would explain a lot.

Was this even the same Súmáí? He'd said we were headed to the place we'd met, so I knew this Súmáí was the one who'd been there that first time. Last night at dinner, he'd smiled at the face I'd made at the food, like it was payback for my toying with him in the cabin. But that could just have been coincidence. I remembered the hat I'd seen on his bed, and, a few minutes ago, when he'd seemed pleased and said, "You remember." Had he also been confirming that *I* was *his* Sovern?

"Have you visited me beyond my time?" My words were careful not to show emotion.

He slowed to let me catch up. "I have seen your land."

"No. I mean a me beyond that. An *us* beyond then."

His head cocked. Silence. I grabbed his arm.

"Have you met a me from a different land?"

His expression showed he understood me completely. His eyes clicked through possible answers, and I knew he understood way more than I did.

"Tell me!" I said.

It took him a minute to decide what to say. "I traveled through the trees, but I did not visit you. Or other Soverns."

He grinned. "I did not want to fight your father. He is big and strong. Like a bear."

The mention of Dad made me feel sick again. I remembered that night Súmáí's face had appeared in the cabin's window while Dad and Wash had been out investigating the noise at the pumps and how afraid I'd been that they'd battle.

"Thanks," I said, sarcastic. I turned and flung out my arm as if I were throwing something—I can't say what. I just needed to throw *something*.

His voice turned gentle. "I also grew weak."

I glanced up the mountain, the direction of the Always spruce. "I know the cure for that. Just eat a lot of salt."

Súmáí snorted. "I began to feel like air."

"In my world, there are places where we could just go buy food and bring it back. They sell *whole containers* of salt." I showed the height of a salt container with my hands. "You don't have to steal." I pictured Sapphire East. "But if you need salt from the lodges, it comes in white paper packets, about this big." I held my finger and thumb about an inch apart. He cocked his head and looked at the ground.

"What?" I said.

"Your shadow. It is like mine."

I looked down and saw the shadow my hand cast was half as dark as the other shadows around. Súmáí held out his hand, and its shadow was similar.

"You have wealth. Yes?" he said, studying our shadows. "Our number is half what it once was, but we are still many stomachs."

"Half?"

He looked away from our hands and said, like giving up, "I do not want to travel through the trees anymore, and if you left, we could not know when you would come again."

"Why don't you want to travel through the trees?"

He shrugged.

"You mean, if I leave today and return, it could be before now, or after?"

"Yes. I might be a child, or an elder. Or another Súmáí."

Or on a reservation, far from here. "So this is why you were so happy to see me?"

He kept his eyes averted but nodded. The careful way he held his torso and arms and the sad cast of his face sent a chill through me. He was guarding every last word he told me. Warrior, indeed.

"So if I leave now … " I spoke carefully. "If I leave, I might never find *you*, this Súmáí, again." I suddenly realized that my being there, just then, with him, was a fixed point on a grid of infinite dimensions. I faced him fully. "Why us?"

He met my gaze. "Why you and me?"

I nodded.

"The quills, I believe. Beyond that, I cannot say."

"What do you mean?"

"Do you remember the day we met? How you … left, and I held your quill?"

I remembered Gage pulling me from that spruce, and my fury. "Yes."

"After that, I could walk in your land."

"Could you walk in any others?"

He shook his head.

Was that why I was here? Tramping around? Because he'd given me his quill?

We resumed our ascent, and I realized I'd probably made Súmáí's vandalism possible—even before I'd met him. Dad would love that. My head searched so hard for a pattern to explain everything, to explain what bound us, that I felt dizzy.

We arrived at the Always spruce. I stood before its trunk and traced Mom's claw marks with my eyes. Súmáí gestured for me to follow and led me to the spruce's other side. He pointed to newly healed claw marks in the rough bark. *Marks for Súmáí + marks for me = weird.* I craved laying a palm on that trunk and going home, but if Súmáí was right, I might never be able to return to this place and time. He'd said he didn't want to travel through the trees anymore, and I definitely wasn't ready to give him up yet.

So it was now or never.

I thought of that guarded way he'd stood moments ago, and I craved every last one of his answers. He'd said that I would return to my world on the same day at the same time. If that was true, what could it hurt, spending more time here? For Dad's sake, I prayed Súmáí was right…and I decided to stay.

I laid my snowshoes against the spruce, picked up my parka, and stuffed my hat into its sleeve. I felt my phone in its pocket, dug it out, and pressed the camera icon.

"Hey," I said.

Súmáí turned from scanning the forest, watching for the Mom-bear, no doubt.

I clicked a photo and brought it up on the screen. "Súmáí, look! This is you!" I stepped to his side.

He sucked in his breath, squinted at his image, and leaned close to it. "My brother! You have captured him!"

"No. That's you! Look at the forest in the background."

He scanned the pines behind him.

"I took it just now," I said.

"You have imprisoned my spirit?"

"No. It's just a picture."

He looked at the image, then me, then my phone's shape, and something seemed to register. I made a mental note to get that scrap of information too.

"Your spirit is free," I said. "I promise. Look." I held the phone at arms' length, the choice to stay with him fresh and raw in my chest as I snapped another photo. I held the image before him.

He looked from me to the photo. "Why do people do this?"

I shrugged. "To remember, I guess."

"Remember?" He said it like the greatest irony.

A lump filled my throat, and I worked to swallow it just as the last thing I'd expected hit me full on and defenseless: Mom's dying moment. Metal and gas smell, distant sirens, hair curtaining her cheek, and her wrist's pulse beneath my fingertips diminishing—fainter, fainter, gone. And then screams erupting in my gut as I pressed my lips to stop them. I'd pressed my palms to my ears against the *tick, tick, tick* of the hot crushed engine and sealed the sound of her pulse in my memory.

"You're right," I said. "The important things you never forget."

I took Súmáí's hand, pressed his palm to mine, and held our pressed hands up to the sun. His was a little bigger and wider. A string of light lined the back side of our joined hands, but their fronts and our thumbs met in a line of shadow. I thought of Cairn's research. Were our particles connected? Could something from that tiny realm have drawn me here?

I bumped my fingertip over the four bones on the back of his hand. "Spooky action," I said. I turned his hand and studied his wrist where his heart pulsed. "Entanglement," I said. All this would lead to a breathing Mom restored to my life. I knew it.

I slung my parka over my arm. "Let's go."

We crested the ridge, me huffing, and crossed west from Gold Bowl into Platinum Bowl. In summer a mountain bike trail snaked around this spot. In winter it was a run called Fool's Gold. The wind blew over its top and formed cornices that tourists skied off in droves—hooting, crashing, cheering. When the cornices got lethal, Dad dynamited them. Now a family of marmots whistled their way beneath a pile of rocks. We skirted the forest where Last Chance would exist and dropped into Shangri-La.

In Súmáí's world, the meadow forming Shangri-La was larger. He slunk along its edge, and I followed till he crouched in the grass near the spruce I'd collided with. I looked up at it, realizing that in this world the tree was still big, but with less girth and height. When I'd traveled to Mom's universe from this spot, it had seemed the same size as it was in mine. I was definitely in the past.

"We wait," Súmáí whispered. He pressed his finger to his lips, gesturing quiet, but now seemed a perfect chance to grill him.

"Why—?"

"Shhh!"

"Súmáí—"

He glared at me.

With my soreness, crouching was impossible, so I sat down, not graceful at all, my long legs resembling the grasshoppers that I scared to clacking leaps. I listened to the missing hum of tires on the valley floor, the lack of rumble from planes overhead. I started to make a list of what I wanted to learn from him. I heard instead the drone of bees and flies. A squirrel scolded us. In the distance, a crow seemed to speak a sentence. I looked over to where the Mom and little-me had sat on a blanket in that other universe. What would have happened if Súmáí hadn't stopped me? The sun was warm, and, though I tried to finish that list, the world turned syrupy.

I woke to an odd warbling. I'd collapsed to my side, and I rose on an elbow, wiping drool from my mouth.

Súmáí held a folded aspen leaf in his lips, and he was blowing on it. His bow was cocked, arrow ready. I looked into the meadow just as two velvety does lifted their heads.

He shot, and one collapsed to its forelegs, and then to its side. The other bounded away.

Súmáí sprang up and stood over the deer faster than seemed possible. I maneuvered myself to my feet like the Tin Man and walked to him, palming back my hair. Súmáí drew his knife and knelt over the deer, reciting something in Ute. He leaned toward its throat and I turned away, picturing him moving the same way over yesterday's miners. My hand traced the scabs on my chest. I pressed each one, concentrating on its sting to keep from retching.

When I heard him rise, I said without looking, "What was that sound you made?"

"A fawn's cry."

My legs wobbled and gave out. I landed on my knees in the grass.

Súmáí frowned. "The Great Spirit smiles on us. Game is scarce."

"Why is it scarce?" I asked.

He shrugged, not like he didn't know but like he didn't want to answer, and glanced down the valley.

The half-formed, early-afternoon face on Phantom Peak resembled the line of shadow that had existed between Súmáí's and my pressed hands. I'd screamed at this valley on 2/22: my silence's end. I estimated the place on the highway where Mom and I had sat trapped in that Honda. I squinted, looking closer. Smoke rose from the chimneys of a cluster of three cabins. Around them stretched furrowed green fields. It all looked wrong. Unnatural.

"That is where my ancestors made summer camp,"

Súmáí said. "That is where my brother died." He strode into the forest.

I sighed and held up my thumb against the valley's image below. Its tip to my knuckle—that was the distance separating where Súmáí's brother and Mom had died.

Cracking and banging came from the forest. Súmáí emerged dragging a long, narrow log, all the branches hatcheted off.

"What are you doing?"

"I need to pull the deer."

"Pull?" I said, keeping my eyes averted.

"Did you not listen?"

"Not really," I said. I'd been focused on getting to that Always spruce. I hadn't even planned to still be here. Now, with an actual deer as big as me—a dead thing I couldn't even look at—the idea of dragging it all the way back to camp was daunting.

"Why didn't we bring a horse?"

"You do not like horses," Súmáí said.

"I might start."

He grunted and returned to the forest. The hacking sound rose again. I just stood there with that dead deer. I dared a glance at its lean body, and then I took a long breath and turned, making myself look. It had delicate-seeming black hooves. My eyes traveled up its legs to its white chest. White like snow, I thought. I followed the shining line of its black nose, its guileless brown eye, its large white-lined ear, its curve down its neck to its strong back, ending in its white rump and lean haunches. This doe had been drawn to a fawn's call. In that Honda, I'd complained—a call for help—and Mom had lifted her hand from the wheel to comfort me. My throat clogged with bile, and I looked down the valley to keep from bawling.

Súmáí emerged, dragging another log. He paused, considered the defeated way I stood, and said, "I also do not like horses. They are white man's animals." He dragged the log to the deer. "Many Ute men love horses—to race them, to bet on them. The killing of Meeker happened because he plowed our race track for farming. My father had many horses. My mother came to him in a bet on a horse race." He snorted. "Now we keep only as many horses as can remain hidden. 'Magic dogs,' we first called them. *Magic?*" He laughed bitterly.

Shoulders back, hands almost clenched against the invisible and unstoppable equations of life, he was so thoroughly Gage that it stole my breath. Gage saying, *Why would I want to go to college? Why would I want someone to teach me how to think?* My mind's eye saw Gage say, *Sovereign, like self-rule? That's fucking cool!*

Sorrow for them both pierced me. Fate's track barreled straight toward us, and, somehow, this, here, seemed the start of it. Súmáí and me, that little point on that profound graph. I looked at the lifeless deer, and suddenly I couldn't handle it all. I turned and shouted, "I hate tests!"

I could feel Súmáí watching me, no doubt wondering at the meaning of my English words. In Spanish, I said, "Life isn't fair."

I heard him move behind me and felt the warmth of his hand on my shoulder.

37

As the western sun cast sturdy shadows, we entered the village, Súmáí dragging the deer. He pulled it to his tepee, and his mother emerged, beaming. An ancient woman was with her. They seemed so small and bent, like the scraggy windswept bushes above timberline. The older woman's face resembled a raisin, each wrinkle no doubt containing a story, and her eyes glittered as she beheld the deer. She spoke in Ute, and her voice was surprisingly strong and steady.

"Grandmother says our wedding brings good luck," Súmáí said.

I made a face at him.

Súmáí's mother spoke, and he cocked his head. "She says we must follow her."

The women walked toward camp's western end. The children saw us, and they ran over, cheering and laughing, the dogs barking and leaping. Other women joined till we became a parade. The few men in camp stayed seated around their fires or tending their weapons. A few of them eyed us and chuckled and shook their heads.

Súmáí's breath caught. A tepee stood before us.

Súmáí's grandmother spoke ceremoniously. His mother smiled. Súmáí walked to the tepee's side and looked up at the poles sticking out its top like in KerPlunk. He looked across the gathered faces, even the kids, and spoke. His last word was *towéiyak*.

They looked at me, expectant. I blushed, speechless.

Súmáí stepped to me, took my hand, and led me into the tepee. He closed the flap while muffled giggles from outside drifted through.

"They give us this," he said.

I pivoted in a circle, taking in the tepee's interior. On the far side stretched two willow beds with blankets on top. I couldn't help but remember the twin beds in the cabin's bedroom—one for me, one for Dad. I said another prayer that Súmáí was right and that Dad hadn't lain in the dark last night staring at my empty bed.

Two tall storage baskets stood against the side a little ways over. My snowboarding clothes were folded in a neat pile beside them with my dancing dress on top. My snow boots were there too. Súmáí set his bow and quiver down next to them.

On the opposite wall stood a water basket, dark pitch lining its bowl. In the tepee's center lay a fire ring. I looked at the sky through the tepee's open flap and then at Súmáí.

"They think I'm your wife." My words sounded desperate. I was worn out from the day's emotions and exertion, and my whole body ached.

He sighed. He was tired too.

I bit my lip. "You're sure I'll return to my world on the same day?"

"Yes. You will stay?"

"For a while."

His mouth twisted to hold back a smile. "It is custom that we lie together."

I stepped back. "I can't!"

"I know," he said.

"You don't understand—I'll hurt you." I touched my chest. "Here."

"I know." He stepped closer.

"No really! I'm disaster for everyone I—"

"I am used to these things. I am a warrior." His mouth quirked up on one side.

This weird thing happened then. Maybe *fatigue + learning all he'd lost and would still lose = hallucination.* All I know is he transformed to the one person—anywhere—who understood how I felt. I lunged to him and hugged him.

I must have stunned him, because it took a minute for his arms to circle me. When we pulled apart, he touched the freckle on my lip.

"I like this," he said.

I hated that freckle, and, embarrassed, I pressed my face into his chest.

I washed my bra and underwear every several days. Each day, Súmáí and I hunted, and I grilled him with questions, which he mostly evaded. It became obvious that I wasn't going to hang out with the women and learn their responsibilities, so Chief Úwápaa, with Súmáí's uncle and cousins flanking him, presented me with a bow. A left-handed one.

I forced my mouth closed and accepted it and the quiver of arrows. I studied it in wonder, and its shape felt so natural in my hands that I sighed. "*Towéiyak,*" I said, meaning it.

Súmáí taught me to hunt—how to track, move soundlessly, make low signal whistles to a partner, and shoot. At first drawing a bow's string made my ribs, arm, and fingers ache, but one day that ache was gone. The heft and shape of the bow and aiming down an arrow became second nature. Sometimes, after I'd pierce a flower petal Súmáí had pressed against a tree's trunk, he'd tackle me right there in the grass and kiss me. The two younger guys with Chief Úwápaa that day I'd arrived were Súmáí's cousins—Panákwas and Mú'ú'nap—and on the days they joined us, they'd just shake their heads and walk away.

I never let things go farther than that, though. Out there, or in our tepee. Nights, we'd lie in those willow beds, craving strong between us, but I just couldn't give myself like that.

I ate meat every day—deer, elk, buffalo, rabbit, squirrel, beaver, badger, marmot—and I got used to hunting with Súmáí, yet I could not bring myself to *kill*. I sensed that this bugged him, but he didn't say anything.

All around me, people spoke Ute. Súmáí started teaching me words. I'd hear them sprinkled through conversations, and I started to detect patterns. One day, those patterns focused. I still spoke it like a three-year-old, but I understood it well enough to get by, and it was crazy how just understanding what people were saying changed them from seeming like characters in a movie to real people. Súmáí's mom seemed not to mind me so much. His grandmother got a kick out of me, and she walked around laughing this low *he-he-he* and shaking her head at the dorky things I did. Panákwas and Mú'ú'nap's wives grew chummy with me as the guys played gambling games with the hulls of yucca seeds. Chief Úwápaa, though, always kept his distance.

As they got used to me, I'd hear people singing to themselves or humming as they worked. I'd see their voices in soothing waves. I started singing too. "Blackbird" mostly, the tune Mom always sang when I was little. It would remind me that I'd thought there was a way to bring her back, and I needed to find it. A good reminder, because with Súmáí and his people, I was starting to forget. At first I notched each sunrise on a stick, but each day stretched long, and joined to the next in a contented blur. As I started to make my eighth notch, I couldn't see the point of tracking time in this world like I did in mine, especially if I was going to return at the same moment I'd left. So I stopped. Before I knew it, one full moon had passed. Then another. Light, dark, and the moon were the only clocks.

Practically every night, they told stories around the fire, or sang, or danced. The dancing and singing were better than any movie. They had these rattles that would light up in the dark. Súmáí said they were made from buffalo hide with pieces of sacred quartz inside, and that this quartz called the spirits. I reasoned that the rock chips sparked off one another, but, honestly, around that campfire, with the singing and the starscape, those rattles *were* magic. His family also played flutes made from yucca stalks, which raised the hair on my arms and neck. And drums that echoed in my bones.

Everyone told stories around the campfire. Even kids got up a few times, and I liked that because I could understand their sentences without Súmáí's help. My eyes would seek Túwámúpúch, wherever she sat, and I'd watch her rock her son and think how my presence was blocking her happiness. It was like pressing on a splinter beneath my skin, and this, too, reminded me to keep gathering information. That sometime soon I should return home.

But then I'd start a new day with Súmáí and I'd forget. Some nights, I'd watch the campfire's smoke waver and spiral up, and that Sovern back home seemed like another person. Like looking at one of those other Soverns in the universes through the spruce.

One night, Panákwas told a story about a bear, and I peered between the gaps in the tepees, looking for Mom. I hadn't seen her since that first day, and I was starting to wonder if maybe I'd had things wrong. Then Súmáí squeezed my hand, and my worries faded in the warmth of his arm pressing mine.

Halfway between the first and second full moons, when

it came time to decide who would tell the next story, Chief Úwápaa said, "Bear Necklace," and all eyes veered to me.

"I can't," I said. "I'm bad at your language."

"Tell it in Spanish," he said, "and Súmáí will translate."

"We will help you," Súmáí said and glanced at his father, who nodded.

I wanted to run to the forest, but I sensed this was a matter of honor, and when I stood, the gleam in Súmáí's eye confirmed it. I could also see worry: What would I tell his people? Would I bring ugliness from my own world?

As I searched my mind for what to say, I realized he was right to worry. Then my gaze caught on the feathers adorning the tops of Chief Úwápaa's braids. Mom began singing "Blackbird" in my head, and Angelou's *I Know Why the Caged Bird Sings* was right there, ready.

"This is the story of a girl who was like a caged bird. A girl who whites did not like because of her dark skin. She lived halfway between my time and yours, when people with dark skin suffered many injustices at the hands of whites."

Chief Úwápaa nodded. "There was a great war in the East."

"The Civil War?" I said, and then corrected it to what people might call it in this time. "The War Between the States?"

"I do not know this name," Chief Úwápaa said. "Only that the whites had a great war that has made them too poor to pay our treaties."

"The black-skinned people," I said, "came to this country as slaves. The great war was to free them. After the war, slavery was not allowed, but many whites still treated them cruelly."

The chief shook his head. "Buffalo soldiers."

"What?" I said.

Súmáí said, "Black-skinned soldiers with the buffalo's tight curly hair. Scouts say they came to avenge the killing of Meeker. But the Utes had already left."

People around the campfire nodded.

"Two of our family have been stolen as slaves," Súmáí said.

"By whites?"

"Arapaho, we think. We cannot find them," he said.

Everything, regardless of time, seemed a tangled web of wrongs, deceptions, and resentments. I remembered Lindholm saying the Utes had warred with the Arapaho, and suddenly my own world hovered close around me. I swallowed and continued. "The girl in my story was named Maya, and her brother was named Bailey. When Maya and Bailey were small, they were sent to live with their grandmother, who owned a...trading post and had much...religion."

Sniggers erupted from my audience.

"We know religion," Súmáí said. "It makes us laugh."

"Maya and Bailey were sad that their mother and father had sent them away, but they liked living with their grandmother. She was a strong woman, like Súmáí's mother, and people looked to her for strength and wisdom."

Súmáí's mother grinned and rocked on her log. I nodded to her, and she nodded back.

"Always, Maya felt she was balancing on a blade's edge. Her parents sending her away made her feel unworthy. She felt she was ugly, and she thought white girls were pretty and wanted to look like them."

A couple grunts carried across the fire.

"But Maya's grandmother taught her that she was smart." I tapped my temple yet didn't mention how much she loved to read. Súmáí's people wouldn't understand what reading meant. "From watching her grandmother endure white cruelty, Maya learned to be strong *here*." I pressed my hand over my heart, felt my amulet bag beneath, and remembered standing like this on the day I'd retraced my steps in Shangri-La and found Súmáí. How did I appear to these people, a white telling this story? I didn't belong here.

I glanced at Súmáí, who nodded. I took a deep breath and said. "From watching her people's strength—cotton pickers who came to her grandmother's trading post, who worked day after long day with no hope of a better life— she learned pride. Though she was surrounded by white injustice, Maya grew strong with her grandmother."

"The Navajo grow this cotton," Chief Úwápaa said.

I thought of the blankets on our willow beds, had heard they'd come from the Navajo.

"One day, Maya's father came to her grandmother's trading post, and he took Maya and Bailey to live with their mother in a city called St. Louis. In a state called Missouri."

Chief Úwápaa nodded. "This is near the Trail Where They Cried?"

I blinked.

"I heard a story of many Cherokee dead on that trail," the chief said. "They tried white ways, and still they were forced from the land the Great Spirit gave their ancestors."

I realized he meant the Trail of Tears and felt embarrassed

not to know more. "It's near there, I think. Missouri isn't so bad in my time, but for Maya it wasn't good. In Missouri, she suffered at the hands of her own people. Her mother was very beautiful. She worked in a gambling house." My audience's interest was sharp. I thought of Súmáí, Panákwas, and Mú'ú'nap playing shell games, and how often I saw the other men playing similar games and betting on them. "She was gone often, and she had a boyfriend who lived with them."

"*Boyfriend?*" Súmáí said.

"Man who lived with them but was not her husband."

He nodded seriously and several hisses rose from the faces around the fire.

I looked across the children and realized I needed to curb my words. I hadn't seen a single Ute kid spanked. I *had* seen an adult say a simple harsh word, and that kid shaped right up. Mostly, I'd noticed the softening of people's expressions when they looked at the kids.

"He was bad to Maya," I said. "He … shamed her." That seemed to work; the kid's eyes turned to saucers, their imaginations stampeding, and the adults sat at attention with appalled expressions.

"When Maya finally found courage to speak about it, the boyfriend was killed." The adults nodded. The kids grinned. "Maya never knew who did it, but she was sure it was someone in her family. She felt her words had killed the man. For many moons she did not speak because she did not want to harm anyone else." I swallowed hard on those words.

Chief Úwápaa's bottom lip pushed out. I could tell he

didn't like this turn or the adults in the story. I wondered what he'd think of my silence after Mom died.

I hadn't finished listening to the book. How should I end it? With Maya not talking and regretting what the Utes saw as justice?

"Finally, Maya understood that … " My voice cracked and I looked down. I'd become that desperate Sovern again, and it felt like saying the next part would change my own equation. Shangri-La's cold surrounded me, and I heard myself yell *Coward!* I felt anger's heat and Handler say, *She's gone.* My skin turned clammy, and my pulse was faint and fast. All those gazes were fixed on me. Chief Úwápaa nodded, encouraging.

I looked up at these people, snared in a rebellion they could not win. My gaze landed on Túwámúpǔch, who held her baby and watched me intently. I straightened.

"She understood she could not control the lives of other people. She understood that her words had not killed the man. She saw that her silence hurt her family. She began to speak again."

Nobody reacted.

Finally, Chief Úwápaa grunted. He slapped his thigh, rose, and strode to my side. "It is a good story. But there are no animals. Where is the bird?"

"Maya is like a caged bird," I said.

"A bird that is freed?" he said.

"No. A bird that still sings though her life is a prison."

He looked out across the faces cast in firelight, and they looked back.

38

After that evening I told the story, the tribe seemed less awed by Bear Necklace. They seemed to welcome me more. Maybe actually like me.

One afternoon, when Súmáí and I returned from hunting, unsuccessful, his mother sat, as she often did, on a log, legs crossed, stitching beads onto a lap-sized piece of elk skin. She eyed the cloudless sky. "The Great Spirit is angry. No game. No rain."

I realized then that it hadn't rained but for a sprinkle since I'd arrived. I remembered the yellow snap of the grass beneath my slippers as Súmáí and I had descended the mountainside.

"You should travel through the trees to hunt again."

Súmáí shot her a look.

His mom eyed me. "She will be fine here without you."

He shook his head. "I do not know the way of the trees about this. We are here, now. I will not gamble."

She sighed and said to me, "I will teach you to bead?"

I must have looked stunned, because Súmáí nodded like *It'll be okay*. Not wanting to add to his mother's resentment, I settled beside her on the log and crossed my legs. She eyed the cloudless sky once more and handed me a piece of fine thread and a needle made from a porcupine quill. She passed me a hand-sized scrap of elk skin with a grid traced in charcoal.

She took a chunk of wax and said, "Do this." She held a piece of thread down against the wax with her thumb and pulled the thread across it. "It makes the thread strong."

I watched Súmáí walk to our tepee, longing to follow. I took the wax from her and mirrored her movement. It released a fresh, sweet scent. She threaded her needle, so I threaded my needle.

"Make a knot in the end." She demonstrated how to twist and tie off the thread. "Begin at one corner, and then slide on the beads you desire." She modeled this, pushing the needle through a piece of rawhide and then dipping it into a bowl of tiny orangey-red beads and loading it full. "Draw the needle back through." She returned the needle through the rawhide. "Take a second needle and thread"— she waxed and threaded a second needle—"and stitch down the beads." With the second needle, she moved horizontally, stitching down the string every two beads.

"For a pattern, you must plan. You can draw it in the dirt first."

I repressed a laugh. Fully formed patterns and equations cluttered my head. I stared at the grid on the elk skin and it seemed like a gateway. What did I want to create? Alternating colors? A diamond shape? I surveyed the beads to choose from: white, blue, orangy-red, and purply-black. A robin swooped down and pecked at the dry ground. I pictured the cover of Angelou's book, that blackbird flying straight up in silhouette.

I loaded the needle with red beads for the border. Súmáí's mom watched me, leaning in, the closest we'd ever been since she'd dressed me that first night. I bit my lip at how it conjured Mom leaning close to pat my leg.

Súmáí's mom nodded when I completed the first row. For the next row, I loaded one red, then filled the needle with blue beads for the sky. Nine beads in, I loaded a white one as outline and mirrored the rest back out to the other border. On the next row, the white beads moved out in a narrow triangle, two black beads between for the beak. When I started on the bird's wings, Súmáí's mom watched closer.

My stitches were tight and the image clear. I felt proud, but my brain was also running full-tilt, happy to be turned loose in the task. I finished the spread wings and moved down the silhouette to the tail. I finished off a last row of all-red border along the bottom as the day's light began to fade and Súmáí returned.

"You have been working long." He crouched beside me at the log's end. "You like beadwork?" We still spoke Spanish since I was better at it.

"Once I start a thing, I get into it." I tied off the last bead, cut the thread with a knife, and smoothed the scrap on my knee.

"I have sharpened your knife and arrows, and—" He ran his finger down the bird. "*You* made this?"

I shrugged.

"I have never seen its like." He looked at his mother, who had long since gotten up and started cooking dinner.

"Right," I said, sarcastic.

He eyed me with a puzzled expression. "You have not learned beadwork before?"

"No. Why?"

His mother came to stand behind me and looked down at the scrap resting on my leg. "She has a gift," she said.

"*Gift?*" I said, sarcastic again. But I did have to admit that it had turned out cool. The relaxed way my brain felt was even better.

"Thank you for teaching me. It is only good because you made the lines," I said to her.

She smiled then and touched my head. It's hard to explain how that touch felt. The closest I can come is *her touch + looking at that beaded bird = forgiveness for killing Mom.*

"It will become a tobacco pouch for your father," she said.

Dad doesn't smoke, I thought, and then realized she meant Chief Úwápaa. I blurted a laugh, and they both looked at me. I pressed my lips tight to keep from making another noise I'd regret.

Moving to the fire's far side, Súmáí's mom bent down to

the pot and stirred it. "It is okay to accept a gift." Her eyes were dark and sure, despite the wavering heat rising from the flames. "You must choose which battles are worth fighting." Her gaze darted from Súmáí to me with an expression that held years of suffering and loss. But then she smiled, and I saw it held happiness too. "Tomorrow, daughter, I will teach you to make the pouch."

It took me forever to work up the courage to present the pouch to Chief Úwápaa.

"He can be difficult, but it will be fine," Súmáí said.

"I know," I said. "It's not that. I'm out of practice at... this kind of thing." Accepting a gift takes a certain strength, but to give one, I was realizing, was much harder. Each day I'd hunt with Súmáí and try to picture myself standing before his village, giving their chief that pouch, and I just couldn't. Such a simple thing, yet it drove me crazy.

Finally, I said, "Okay, I'll do it," because I realized I'd never feel ready. It happened under the third full moon, around the campfire, before the stories began.

"For the kindness you've shown me," I said.

Chief Úwápaa accepted the pouch and stared at it so long that the kids started to squirm. He held it up for the audience, its soaring beak aimed heavenward.

A few people said, "Oh!" A bunch nodded.

"Thank you, daughter," he said.

I shuffled to the back of the circle, to a seat beside Súmáí. He took my hand and squeezed it. He kept hold of my hand, turned it up, and while his uncle started a story, he ran his fingers across my palm and then across my wrist. I blushed as a few faces turned to us. Súmáí rose and led me away from the fire, through camp, and out its eastern side.

"Where are we going?" I said.

He only smiled back at me.

The moon was a spotlight, and I'd grown used to seeing at night, so walking was no problem. When he crossed over the tributary from Silver Bowl, I guessed we were headed to the pool from my first day here.

We arrived, and Súmáí stripped to just his breechcloth, so I did. We lay our amulet bags together. At the water's edge, my reflection stared back. Each time I'd filled our water basket, my reflection had lurked, but I'd avoided it. Now I studied it.

After so much time with the Utes, seeing my light hair and skin startled me. I saw myself as Súmáí must, and realized that when we'd first met, I must have been as unappealing to him as he'd been to me. My hair had grown easily three inches since then—the mornings now held crispness, and the Indian paintbrush had given way to late summer's purple asters. Aspens here and there were yellowing.

I leaned out over the water to view my reflected chest. I went to roll back my shoulders but realized they were already back: I no longer hunched. The bruises had faded, and the scabs had evolved to a necklace of rose-colored scars. I bumped my fingers along them, from one clavicle to the next. I looked back at Súmáí. He watched, his edges lit by the moon.

"Don't move," I said. I stood before him and, starting at his feet, traced his outlines. "I want my hands to remember your shape."

"Remember? I am here. Now."

"Just let me finish," I said. I ran my fingers over the muscled curve of his forearm, the knob of bone at his elbow, the undulation in his biceps and into his shoulder. I traced up his Adam's apple. I put a lock of his hair into my mouth, pulled it out the far side, and kissed him. Though we'd kissed plenty, I'd always stopped things before they went too far. Now I didn't want to stop the intimacy.

Night's chill pressed my skin, but his palm against my lower back was warm. Instead of pulling back after the kiss like I usually did, I molded myself against him. His face held surprise and gladness and a tenderness that made me gnaw my lip.

———

Súmáí rose and moved to the illuminated side of the rock. He picked up the hip pouch he always wore and pulled something pencil-shaped and white from it. He started scraping on the rock with its tip. I stepped behind him, wrapped my arms around his waist, and rested my chin on his shoulder, watching.

"What's that in your hand?" I said.

"Elk bone."

His muscles tensed as he pressed hard into the sandstone. It became a figure in pants and a shirt with hair my length. Around its neck, he ground dots.

"That's me!" I said.

At the end of one sleeve, he ground a knot, and from that started another arm that moved up to become another shirt, pants, and person with even longer hair.

"That's you!" I kissed the tip of his ear poking through his hair.

He scraped bows over our shoulders and strings across our chests. Beside him, he scraped a tree. In its branches, he ground a round shape with spikes coming out. Beside me, he scraped a bear. He stepped back.

"You're pretty good," I said.

He scraped, in the space above our joined hands, the shape of my heaven-bound bird. The whole drawing looked like a first-grader had made it, yet it was the most beautiful thing I'd ever seen.

He turned to me. "A wedding gift," he said.

I literally jumped into his arms and wrapped my legs around his waist. He took two steps forward, pressing me into the drawing. I held up two crossed fingers, and he pressed his head against them.

He carried me to the pool, careful with his footing off the bank into sand that had been submerged in the swollen runoff of early summer. Even in this light, the pool was transparent. I lay back and the stars pressed down. Súmáí's hands came to my neck and butt, holding me suspended.

From the darkness came the snap of a branch and snuffling.

We waded to the pool's far side and slunk behind the boulder. I shivered, thankful that the rock still radiated the day's heat. A bear sauntered out of the forest, nose lifted to the air. It looked toward where we hid and grunted.

I sucked in my breath. My hand came to my scars and traced each healed indentation as the bear moved to the pool's edge. Above her left eye curved a crescent scar, and I searched for her cub, straining to hear its bark. I willed her to call for it, but she didn't.

She lapped water from the pool, her tongue rapid and translated gray by the light. She drank for a long time. Súmáí took my hand and squeezed it. She glanced at our movement but returned to drinking. Finished, she stared at us.

"Where's your baby?" I said.

Her head tilted. She sort of sneezed, yet not a sneeze, more like a furious *Uh!* She lashed the shore with her claws.

Súmáí stepped back, drawing his knife, but I stayed right there.

She tilted her head to the side and then plopped down like a dog, revealing dried-up teats and a blood-hardened slash, long as my forearm, across her chest.

"Oh, Mom!" I stepped forward. "What happened?" My first English in so long.

"Sovern!" Súmáí said.

The bear lashed out at air, roared drunkenly, and collapsed to her side. I ran above the pool and crossed the creek on three stones.

"Sovern!" Súmáí said.

"It's Mom!"

He loped above the pool and crossed on the stones.

I reached Mom and kneeled beside her. She grunted but didn't move. I ran my fingers along the slash on her chest. Up close, it was infected and smelled rancid.

"Súmáí, you stole medicine from my world too. Yes?"

"*Medicine?*" he said. "There were things that were not food."

"Do you still have them?"

"Yes."

"Can you bring them to me?" I said.

"I will not leave you."

"Súmáí! This is my mother!"

He bowed his head, no doubt struggling with the thought of leaving me alone with a bear, Mom or not. He crouched beside me and kissed my forehead.

"And a needle and thread," I said.

He sprinted off.

"You'll be okay, Mom," I said. "Where's your cub? Is she dead?"

I pictured Súmáí the second time we'd met, miming an explosion. I saw how pale Gage had been when Súmáí had visited our world. Suddenly I understood: two Soverns could not exist in the same world. One me had to die, and I'd erased her cub.

I heard Dad say, *This is our life. This is what we've been dealt.* What had I done? I moaned and rocked myself.

After a time, I returned to our clothes on the pool's other side. I slid on my bra and tied on my leggings. I gathered my shirt, Súmáí's clothes, and our amulet bags. I hopped across the three stones at the pool's top. I tied the sleeves of my shirt around my waist and shaped its body into a bowl. Kneeling at the water's edge, I filled it and shuffled to Mom, emptying it along the slash. Mom whined and weakly lifted a paw.

I returned to the pool and rinsed the slice again. The

wound's edges softened, so I drew my knife from its sheath at my belt and stared at its blade, gathering courage. I hummed "Blackbird" as I scraped, sometimes cut, along the places where the wound had grown infected. I gagged on the smell as I wiped off her infected flesh in the grass.

Mom's breathing stayed shallow, and she'd grunt or lift her paw, trying to wake, but each time she fell back into unconsciousness.

I filled my shirt and rinsed the scraped-out wound. Coyotes howled—loud and close—and I readied for action, but their eerie yips skirted us and trailed up the mountain. I knelt back down and studied Mom's face, with her slack lip caught on her fang. I reached out and ran my finger over her crescent scar. "I'm not letting you die this time."

A rush of movement and a thump at my side made me flinch. Súmáí stood over two boxes. The top one had a porcupine needle stuck into the cardboard, next to a stick with thread spooled around it. Beside the boxes, he dropped our bows and arrow quivers.

The cardboard and the boxes' hard rectangular lines seemed so out of place. It brought to mind the Condo. The red "+" sign that labeled all ski-patrol shipments marked their tops. Below that, also in red, Wash had written *Sapphire East*. I ran my fingers over his writing. *Dad – Mom = y. Me + Mom-bear = x.* The symmetry of this box being here, now, made variables seem part of some great plan. Probability, one test in fate's game.

I tore open the top box and found bandages, Band-Aids, aspirin, ibuprofen, and hot-cold packs. I tore open the second box. Among other supplies were two bottles of hydrogen peroxide and two tubes of antibiotic ointment. "Thank you, Wash," I whispered.

Behind me, Súmáí dressed. He moved to my shoulder as I opened one bottle of hydrogen peroxide.

"Careful," I said. "This is going to sting."

I sloshed hydrogen peroxide onto Mom's wound. It foamed like crazy in her raw flesh. I leapt back as she growled and lashed with her front and back paws. I sloshed it again, and she lashed out again. The third and fourth times, she just rumbled and lifted her lip to feebly bare her fangs.

Súmáí watched, wide-eyed.

"What *is* that?" he whispered.

"It kills the sickness in her wound."

"It is magic?"

"No. Just science," I said.

"*Science?*"

I sighed, letting the hydrogen peroxide do its work. "It's one of the things people have figured out about how the world works."

"In your world, man can stop death?"

I started to say no, but stopped. I considered antibiotics, immunizations, surgeries, chemotherapies, tracheotomies. "Sometimes. We can stop death for a while, but everyone still dies."

"Sovern," Súmáí said tenderly. "I saw her once when you were very young."

I bowed my head and nodded. "I remember. After that, you became the scary monster of my childhood."

I could feel him brace behind me. "You have known me many years then."

I blinked, seeing that memory. I saw all of us—Gage, me, Mom, Dad, my ski-patrol family, Súmáí, his mother, Chief Úwápaa, and Túwámúpúch—caught up in time's vortex.

Súmáí rested his hand on my shoulder. "I did not see your mother beyond when you were young. Did something happen to her?"

"Uh-huh." I couldn't look at Súmáí and say it, so I peered to where the moonlight gave way to darkness. That dead deer, from the first day we'd hunted, was right there with me. So was Súmáí's mom, gazing over the fire, her eyes sure despite the wavering heat. *You must choose which battles are worth fighting.* I brought my hand to my stomach, and beneath it my innards calmed in a way that I knew would last. "She died," I said.

"This is why you came to the tree? Seeking your mother?"

"Uh-huh."

Súmáí ran his thumb along his jaw. "I sought my brother."

"Did you find him?"

He thought for a moment. His mouth set, and I knew he'd decided against telling me something.

I wanted to press him for information, but instead I said, "What was your brother like?"

"He laughed often. His smile..." Súmáí shook his head.

"His eyebrow dove and his lip soared—he made me laugh, even when anger took me."

"You miss him."

Súmáí looked at me hard. "I live to honor him. To honor all my people who have died."

I reached for the antibiotic ointment and squeezed the tube's contents into my palm. I spread it down the wound's length. Mom had settled into sleep's even breathing. I grabbed the needle from the box, held it up against the moon's orb, and threaded it. I tied a knot in one end, like Súmáí's mother had shown me. I took a deep breath and pressed the wound's edges together. Mom's skin was tougher than I'd expected as I pushed the needle through. She moaned but didn't rouse, and I remembered the night I'd brought Dad to Mom through the recreation path spruce, how my body, strained beyond its limits, had forced me into unconsciousness despite how hard I'd fought it.

I pushed the needle through the other side and tugged the thread tight. I repeated the process forty-six times, careful to space the stitches so the wound could ooze. I tied off the thread at the end and cut it with my knife. I found a bottle of antibacterial soap in the box and washed my hands in the pool.

"We will need to protect her while she sleeps," Súmáí said.

I nodded.

"A blade made that wound. A blade not from my people. This is not the way of a Ute. In the morning, I must warn my father."

39

Just past dawn, Chief Úwápaa and Súmáí's uncle found us, their faces pasted with horror and wonder. Súmáí pressed his finger to his lips and gestured for them to move with him into the forest, toward where they'd left their horses. Mom slept on. I wondered how long she'd snooze. It didn't matter. I'd stay to protect her for as long as it took.

I scanned around the clearing, seeing it and Súmáí's world through practical eyes. It had been about three months since he'd scalped those scumbags right where Mom lay now. I'd pushed them way back in my memory, but the revulsion I'd felt surged back, and I considered that someone might have come looking for them.

Súmáí returned, face grim, and stood at the forest's edge. I walked to him.

"My father and uncle will ride to Big Ridge to scout the next valley."

"Súmáí, what happened to those men we killed here?" I whispered.

"The women prepared and burned them."

"Do you think more whites are coming?"

"The whites in the log dwellings you saw may have cut the bear." He nodded toward the western valley. "We need to be sure." He looked over his shoulder at the sound of his father and uncle preparing to leave. I could tell it killed him, not going.

"Go with them," I whispered.

He eyed me intently. He ran his finger up my jaw, lifted my chin, and kissed my jawbone, then just in front of my ear, and I caught my breath at how it conjured Gage.

"I will send Mother," Súmáí whispered and was gone.

Whites were coming, I was sure of it, and my own world was beckoning me home. I pressed my lips against the scream that longed to bust out.

I crept to Mom, knelt at her ears, and studied her upside-down head. Her brown snout was long, ending in a black nose that exhaled air and rustled the short blades of grass before it. Here, at the creek's edge, the grass was soft, its green glistening with dew in the soft light. Near what I could only call her cheeks, light fur flared out. I held up my hair, hovered close, and compared their like colors. As I looked down her body, most of her fur had an outer layer the color of my hair, and a dark inner layer the hue of her snout.

"Hang on, Mom," I said. "I know you can." Above, the Milky Way was fading to day, and it felt like those stars watched us. "Is this why I'm here?" I said. After a bit, I said to Mom, "They never answer." I rested my hand on her ribs' rise and fall and patted her in the rhythm she'd always used to comfort me.

An intake of air caught my attention, and I snapped straight and alert. Súmáí's mom stood at the clearing's edge. We eyed one another. She nodded to me. A little back and to my side, she set down a hatchet, lowered a bow from her shoulder, and sat. I could feel her studying Mom, then me, and I wondered what she saw.

The air warmed enough that a brown butterfly emerged and passed so close to my face that I felt the breeze of its wings. The grasshoppers started clacking. When our shadows pulled tight beneath us, Mom's breathing changed. She lifted her head but lay it back down like it was too heavy. She lifted it again and heaved up onto her side.

Súmáí's mom shifted from sitting cross-legged to a crouch. I moved to kneeling. Mom looked around like her surroundings were a surprise. She saw us, focused on me, and grunted. She sniffed her chest, lifted her paw, and investigated my needlework. She licked it a long time. As I listened to her loud tongue, I thought, Good, get some of that antibiotic inside you.

Finally, she stood and wobbled to the pool's edge. She drank, the sound of her lapping taking over the air. She turned, still wobbly, and walked toward us. I glanced at Súmáí's mom, who sat straight as an arrow.

When Mom was five feet away, she lowered her head

and rocked slowly from foot to foot on her front paws. I held out my hand. She took a step toward me. I leaned toward her. She took a step closer. I reached till I had to lean on my other arm. Her cool nose wet my palm. She blew out hard, and I yanked back my hand, but then returned it. Maybe she smelled the medicine, but I like to think it was just me, because she licked that lifeline.

She shook her head, then sauntered past Súmáí's mom and into the trees. I kept watching even after I couldn't see her anymore.

"*Towéiyak*," I said over my shoulder.

"*Towéiyak*?" Súmáí's mom said.

"For teaching me to sew." I smashed a tear from my cheek. "That is my mother."

Súmáí's mom nodded. "She is beautiful."

I smiled and said in English. "Did you hear that, Mom? *Beautiful*."

40

That evening, I sat on one of the willow beds in our tepee, staring at nothing. Once, the space Súmáí and I inhabited had held only two words, but it had never, ever, been simple. Now, it spanned three languages, and I was more confused than ever. Always, beyond any words, I'd felt drawn to him. Just then it seemed we were connected by a bungee that was stretched to its limit, and I sensed it preparing to recoil, to hurtle us toward something we could not control.

"Come home, Súmáí," I said for the hundredth time. This was our first separation since I'd arrived in his world. I picked up the water basket and headed to the creek, glad our tepee was on the camp's tip, where there were fewer eyes to follow me.

At the grassy bank, I knelt down and, gripping the basket tight against the current, dipped it in and watched water eddy into its pine-pitch lining. Would this water live on?

Had I drunk it 136 years later? I set the heavy basket beside me and spit into the creek. I watched my bubbly saliva wash downstream. Maybe someday I'll drink a molecule of that, I thought and looked at the sky. Maybe a falling drop of it will hit me. I held up my palm and studied my lifeline for signs of this world.

"Sovern."

I flinched. "Don't do that!"

Súmáí's face was grim. "Whites camp over Big Ridge. Whites that seek the shiny rocks."

"Miners?"

"And soldiers."

My hand flew to my mouth. I rose, facing him.

"The men gather in my father's tepee to smoke and consult the spirits."

"Can I come?" I spoke through my fingers.

He shook his head. His eyes held a thousand words, yet he just turned and walked toward his father's tepee.

———

While Súmáí's mother, aunt, and Túwámúpúch prepared the evening meal, I stitched beads—a new amulet bag for Súmáí—with my ears tuned on the voices in the tepee. All I could make out were muffled words. Túwámúpúch took her baby from its cradleboard and, folding down one side of her dress, nursed him. His little hand reached up, his fingers so tiny, even down to his miniature fingernails. Túwámúpúch held out her finger and he gripped it.

"He is handsome," I said.

She actually smiled, sort of.

Súmáí stormed out of the tepee.

"Súmáí!" his mother scolded.

"I am no longer a child, Mother!" he snapped. Then he looked at me like someone had stabbed him, and my pulse skipped a beat. He spun on his heel and stormed toward our tepee. I looked at his mother.

"He always battled his cradleboard," she said.

I packed up my beadwork, pulse pounding as Súmáí's uncle emerged, followed by Panákwas and Mú'ú'nap, who walked, stern-faced, toward their tepees.

"We will move camp at dawn," his uncle said. "Panákwas and Mú'ú'nap will keep watch tonight."

The other women seemed to expect this news. I just about choked. I looked at Túwámúpúch, and she nodded toward our tepee.

I found Súmáí inside, on a willow-bough bed, glowering as he sharpened his knife against a stone. I'd never seen him so tense, such an echo of Gage it froze me. I'd always wondered why Gage, who had both parents, money, and intellect, was so angry with the world. Was it a ripple of this self?

After a while, I moved behind Súmáí and slid my arm around his waist. I kissed the tip of his ear and lay my cheek against his back. "I heard."

He swiveled to me and cut a lock of my hair with his knife. He opened his amulet bag and folded it in.

"Why won't you look at me?" I said.

His eyes met mine, and their barely contained fury stole my breath. "You must go."

"What?"

"I was wrong to keep you. Return to your world. I do not know where my people will make camp. There could be no trees. Or different trees."

"I'm not ready!"

"Sovern, my father will not fight! We have no *hope*."

Whatever equation existed for this moment, it was the inverse of when I'd arrived here. "Come with me."

He shook his head.

"Please!"

I took his hand, and he looked down at my grip.

"You'd get used to my world," I said. "We could buy some land, live where there aren't so many people. There's lots of places like that. We could hunt. There's deer and elk everywhere."

"Gage lives in your world."

How could I have forgotten! I swallowed back the guilt of killing my cub-self.

"Dammit," I said and nudged Súmáí, hoping he'd get the joke. "Okay... we could find a world where you and I didn't exist. One with lots of game for hunting."

"That is not the way of the trees."

"We'll figure out a way!"

"How would we walk in that world?"

"I don't know! We'll figure it out!"

He returned to honing his knife. "My place is with my people."

"Dammit, Súmáí! There's so much you haven't told me! Tell me!" I took a deep breath, felt I teetered on a thin line. I was furious with myself for settling into life here, for not hounding him relentlessly for information. Now we were out of time. "Remember science? The things we've figured out about how things work in my world? I'm really good at a type of it. Sort of. Maybe. I'm good at math."

He looked at me blankly.

"Come with me for now. We'll get you someplace safe while I figure this out." I had no idea if I could *really* figure *anything* out, but I had to get Súmáí somewhere safe. "Then we can be together. It might take some time, but—"

The flat of his knife's blade pressed against my lips.

I swatted his hand away. "You mean to *die* with your people?"

"Would you not do the same?"

That stopped me. I considered the last year, how I'd self-destructed, refusing to accept Mom's death. Wishing I'd died with her. Or instead of her. I heard Handler say, so kind it hurt, *Your mother's gone, Sovern.* I heard Dad say, *You're destroying yourself trying to keep her alive.*

Out the hole at our tepee's top, the sky was twilight. I'd felt like I was healing, like maybe I could accept Mom dying after all. Now I faced losing Súmáí? His tribe? Loving them all as dead things? My pain intensified by a power of ten, and I screamed. With all I had. At dreams and beliefs and love and happiness and the orderly lie of math. At tests. At fate.

Súmáí wrapped me in his arms. He rocked me, and my screams diminished to wails. I started saying "Never!" over and over. When I couldn't say it anymore, I filled my mouth with his hair and bit down. After a time, I fell asleep with his wrist's pulse beating beneath my cheek, our legs tangled, the fingers of his other hand weaved into mine.

I woke to something pulling the corners of my mouth and jostling the back of my head. I sat up as my hands were drawn behind me and bound. I wanted to scream but was afraid. Had the whites invaded in the night? Had my screams revealed the village? Súmáí appeared and pressed his finger to his lips, gesturing silence.

He held my snowboard pants to my feet. I knew what he was up to then, and I kicked like crazy. He was so strong, though, and my balance was off from my bound arms. Before I knew it, he'd rolled me onto my side and gotten my pants to my knees. He stood me up, tugged the pants to my waist, and bound them with my belt. He pulled my underwear shirt, long-since washed of blood, over my head. He didn't bother with the arms.

I itched to slug him, but the rawhide binding my wrists wouldn't give. He tugged on my snow boots without much trouble. He stepped back and looked at me as I shot arrows with my eyes. He smiled sadly and kissed my forehead. I stamped my foot and screamed behind my gag, a weak, useless noise. He tied a rope around my waist, slung our bows and quivers over his shoulder, and led me by the rope out the tepee.

A horse waited with my parka draped across its back.

He crouched and held out his clasped hands as a step. No doubt he'd toss me across the beast—sack-of-potatoes style—if I didn't cooperate.

I sucked a long breath. I was going to kill him when I had the chance. He chuckled at my expression as I stepped into his hands, and he hoisted me. My butt plopped onto my parka, and my phone in its pocket—long since drained of battery—pressed the back of my thigh. The horse took a sideways step. I'd never sat on a horse, and the sensation of sitting on something alive stole my attention.

Súmáí gripped a piece of mane and swung onto the horse effortlessly in front of me. He tied my rope's other end around his waist. He steered the horse up the path I'd first arrived on. I laid my head against Súmáí's back and tugged furiously at my bound hands. He glanced over his shoulder. I let out a noise that sounded like a wild animal.

"This is how it must be," he said.

Whatever. He was *not* winning this battle.

I finally settled down and molded my body against his. My stomach growled. We'd missed dinner. I glanced at the moon, a spotlight overhead. I'd never realized how unreliable the moon was until I lived here. It was always moving, setting early some nights, late others. I didn't trust it.

When I felt Súmáí finally relax, I chose an area ahead clear of bushes and rocks. I counted down, gathering courage—six, five, four, three, two, one! I swung my leg behind me and slid off the horse.

Súmáí grunted, yanked backward, and landed on top of me, our bows and arrows brutal lines of impact. I squeaked pain but kicked at him with all I had. I rolled up and started to run, but the short rope stopped me in a one-kneed crouch, like I was starting a sprint.

"Are you hurt?" His voice was so soft, so caring.

My chin dropped to my chest.

He leaned closer—I knew he would—and rested his palm on my shoulder. I'd thought my next move would be harder, but I was driven by rage. I swung my head, clocking him in the temple. He toppled back, the rope pulling me onto him. He was out cold.

I rolled onto my back, falling halfway off his body, and groped for his knife. So that I wouldn't cut him, I eased carefully onto my side before drawing it from its sheath. It took a while, but I rotated the blade till it faced up. Freshly sharpened, it sliced through the rawhide binding my wrists with hardly any pressure. I slid my arms into my long underwear's sleeves and pried the gag out of my mouth.

Our bows rested along his side with his arm through them. I extracted mine and then slugged him. "You're *not* getting rid of me that easy," I said. I fled to the aspens.

41

About fifty yards into the aspen grove, I looked back at Súmáí. I couldn't leave him lying there unconscious. I trudged to a log and plopped down. I rested my chin in my hands and pressed the tips of my ring fingers against the inside corners of my eyes to dam them, but water still leaked out. I heaved a breath, and my whole body shook.

Who did he think he was? I wasn't his property! Whether I went back or not was *my* decision. Not his. I clenched my fists. Then Tara's black eye and stitched forehead rose in my memory. I heard him say, *We are at war with the white enemy,* and it hit me one hundred percent that he wasn't planning to live. He really believed his people would be massacred or dragged to a reservation. He was probably right, and he would never let himself be forced into captivity. He'd die fighting. He was sending me off before that happened.

I heard a faint noise and movement. My ears strained and made out the scuff of a hoof against rock, a low whisper, and leather's squeak. I rose, head swinging from the noise to Súmáí and back. I glimpsed motion downhill. I whistled low—the hunting signal Súmáí had taught me.

Mú'ú'nap stepped out from behind a tree and I rushed to him, both of us whispering, "Soldiers!"

My eyes darted to Súmáí, and Mú'ú'nap's gaze followed. He sucked in his breath.

"He's fine." I hiked my bow higher on my shoulder.

"He does not look fine."

"We had a fight. I'll wake him. We will distract the soldiers."

Mú'ú'nap smirked and glanced at Súmáí once more, and I knew Súmáí would never hear the end of this. If we lived.

Mú'ú'nap nodded. "Panákwas tracks the soldiers on the other side." He sprinted off.

I scurried to Súmáí. For a moment, all I could do was stare at him. I needed to burn him into my memory. "Súmáí, soldiers!" I whispered.

He sat up, rubbing the side of his head. His eyes weren't focused.

"Soldiers are coming. Now!"

He scrambled to his knees, felt his knife was out of its sheath, picked it up, and replaced it.

"Mú'ú'nap has gone to warn the village! We need to distract the soldiers!"

He rose, wobbling, and whispered, "You must go! Go now to the tree!" He led the horse to me and held out one

327

rein. I noticed it was that first horse I'd led, the one with the white oval on its forehead.

"Dammit, Súmáí! This isn't your choice!"

"You are not meant to die here!" he whispered.

"Maybe I am! Maybe that was the plan all along. How do you know?"

His piercing gaze reeled back a million miles and a sort of understanding settled in his face as a frown. Resignation moved down his body. His expression scared me more than anything I'd seen in his world. More than the approaching soldiers.

"What?" I whispered. "Please, tell me!"

He half-nodded, half shook his head, closed the distance between us, and held me so tight I lost all my air. He touched that freckle riding my lip and looked up at the moon. He held up his crossed fingers. I held up mine and pressed my wrist to his.

"This way," I whispered.

At the log I'd been sitting on, I could hear the soldiers again. Súmáí cocked his head, listening too. The horses gave them away, and I realized how wise Súmáí had been to leave our horse behind. We moved diagonally up the hill, and the soldiers' sounds grew louder.

My hunting lessons paid off. I moved almost silently except for the crackling yellow grass, despite my clunky snow boots. The sounds were suddenly close, and I smelled, of all things, Ivory soap. Súmáí slid behind an aspen trunk. I slid behind one a few feet away.

Soldiers were descending, bodies swaying side-to-side from riding horses downhill. Over every shoulder bobbed a rifle. I hadn't considered guns. I knew Chief Úwápaa kept rifles in his tepee and that probably every Ute brave but Súmáí, the purist, had at least one firearm in his tent.

I'd counted twenty-three soldiers when Súmáí eased his bow off his shoulder and notched an arrow in its string. I did the same. Our eyes met, and he nodded. We both turned and shot. Shot again. Four soldiers fell, and their horses lurched to the side or trotted a few steps. One whinnied.

The soldiers just ahead of them spun their horses, rifles sliding to the ready.

"Attack!" someone called.

Súmáí took off up the mountain, and I sprinted behind him. At our heels came the sounds of horses moving fast and men's shouts. One voice yelled, "Steady, men!"

"Indians, there, sir!"

"Steady!" the voice yelled again. "Cover that direction!"

The forest turned from aspens to pines. Súmáí stopped behind one. I stopped behind another. We rested our hands on our knees, panting. Our eyes met, and I chewed my lip. I'd just *shot* two guys. Guys on a mission to kill us, but still.

Súmáí slunk forward. I followed. We got close enough to spy four soldiers scanning our direction down their rifles' barrels. How dumb could they be, just sitting on their horses in the open?

Súmáí notched an arrow, and so I did. He shot. I shot. Two men fell. He shot and I shot, and one man fell. Súmáí had missed, and I hadn't. A bullet grazed Súmáí's tree, and he flinched in a spray of bark. Bullets sailed between us, and one thudded into my tree.

A war whoop rang out, and suddenly there were shots on shots. I flinched as death cries pierced the night. Gunpowder's sulfur scent floated on the air, tinged by blood's metallic one. And a sweet scent too, that I recognized as terror.

Súmáí took off and I followed. He ran this time till we stopped behind two trees grown together. Below us, the gunshots and the death cries continued.

"No one can pass us," Súmáí whispered.

I nodded. If one of the soldiers escaped, he would tell others what had happened. A full-on army would come. I bit my lip against this futility. There was no stopping the white invasion.

I notched an arrow in my bow and prepared to skirt the sound of fighting, but Súmáí whispered, "You are a great hunter now." He watched me intently as my throat clogged with bile.

He chin-pointed up the mountain, so I moved uphill, toward the route back to Big Ridge, and he mirrored my progress fifty yards above.

A ways off, too far for arrows, a soldier streaked away from the battle on foot. Súmáí lit off after him, letting out a whoop I'd never heard. As I followed, a second echoing whoop sounded. I thought of my low whistle to Mú'ú'nap earlier and realized I was learning a fourth tongue: the language of battle. I pushed back the images of the guys I'd shot falling from their mounts, glad their faces had been obscured by their hats' night shadows.

Behind us, the sounds of fighting stopped. Moments later, victory whoops filled the night. So cliché, so big-screen, yet I'd never considered they could be communication.

The soldier was fast. We pursued him over the ridge marking the boundary from Gold Bowl into Silver Bowl. Súmáí reached down and touched a footprint in the loose soil around a pine. "Indian."

"How do you know?"

He pointed at the track. "Moccasin. A scout."

"Then we can let him go."

Súmáí shook his head. He looked at his own moccasins. "Will you at least wait at camp?"

"No! You just said I'm a great hunter."

"To hunt you must accept death," he said.

My mouth dropped open, but I could find nothing to say. He took off again with more caution. He didn't look back, but I followed.

———

We chased that scout diagonally up the mountain for what seemed like forever. I'd catch glimpses of him—tall, military pants, flannel shirt, buckskin vest, hair in a single braid down his back. No bow or rifle rode his shoulder, and I took heart in that. Obviously the scout knew this area, but he couldn't know it nearly so well as Súmáí and me. Especially me, because I'd snowboarded every contour of this bowl seeking entertainment and adventure. Now I ascended it, life on the line.

I glanced at Big Ridge, at where Sapphire East lodge

perched in my world. Inside it, greeters held out tissues for entering guests to wipe runny noses before they headed to the restaurant to select gourmet meals. Calm music wafted down from speakers mounted in the vaulted ceiling. Sometimes it was Native American flutes and singing. In the women's bathroom, there were hair dryers, hair spray, and lotion. Out front, on a little rise beyond the racks of skis and boards, stood a bronze statue of a bear that people from all over the world would pose with for photos. Out the other side stood a glittering ice sculpture that would change every year—mountain lion, eagle, skier, Ute. Even though it was more spectacular than the bronze one, this statue wasn't in as many photos because it required tourists to exit out the lodge's inconvenient far side and walk thirty yards to the right.

I hadn't come to Sapphire East with Súmáí, and seeing it for the first time, I was amazed again by how many more trees there were here than in my world. Yet I still recognized the hollow before the rise to the ridge, a spot where I always had to maintain my speed from above, which was hard because a sandstone cliff band striped it. I'd always hated those cliffs. They were higher than I was comfortable jumping, but I'd found a spot toward their outermost edge where I could negotiate halfway down and, pulse pounding, launch the last ten feet.

Súmáí stopped and scanned around.

"Do you see him?" I whispered and wished I hadn't been gazing at the imaginary lodge.

Súmáí pressed a finger to his lips—*Shh!*—and shook his head.

I eyed the cliffs, glad for them now. The scout wouldn't be over there. But where had he gone?

Before the final rise to Big Ridge lay an open stretch, then a teardrop-shaped grove of pines. In my time, one of those charred trunks stood alone there, and a chairlift carried skiers straight over it. Between us and the pines was an open stretch.

Súmáí jogged, hunching low, along the forest's edge, and then he paused, scanned the open area, and sprinted. I sprinted right behind him. We entered the grove, moving cautiously, searching. Had we come all this way just to lose the guy?

The moon had shifted toward the horizon and now painted everything in long shadows. One side of the trees' trunks were lit in stark relief, and I recognized a spruce with yellow spots. It had an Upward Dog shape. I peered into its branches and made out a brown-gray lump.

"Súmáí! Another tree!" I whispered.

He circled back to me, finger pressed to his lips again in frustration—*Shh!* He studied the trunk and squinted up into the branches. He looked at me, eyebrows raised.

I blurted, "I can't—"

I will never forget the clean sound of that airborne blade piercing his flesh. A knife sunk to its hilt just above the waist of his pants. He stumbled back, notching an arrow, and shot. There was movement—fast—maybe twenty feet away. In the striping shadows, I couldn't see whether the arrow found its mark. Súmáí collapsed against a tree trunk.

"Súmáí!" Over his shallow breaths, I heard a snap and

movement heading out of the grove. A fury shot through me, so potent it sparked out my fingertips. I bolted after the sound.

The scout loped with an arrow stuck in his thigh, so, despite those snow boots, I gained on him as he traveled west, toward the cliffs. I followed, lower on the mountain. He must have forgotten the cliffs, because he reached their edge and had to scramble straight up. I beelined to their base, knowing my shortcut well. I could hear him above, to my right, still ascending as I scaled the ten feet I usually launched. I worked to silence my breaths as I scurried over the top. I set my feet and notched an arrow.

The scout rounded the cliffs, looking over his shoulder as he hobbled toward me. Pulse deafening in my ears, I sighted his chest. The scout looked ahead, saw me, and his moonlit face converted to shock. I shot.

"White? Woman?" he said in English, and he slumped to the ground. The arrow in his thigh hit first, rolling his leg inward, and he cried out.

I strode to him. His hand gripped my arrow in his chest, and his eyes spewed hate. At his hip, his knife sheath was empty. I wanted to kick him, kick him right off that cliff. But I couldn't.

"You are a traitor," I said in Spanish.

He *laughed*, a ghastly rasping sound. "And? You?" I can't remember which language he used. His eyes closed and he fell into unconsciousness.

I turned to the moon. I looked down the valley to where Phantom Peak loomed, the shadow-face now cast by lunar light. Its eyes watched me, harsh with judgment. My voice had given us away when I'd spoken in the grove. Súmáí had warned me, and still I'd spoken.

I looked to the stars and opened my mouth, but no scream came. I drew from my guts, bent double with the effort, but still no scream. I dry-heaved on silence.

I sprinted back to Súmáí. He sat slumped against the pine. He'd pulled the knife out. Blood—black in the moonlight—bloomed against his shirt.

"Oh, Súmáí, what should I do?"

"Do you have a needle and thread?" His face contorted in pain as he tried to smile.

I kissed him and he kissed me back, hard.

"Súmáí, there's a tree. Right here! We could travel to the tree near the village. I'll get the horse and bring you down."

He shook his head. "That is not the way of the trees."

"Okay, then we'll go to my world. They have magic there, remember? Dad can save you! He's right on the other side!" As I said it, I knew it was the right idea.

Súmáí shook his head.

"You'll die!"

He shook his head.

"Can't we at least try?"

He smiled weakly, reached up, and touched that freckle riding my lip. "Wife." His eyes fluttered closed.

"Súmáí! No!"

Blood had glued his shirt to his skin. I peeled it back. A two-inch mouth above his hip burbled blood. Whimpering, I pinched it closed. There was so much blood.

"Súmáí, wake up! Súmáí!"

He didn't stir. I kissed him, and still he didn't stir. I sobbed and slid my hand behind his head, sat him up, pulled his arm over my shoulder, and wobbled us to standing. Seven steps, me dragging him, brought us to the spruce.

I hugged and lowered him against it, setting him down too hard, and then kneeled, straddling his legs. Smearing aside his hair that had stuck to my cheek, I took his hand, wiped his palm off on my snow pants, and pressed it against the spruce. I filled my mouth with a lock of his hair. I wiped off my other palm and pressed it to the trunk.

The plucked-cello-string sound reverberated through me. It grew louder, intensifying till it felt like a volcano was vibrating beneath my hands and through my body. Súmáí shook. The spruce's roots rumbled beneath my knees. An electric jolt shot through me, and Súmáí jerked like a puppet as I cried out. The sound's frequency rose so high I wanted to cover my ears.

"Sovern," Súmáí said just as a jolt shot up the spruce. A deafening crack sounded, and the top ignited. Needles rained down as our eyes latched. A porcupine thumped to the ground, grunting in pain and sending out a spray of quills that pierced our pants. Súmáí's hair yanked from my lips.

Blinding white. Charcoal's blunt scent. Cold.

My palms pressed against smooth black. The chairlift hummed overhead, voices falling from it—chit-chat, banter, laughter. Snow schussed against turning skis. Súmáí was gone.

"What the hell?" fell from overhead.

336

"Get a picture of that!"

"Is she drunk?"

"Post it on Instagram!"

The heavy scent of shampoo and perfume arrived. "Miss? Are you all right?"

Out the corner of my eye, I saw pale cheeks and a mouth coated with stark red lipstick. Her skis and poles crunched snow as she backed up.

"What's the matter, Helen?"

"Norman, call 911!"

42

"S overn?" Sarge crouched in the charred trunk's well beside me. "Sov?"

I'd made a grave mistake—I should have fled when that couple called 911. I was covered in blood but not hurt. There'd be no explaining it. I rocked my forehead against the dead spruce, unable to pull myself away from that link—any link—to Súmáí.

"*Lo siento!*" I whispered. *Sorry*, indeed. Why couldn't I have listened to his warning?

"Sov?" Sarge touched my back. A moment later, I heard him pull his radio from its Velcro holster. He was calling for a sled, and the thought of that humiliation gave me the strength I needed.

"*Lo siento*," I said, this time to Sarge. I spun away and sprinted across groomed corduroy toward the cliffs, on the same path the scout must have taken. I could hear Sarge pursuing me, but his steps died out as I adjusted my route, heading up so I'd come out above the cliffs. Over three months in Súmáí's world had left me fit. I hit the road to Sapphire East lodge, against the rush of post-lunch skiers and boarders heading into the bowl. I'd left this world for Súmáí's in the early afternoon, so maybe I *had* returned at the same time— just through a different spruce.

I looked over my shoulder and spotted Sarge watching me with the saddest expression. He'd call Dad, no doubt.

People skied past, horror all over their faces. I took in my bloody clothes and felt the drying blood on my face. I couldn't care less what these idiots thought of me. I did care about Dad, though, and I needed not to make a scene. I needed to get to the cabin.

I followed the road halfway up and then cut across Silver Bowl. I'd forgotten I'd left on a powder day, and the cut-up snow off the groomed section was thigh deep. With each step, I tinged the snow pink. I found tracks that traversed horizontally across the slope, and I followed them into a stand of pines where I paused to catch my breath and think.

Once Dad heard, he would no doubt tell Wash, Big John, Tucker, and Crispy that I was on the loose. I couldn't handle facing any one of them with the touch of Súmáí's lips still fresh on mine, and his blood against my body still warm. I hugged my sticky chest, pressing all I had left of him nearer. I sat down, rocked myself, and bawled.

After a while, cold made me rise, and it occurred to me that I *could* rise—that I wasn't weak, like I'd been after my visits to Mom's universes. Another sign that it really was this world's past I'd been in.

Above and to the left was the lift that followed the ridge between Gold and Silver Bowls. I prayed that the liftie working the top was a snowboarder. Across from that lifthouse stretched the service road between Sapphire East and City Center. Used by snowcats and snowmobiles, it was U-shaped, rising to both locations. If I could borrow the liftie's board, I could glide in seconds half a mile toward the cabin.

I looked out at the lifthouse from the pines that stopped just before the ridge. A snowboard leaned against a railing at the top of three stairs leading to the door. Beyond the lifthouse stretched an open area, with skiers and boarders gliding away from the chairs. I couldn't make it across that open space without the liftie seeing that I'd heisted his board, so I'd have to backtrack.

I slunk to the board, maneuvered it under the rail, and retreated into the pines. I followed the forest, staying high. After watching for someone watching for me, I sprinted across the no-man's land of the scoured ridge and crested over into the scraggly trees on its other side.

I stepped onto the road, threw down the board, and ratcheted its bindings tight against my snow boots. The liftie must have been huge, because his board was a beast, and his bindings were so far apart that standing in them felt like starting the splits. It would carry me far and fast, though.

I ran, in crazy strapped-in steps—one, two, three, four—and jumped, landing with momentum, right foot forward. I hunched in an aerodynamic tuck and felt the bow and quiver press my back in the sore line I'd gotten from falling off the horse. I locked my freezing hands behind me. Speed. I needed speed to carry me far up the other side.

The road was steep on this first part, and my pulse revved at my acceleration. I gulped panic, willed myself not to change my balance heel to toe, and the world blurred. I sobbed as Súmáí's blood lost its last warmth in the icy wind. I raced into the hill's bottom and leaned hard on my back foot—my front foot lifting—to force a last bit of acceleration.

About a third of the way up the other side, I lost momentum and stopped. I hopped sideways to keep from sliding backward. I unbuckled my boots and turned the board over in the road's center, digging its bindings into the snow so it wouldn't glide away. Maybe the liftie would get it back before his shift was over.

A snowmobile approached, and I sprinted into the pines. I didn't look to see who drove it. If it was one of my ski-patrol family, I'd feel so guilty. I kept grinding through the deep snow, diagonally and up, toward the cabin.

I skirted the edge of the runs that sprayed off City Center like a wheel's spokes. I came to one of the busiest runs on the mountain, and, hiking my bow and quiver higher on my shoulder, turned my less-bloody back to the traffic and ran. I still heard gasps. A "what the hell?" An "is there hunting season in March?" That made me snort as I considered Súmáí's hungry family.

I entered the cupped hand of pines, and everything that had happened over the last few hours—my fight with Súmáí, our battle with the soldiers and our pursuit of the scout, then my own pursuit of him, my attempt to save Súmáí, and the cold flight from that blackened spruce to the cabin—settled into my legs like lead. I trudged till I spied the cabin's door. It was ajar, and Dad's skis leaned next to it.

He never left his skis out there. He was waiting.

I fell to my knees and squinted at the sky. I thought of Chief Úwápaa, Súmáí's mother, Túwámúpúch, her baby, Panákwas and Mú'ú'nap, their wives. Had they survived the attack? No doubt Súmáí had died at that burning spruce. I saw the men I'd killed topple from their horses and saw hate spew from the scout's eyes. *And? You?*

I felt my needle push through Mom's bear flesh and her tongue lick my palm. My hand, the one Mom had licked, came to my scar necklace and traced it. I was Bear Necklace, Woman of the Trees. I shut my eyes, sealing those memories before I faced Dad. I rose and strode toward the cabin.

My steps were soundless up and across the deck. I peeked in the door's open wedge. Dad sat, elbows on his knees, hands clasped, head down. His shirt sleeves were pushed up, and his one wrist was lily white from the newly removed cast. I nudged open the door.

His face shifted from grim to horrified. I could see him forcing himself still as he looked past the blood to my longer hair and the bow and arrows jutting above my shoulder.

"Sovern?"

I stumbled back, hitting the open door, and it slammed closed behind me. I banged to the floor, my arrow and quiver clunking at my side. I tried to speak—I owed him that—but my words had killed Súmáí now too, and my mouth wouldn't budge.

―――――――――

The sun had moved across the living room window when steps sounded on the deck, followed by a knock.

"Hang on," Dad called.

He slid me from his lap, hobbled on legs obviously filled with pins and needles, and nudged aside my bow and quiver. He opened the door, stopping it before it hit my knee.

"Hey!" Wash said, and I watched his snow boots maneuver around Dad. "Ah, Sov! What the hell's happened?"

I looked up at him, chin trembling.

Dad reached down and scooped an arm around me. "We'll find out later," he said to Wash. "Help me, will you?"

Wash lunged to my other side.

"Bathroom," Dad said.

"Hoo, Sov!" Wash waved his hand past his nose. "Where have you been?"

I couldn't make my legs or arms help them. In the bathroom, after closing the door halfway, Dad peeled off my long underwear shirt, and it was like I was watching from somewhere else. I felt an extra tug as my amulet bag caught my hair, and I knew Súmáí's blood glued it to my shirt. I blinked back the memory of him in the pool, removing this same shirt, saturated with *my* blood. Dad dropped it onto the floor and gingerly tugged off my snowboard pants, avoiding touching the quills. I glimpsed a red-faced horror in the mirror and looked away as Dad investigated me for injuries. His mouth dropped open when he noticed my scar necklace.

"You went through the spruce, didn't you?" he said.

I tried to speak. Really, I did. Words just wouldn't come, so I looked up with eyes that said yes.

He tilted his head, sighed, and turned on the shower. He tested the temperature and adjusted it. He pulled a washcloth from the shelf of towels and draped it over the tub's side.

"Can you wash yourself?"

I stared at that washcloth. I didn't want to use it.

"Sov?" Dad finally said. I could hear him struggling to keep control. You could kill a person in a thousand different ways—in self-defense, in revenge, in love.

My sight glanced off him, and I barely forced a nod. He put his hand on my shoulder, all awkward. He started to gather my clothes, and then I did move: I yanked the clothes right from his hands.

Dad looked at me like I was a wild animal, and then he shut the door behind him. Wash's whisper slid underneath it. "Shite!"

I pushed aside the clear shower curtain and stepped in. Hot water felt ridiculously good, yet also like a betrayal, a decadent lie. Pink rushed past my feet toward the drain, and I heard Súmáí say my name. I felt his eyes on me that last instant and his legs beneath mine. I fell to my knees.

After a while, I wet the washcloth. I took the bar of soap, its Ivory scent releasing, conjuring the moment I'd sighted the soldiers down my arrow's shaft. The soap banged against the tub's bottom.

I squeezed my honeysuckle-scented shampoo into the washcloth, held it to my nose, and inhaled. I scrubbed. And scrubbed. Inside my belly button, Súmáí's blood had pooled and dried. I left that.

Bookmark:
Albert Einstein

———

"God does not throw dice."

43

I sat on the deck and leaned against the cabin's wall, letting the sun drench me and rubbing my thumb over my amulet bag. Súmáí's blood had dyed it red. The way it rested against my chest was a comfort. Warm March days had always been my favorite, but I strained to feel pleasure. Time was, Mom would have had some comfy patio chairs for us out here. But Mom was dead, and I wasn't Mom.

I ran my tongue over my teeth. After Mom, I'd chosen not to talk to seal in the sound of her pulse in my memory and to save anyone else from being hurt by my words. Now I tried like hell to talk, but my mouth just would not speak. For the last five days, Dad had pleaded, "Please, Sov, tell me what happened," but I could not make myself respond.

A snowmobile drew close and loud. Which of the guys was checking on me this time? One stopped by every hour. Mostly,

I was sitting out here no matter the weather. This was where I'd first seen Súmáí, and inside the cabin felt confining. I scanned the clearing, waiting for the snowmobile to appear, wondering if Dad had inserted *Visit Sovern* on the schedule.

But really, I was lucky. Crispy would arrive bearing a constant supply of baked goods. Big John would just sit with me, his hulking presence a comfort as he told stories of what his sons had done. Even Tucker visited, never sitting, but saying hey. He wasn't so good at improvising with a mute, and he usually left pretty quick. Tara stopped by, her black eye healed to a faint purple swoosh, and her forehead's cut to a short red line. She had no problem with silence. We'd just sit and she'd pat my leg before leaving. One day, Sarge even made it over from Sapphire East. He'd sat in one of the leather chairs, not mentioning how he'd found me blood-soaked and hugging that charred trunk, how I'd fled from him. Instead, he talked about the trip he and his wife would take to the Mexican Riviera once the mountain closed. He left with a salute.

I couldn't get my head around turquoise waves and white sand. I lived for Upward Dog spruce, yet couldn't even consider laying a palm on one. To only be able to look at a world and not take my hand from a trunk seemed so limiting now. And to return to Súmáí's world? I couldn't do it. *Me + anyone I loved = disaster.*

Wash had slept in the cabin every night, leaving two hours after Dad. Mornings, he'd grin at me and say, "Man, all this beauty rest. Any lady crossing my path is toast!"

At least someone was sleeping. My bed was too soft and

the room stifling. I hung my bow and arrow on the log wall over my bed, and I'd stare at it for hours, listening to how Dad's breathing was so different from Súmáí's. That difference seemed to mock me, hour after dark hour. Always, there was the distant hum of tires on asphalt and jet engines in the sky. Combined with snowcats, phones ringing, chairlifts gliding, music playing, and voices, voices, voices. Mostly in English. When I'd hear Spanish, my heart would lurch.

Mornings, I'd wash my face, brush my teeth, and stare at my scar necklace in the mirror like it held an answer. But no answer came. It was assurance, though, that none of it had been a dream.

One morning, I took the kitchen shears and, with no regard for symmetry, cut my hair the same length as Túwámúpúch's. When Dad saw it, I thought he was going to cry. Wash guided me to the bathroom mirror, shaking his head and saying "Shite!" He tried to repair what I'd done.

A snowmobile appeared around the pines' edge. Wash drove, and behind him sat a guy in an orange down coat, sunglasses, loafers, and chinos. Wash bounded off the snowmobile and up the steps. "Got company, Sov."

The man stepped onto the porch and pulled off his sunglasses. It was Handler. I braced.

"Morning, Sovern." His voice yanked me toward this world's reality. I trained my gaze on Phantom Peak.

"I'll leave you to it," Wash said. "When you're finished, just head over to ski patrol, on the first floor of the lodge there." He pointed the direction of headquarters.

"Thank you, Mr. Washington," Handler said.

"*Mis-ter Washington*? That's my father. Call me Wash."
He grinned in that crazy way, making me smile a little.

Handler chuckled. "Wash."

Wash bounded off the deck, hopped on the snowmobile, and drove away. When quiet returned, Handler strolled to the wall and leaned against it, hands in his chino's pockets.

"I've always liked these sparkling spring days. They seem to hold hope."

Silence.

"I hear you're not talking again. Don't feel like I came to make you talk. I didn't." He settled on the deck beside me. "I came to check on you."

He rested his elbows on his knees and clasped his hands together. "I'd hate to see you lose credits this semester. Prolong your high school experience, what with how you love it and all."

I snorted.

"I've talked to your teachers. If you'll email them, you can get your missing assignments and keep up while you're at home." He scanned around to see what home was. "My only concern is Spanish."

I loosed a silent laugh. Handler watched me. He shrugged off his coat and laid it beside him.

"Also, I had an email from a scientist—Cairn Hart, at MIT. Apparently you met her here, on the lift?" He had my full attention now. "She wrote that you helped with her research, and she wonders if you might be interested in a summer internship." He held my gaze and nodded. "Apparently she tracked me down because she's worried she doesn't have your email right. You haven't responded to her email, maybe?"

I hadn't even been able to *look* at my computer, let alone turn it on. Doing that would somehow wipe out the close sense I still had of Súmáí. Yet this news altered the light, and I felt pulled between two selves.

"I've seen a lot of sharp students in my day," Handler said. "Some buy into school and some don't. But I've never had an honor like this come along for anyone, let alone a junior. Your mother would be so proud."

He looked out across Gold Bowl to Phantom Peak, and for a while we sat in silence.

He inhaled deep. "It smells so fresh up here. Must be a nice feeling, knowing this is home." He took another breath and let it out. "Well, back to work."

He rose. On his red golf shirt was the logo of a toma-hawk. He strolled down the steps and across the groomed space to the right, his parka held against his hip.

I closed my eyes, and my zombie brain sparked toward solving Cairn's equation.

Bookmark:
Niels Bohr

———

"Einstein, stop telling God what to do."

44

Handler's visit left me straddling two worlds, two selves. Cairn's equation whispered in my mind while the rhythm of Súmáí's pulse echoed against my lips. My need to seek Mom had calmed in Súmáí's world, yet here it felt like hollowness. In its space, that scout's voice rasped *And? You?* over and over, like a summoning drum.

After three days, I realized I had to merge those selves or go mad. First, though, I needed to see *my* world. I needed to confirm that Súmáí's lay in its past. I needed to see how it felt to exist here with that knowledge. Snowboarding was the most efficient way to accomplish this.

My parka was gone, my phone in its pocket, so I zipped on my light Nordic skiing jacket, slid into my exercise tights—my snowboard pants had been banished to the lodge's dumpster—and grabbed my snowboard. I walked through a bright

March afternoon to the beginning of Always, ratcheted down my bindings, and took off, retracing my route from the day I'd discovered the spruce. My heart lightened at gliding, yet also grew heavy with how frivolous it seemed.

The powder snow of a week ago lay beneath three more storms. At the Always spruce, I peered up, and the porcupine in its branches made my pulse lurch. I scanned around and found the spot in the forest across the clearing where the Mom-bear had emerged. My sight traced where my hand had circled the spruce's trunk, and I felt how sure I'd been that I could lift my hand from the bark and disappear. I felt again the surprise gravity beneath my feet, and then Mom's paws compressing my chest like resuscitation.

At first, I could not find Mom's slash on the trunk, but then I saw it, worn by years, the spaces between the slashes widened by the spruce's increased girth. I traced my jacket, beneath which lay my own scars.

I descended to the road, retracing the path Súmáí had led me down, and closed my eyes to recall his nearness. It was a rare uncrowded afternoon, and I made S-turns, moving slowly, watching us walk down in my memory. Passing the spot where I'd clocked him with my head, I blinked back the sensation of that blow, and of waking him in dread and panic. At the road's last bend, I heard the chairlift. My memory heard the dogs barking and the children shouting and laughing, calling *Súmáí!*

I steered to the side of the lift's maze and removed my board. I strode up the adjacent hillside and surveyed the area. Our tepee had stood right where skiers waited on a blue board to load the chair. My vision traced where Chief Úwápaa's tepee, Súmáí's uncle's tepee, Panákwas's and Mú'ú'nap's tepees had been, all the tepees in the village. I studied the open area where we'd danced and sung and told stories around the fire.

"Coward," I whispered to my fear of pressing my hand against a spruce, of trying to return.

I strapped on my board, maneuvered through the lift's maze, and almost choked as I slid forward, alone, to the blue board. I looked up, to where our tepee's opening would have revealed sky, and saw the lift's thick cable coming round. I watched the chair clamp on as it scooped me to sitting. It carried me out of the lifthouse and accelerated, ascending the bowl at fourteen miles per hour. To my right was our aspen grove, where Súmáí's people assumed we'd married. The chair climbed higher. From this vantage, the sparseness of the trees stunned me. Two charred trunks jutted toward the sky.

At the lift's summit, I headed down the east side of Gold Bowl and entered Eternity. In the aspen glade, I steered right of the rock I usually launched off and sat where Súmáí had made our bed. I felt his palm against my back, heard myself whisper *Too fast!* My shorter hair reached only the corner of my mouth, but I tugged a lock there and held it like I used to hold cigarettes. Gray and black chickadees hopped around in the branches above, issuing little squeaks and sending shadows across me. What did they really see? Had they witnessed that night? Had they heard our pulses, or the distant beat of my dance's drum?

I finally rose, snowboarding along the path Súmáí always

led me down, back toward his village. I turned off it early, though, and entered the maze for the lift leading up the ridge between Gold Bowl and Silver Bowl. The maze had only a few people in it, and I rode the lift alone. Gazing west, I relived our first hunting trip, me so sore and huffing along behind. Three months later, bloody, grieving, and weary from pursuing the scout, I'd still outrun Sarge easily. I'd sat for the last eight days, yet my limbs still held the fitness Súmáí's world had forced into me. That, my bow, and my scar necklace were the proof I clung to. Proof I wasn't insane.

I wished I hadn't left my phone behind. That picture I took of Súmáí would have given me another scrap of him. Maybe it had captured a bit of his spirit after all. I looked down and right, estimating where we'd crossed this ridge while pursuing the scout.

At the lift's top, I peered in the lifthouse's window and raised my hand in a wave to the giant, shaggy-haired guy working there. Against the wall behind him, inside, leaned his beast of a board. "*Towéiyak,*" I said.

I glided as far as I could from the lift and removed my board, to walk across windswept Big Ridge to Sapphire East lodge. At the lodge, I strapped my board back on and glided down the road, keeping my gaze on the cliffs. At their eastern edge, I stood right where I'd shot the arrow that killed the scout.

And? You? His words would not stop repeating in my head, a relentless beat.

I gulped the warm March air and made for that solitary spruce's charred trunk. I kneeled on the perfectly groomed snow and studied its twisted gray and black, the only remnant of a tree left in this whole upper part of Silver Bowl. I felt myself frantically hauling Súmáí to it, the hot wet of his blood. I flinched as I set him down too hard. Body vibrating, he said my name, and his eyes latched onto mine. His hair yanked from my lips.

I pulled off my glove and stared at my palm, squinting to discern flame in my life line. *I* had ignited that spruce by not heeding Súmáí's warning. I couldn't have known the tree would burst into flame, yet he'd warned me, and I'd stubbornly ignored him. And by igniting that spruce, I'd lit the grove of pines and started that long-ago fire that burned the back bowls.

I scanned Silver Bowl, now scoured of trees. A wide corduroy plain. White gold.

Cairn's equation appeared across that white, in thick black numbers and symbols. I pressed my palm hard against my forehead, willing the battle within it to calm. Instead, I heard the spruce ignite. Loosing a growl, I rose and slashed angry turns into the run's smoothed perfection.

At the bottom, I didn't take the Silver Bowl lift. Instead I followed a road paralleling the frozen creek back to the chair that ascended the ridge between Silver Bowl and Gold Bowl. As I boarded along the road, I watched for the house-sized boulder by the pool. It appeared, three feet of snow on top, like a slice of cake with a last new layer bulging over its sides like frosting.

The creek was visible only because of its depression. I took off my board and postholed to the edge. Catching my breath,

I scanned across the snow-blanket panorama. Einstein had discovered that this was how space-time looked, and the depressions in these contours created gravity. Was this what determined fate? Imprints like this creek across the fabric of time?

I navigated along the bank till I stood above the pool and crossed, imagining the three stones under my feet as I'd rushed to help Mom. Eight days ago I'd been in that world. Eight days and 136 years. I paused, head down and afraid. Seeing Súmáí's drawing on the rock, knowing I could not travel through the spruce anymore, would transform him from that pulse against my lips to dead. "Courage," I said, to calm my own loud pulse. I waded through the snow to the boulder's far side.

There we were, edges weathered. Me in my deerskin pants, shirt, and necklace. The knot of our hands leading to Súmáí. Bows over our shoulders. Mom-bear beside me. The spruce beside him. The rising bird between us. I sobbed and laughed and pressed my forehead against Súmáí's figure, as hard as I remembered him pressing the rock with that elk bone.

"Wife," I said.

After a time, skiers glided past, voices loud. I pulled back, wiping my face with my sleeve before I realized they couldn't see me. I'd always have this drawing, at least. *This*, above all else, proved I wasn't insane.

I started back toward my board, arms out for balance as I retraced my deep steps. I looked at the opposite bank, where I'd sewn Mom's wound, prepared to face the guilt of the miners.

I froze. The entire stand of trees that had existed there was gone. Frantic, I peered down the valley. One charred trunk, like a sentry, was all that remained. How could I not have realized this before?

And? You?

The relentless beat of that scout's voice became clear. Not only had I started the fire—that was awful enough—but I'd also burned Súmáí's village. *Me + anyone I loved = disaster.*

Bookmark:
Stephen Hawking

———————

"Not only does God play dice, but...
he sometimes throws them
where they cannot be seen."

45

Grief has no equation. It's just the negative value of what you've lost. Tears are proportional. If you can't cry, they mass, crowding more and more space inside your heart till it's a hard hot place. Cry too much and it sucks your heart emptier and emptier till there's nothing but vastness. When Mom died, I couldn't cry. Crying would have meant she was dead. In Súmáí's world, I'd come to accept death, and now I cried nonstop.

Worry lines creased Dad's face. He, Wash, or one of the guys stayed with me full time. A bunch of mother hens. None of it mattered. Nothing mattered. Till after a week, Tara showed up.

"About time we had that ride," she said, and she led me to her snowcat.

I climbed in and shut the door.

"Buckle up," she said.

Our eyes met, and she took a good long look at my pain. "I'm a woman used to silence, eh?" She chunked the snowcat into gear.

There was no moon, and the snowcat's lights cast a wide circumference as Tara U-turned and rumbled down Sunset Ridge. I blinked at the image of me snowshoeing here that day, Hawking's book playing in my head, and then at me returning the next day, with a breathing piece of time.

"They still have me front-side, after what happened at Sapphire East," she said.

We rendezvoused with two other snowcats, and in staggered formation groomed upper Pride and the runs next to it. The cat's rumble was a comforting rhythm, its motion like being rocked in a cradle. Time seemed to stand still, but when I glanced at the clock in the dash, two hours had passed in this otherworldly space. Then this weird thing happened: *that lit circumference + the dark void = a tunnel to my future.* Down that tunnel, I watched a movie of myself in that driver's seat, grim-faced, determined, and steering into the dark.

Thing was, Hawking's narrator kept playing as its soundtack, and Cairn's equation kept scrawling against the lit snow.

"Briggs tells me you might want to drive a cat someday," Tara said, breaking our silence. She snorted. "School's not your thing, eh? I went to a school with nuns."

I looked at her then.

"Yep, me and the sisters. I was wild, and my parents, desperate, sent me to them, hoping God would straighten me out." She laughed. "It didn't work. You know what finally

362

worked? This." She gestured beyond the windshield with her hand. "I'm addicted. It's like I enter another world, eh?"

I felt lulled, and something about her words struck a chord in me. Before I knew it, I'd said, "Eh."

The snowcat crested the run, Tara turned left, and a flash of movement at the forest's edge sped my pulse. Moments later, Emerald West lodge's outlines came into view. As we drew nearer, Tara sucked air through her teeth. One of the first-floor windows was shattered.

"I'm a magnet," she said, and I suspected she was, in a way. She lifted the radio from the dash and called in the vandalism but kept rolling past the lodge.

"I'm forbidden to get out of the cat," she said to my panicked look. "Besides, I need to get you home. Briggs'll have heard about this and he'll be worried sick." The cat rocked a little, and Tara glanced in the rearview mirror, then the sideview ones. She looked at me and shrugged.

I shrugged back, hoping she couldn't see the red climbing my neck. A snowmobile's headlights appeared, like a star in the distance. It neared and Tara braked the cat.

"Tell Sov to go inside and keep the cabin door locked!" Dad shouted over the vehicles' idling engines.

"You hear that?" Tara said, and I nodded. We idled there for a minute more as she watched Dad speed down Sunset Ridge.

She pulled up next to the cabin. I climbed out and waved from the deck as her snowcat lugged away.

Súmáí swung under the railing and onto its far side. My face must have been ghostly, because he stepped toward me like he thought I was afraid. "Sovern?"

I was at him in two strides, but the expression on his face stopped me from hugging him. He wore the liftie uniform, moccasins, and Dad's hat, though the way he stood there, watching me... he wasn't yet *my* Súmáí.

I inhaled his familiar scent and looked into his face. His brow furrowed at my strong emotion.

The wind kicked up and hurled ice bits. Our hair swirled, and his blew across my face. I longed to catch a chunk and put it in my mouth. He noticed my short hair and frowned at it.

I took his hand, went to the door, and keyed in the code. He followed me in and prowled around, ensuring the place was safe. He glanced into the dark bedroom while I loaded a bagel in the toaster, found the bag of little slices of butter in white paper that Dad and I always heisted from the lodge instead of buying sticks, and ran two glasses of water. I spread the butter on the bagel thick, the way I knew Súmáí liked it. I set the bagel on the table as he stood by the front window, keeping watch.

I sat down. Súmáí joined me and touched a daisy in the bouquet Wash had bought for the table's center. I gestured toward the food. He shook his head, no doubt remembering the brownie, chips, and hot cocoa. But I knew now how hunger clung to you in his world, so I held the bagel up to him. He took it, sniffed it, and bit in. He ate the whole thing in seconds. I scooted the plate to him, and he finished the other half.

I toasted another bagel, careful to make sure he could see the bag. I brought the butter to the table and made a show of peeling off the paper and slathering it on. I had a brainstorm and grabbed a salt packet too and sprinkled it on top. He ate that second bagel and downed the water. I watched his Adam's apple rise and fall.

I got some beef jerky and bit it. I handed a piece to Súmáí. He smelled it, took a bite, and pulled a face. Cow tasted miles different from deer and elk. He pointed at me, then the jerky, and mimed shooting an arrow. I laughed desperately at the irony. Then the memories of how much he loved my accuracy with my bow, and of him tackling me in the grass, disintegrated my composure. Before I realized it, I'd taken his hand. I stroked the bones across its back. I turned it over and felt his pulse.

His brow furrowed. I was wearing a V-neck blouse Mom had bought me ages ago, and his eyes glued to my scar neck-lace. I nodded and lifted my chin. He scooted his chair close and sipped air as he traced the holes.

I leaned across the table, took a lock of his hair, and put it in my mouth, relishing its silky texture. His eyes said *Too fast!* and then darted from my hair to my scars. The distant whine of an approaching snowmobile surrounded us. He moved toward the door.

I followed him onto the deck, wanting to tell him every-thing in Spanish, but I sensed that would alter, maybe even rob us of, the time we'd had in his world. Instead, I pointed from his chest to mine. I crossed my fingers. He cocked his head and crossed his.

He started to leave but turned back and studied me. I pressed my lips to keep silent, but then I couldn't stop myself: I hugged him. I counted—one, two, three, four, five—before his arms lowered and he held me loosely.

The snowmobile grew loud, and he pulled back, squint-ing at me. I kissed his jawbone and that little V appeared between his brows. He swung beneath the rail and jogged across the snow. When he arrived at the forest's edge, close to where my boogieman had stood, he turned, waved, and then disappeared.

The snowmobile rounded the pines, and I blocked its headlights with my palm. Dad and Wash dismounted wearily and trudged onto the stairs. Dad saw me and paused.

"We were fine," Wash said. He walked past me into the cabin and collapsed on the couch. "They didn't even steal anything this time. I'm zonked."

––––––––––

I never slept that night. After Dad and Wash started a snoring symphony, I returned to the front window and peered out through the ice blooms till dawn. When Dad roused, I went into the bathroom and flushed the toilet so he'd think I'd just gotten up. It didn't work.

"You sit by that window all night?"

I opened the covers and slid into my too-soft bed. Dad sat on its edge. My hand beneath the blanket made a little nub, and he studied it. "Sovern, don't shut me out. I can't take this anymore." The expression on his face just about killed me.

"That liftie who helped us to the gondola that night... Súmáí? After I showed you how the trees worked... He was my..." My relationship with Gage would be nothing compared to what I was about to tell him.

At first Dad's face filled with relief at my talking, but his gaze sharpened as he heard what I said. I forced myself not to look away.

"He's not from here. Well, he's from here, 136 years ago." I lost my momentum, and my mind seemed to scramble for footing in air. "I killed him! I killed seven guys, plus him, plus probably his whole village!" I covered my face and started keening.

"Whoa, whoa, whoa!" Dad grabbed his phone from the nightstand. I wiped my tears and runny nose with the back of my hand.

"Tucker, I'm going to be late." He hung up and let out a huge sigh. "Start from the beginning."

A knock rattled the bedroom door and Wash peeked in. Dad nodded, so Wash lay down in Dad's bed, making a show of getting comfy beneath the covers to dispel the tension. I glanced at him and he made that not-smile, the left side of his lip curling up while his left eyebrow pressed down. I smiled despite myself, and Súmáí describing a smile like this rose in my memory: *He made me laugh.* I thought how Wash had no family, thought of Túwámúpúch and the baby I rocked.

Dad squeezed my hand. "Sovern?"

I was subjecting Dad to a slow death. I couldn't kill anyone else. "I first met Súmáí at the spruce where I had my accident."

"Súmáí?" Wash said.

Dad held out his hand, gesturing patience.

"It was the third time I'd traveled through the trees. The first time was a fluke. I fell, and when I touched that spruce getting up, it was late spring and there was Mom. The second time, I just had to know if the first was real." I looked hard at Dad. "Can you blame me?"

He pressed his lips tight and glanced at Wash, who was pushing back the covers and sitting up.

"With that spruce that fell in front of us on Pride, and me crashing into a spruce in Shangri-La—"

"Shangri-La?" Wash said.

Dad waved away his question again, so I went on.

"I was curious, so I snowshoed over to check it out. Except this time, when I put my hand on it, there was Súmáí." I laughed and could hear my hysterical edge. "He was as shocked as me. See, he'd been traveling through the trees for … well, I'm not sure how long before me. He'd gotten quills in his cheek too."

I paused to gather my thoughts. Dad's mouth was set. Wash's hung open.

"The next time, I still wanted to find Mom."

I told them everything. About Mom and little-me on that blanket, about finding the Always spruce, about living with Súmáí's people. When I said that Mom had been a bear, that she'd given me the scars, Dad studied the ones that showed above the loose neck of my T-shirt, but then he held up his hand and said, "No more about her." Wash kept interrupting like he couldn't get his head around it, holding out his hands like *really?*

I looked between Dad and Wash and tried to sound confident as I said, "He's been traveling here to feed his people. They're *starving*. Or they were, or they are. It's hard to explain. They're the last Utes in these mountains!"

Dad said carefully, "Are you talking about the vandalism?"

"Uh-huh," I said.

"Why doesn't he ever steal any meat?" Wash said.

Dad usually never lost his cool, but he did then. "Wash, shut up!" He looked at me. "Go on."

"I ended up back here because we were discovered by whites. They attacked. Súmáí ... died."

"That was *his* blood?" Dad said.

I looked at my lap and nodded.

"I asked you not to go there anym—"

"I know!" I buried my face in my hands. "I know. *I know.* I should have listened. I killed them all!"

"Killed them?" Dad said, like I had it wrong. "There was just a vandal here. That was Súmáí, right?"

I opened my mouth to argue, but then what Dad and I were actually disputing hit me: whether a Ute from 136 years ago had been here or not. The long night added up, and hysteria took me completely. I couldn't stop laughing. Dad and Wash glanced at each other.

"Sovern," Dad said, like *gather yourself.*

I tried to stop, really. I just couldn't. And then the meaning of that movie at the end of last night's snowcat-tunnel dawned on me: *You could change the world.*

Whether I liked it or not, Shelley Millhouse had already helped me.

"What?" Dad and Wash said at the same moment.

I reached out and touched the point in the air where their voices' waves would have overlapped. That point had existed for one moment and was gone, like the point I'd imagined for Súmáí and me together in his world.

I spoke, trancelike. "Time is so much more than one line. It moves from past to present to future, yes, but also in every direction imaginable. There's multiple universes, each with a past, present, and future, and they all overlap. A constant living and changing thing."

Wash was staring, open-mouthed, like a kid in bed hearing a scary story. Dad just watched me.

I looked straight at Dad, pleading. "Remember how you said that spruce falling on Pride saved us? Well, the one from my accident, and that Pride one, and those two whirlwinds—all on February 22, of all days? They more than saved us, Dad. They *chose* us. Chose *me*."

"Sovern, I wake up each morning and blast avalanches, rope off hazards and unsafe sections, do speed checks in traffic areas to avert collisions. I work to keep people from damaging themselves in a world I can see and touch. You're destroying yourself in worlds I can't reach. Please, stop!"

I traced my chest's scars: Bear Necklace, Woman of the Trees. Finally, I understood my name. All the ways I was screwed up comprised *me*, *this* Sovern, who *needed* to travel through those trees. Who *needed* to seek adrenaline, and Mom, and Súmáí. I, not those other normal Soverns, was meant to figure this out.

Part of my own equation became clear, and I knew I'd say yes to Cairn's email.

I covered Dad's hand. "I can't."

Wash blew out his breath.

46

I settled onto the deck, leaning against the cabin's wall, taking in the blue-bird day. Looking out at this world, it was hard to believe all the things that had happened. But then I imagined that sky overlapping an infinity of other skies, an infinity of other lands.

Súmáí had been here again. Had our few meetings been chance or fate? I looked to where I'd seen him when I was five, where he'd stood and waved last night. How many times had he traveled to find the right me in this world? Had his visits ending in vandalism begun as times when he was looking for me? The toll on his body must have been extreme. My body glowed full-time against darkness now, no matter how much salt I choked down. I held out one hand, and it cast a shadow half as dark as my snow boots.

The sound of steps crunched through snow and Dad

appeared, wearing just his flannel shirt and uniform pants. His radio was belted at his waist. He walked to the deck's edge, right across from me, and we were eye level. He still wore an exasperated expression from our talk this morning, but he just said, "Lunch?"

"No thanks."

I listened to him opening kitchen drawers, running water in the sink, opening a cellophane bag. He came out carrying a glass of ice water and a plate with a sandwich and chips. He sat next to me and set the plate between us, chips close to me, hoping, no doubt, I'd have some. I wasn't much of an eater lately.

We didn't talk. I just listened to him chew or gulp.

Dad looked haggard and dark circles hung below his eyes. He reminded me of Chief Úwápaa. They both had their battles for what they believed was right. Chief Úwápaa looked out for the welfare of his people, and Dad looked out for me, but also for all his ski-patrol employees and all the guests schussing through the resort. They struck me as similar, too, in how they held on to ways of seeing the world that would soon be dead. For Chief Úwápaa, it was the Ute way of life that had existed for thousands of years. For Dad, it was his narrow linear perspective that the world before us was all there was, and the rest was magic.

"Wash keeps walking around shaking his head and muttering," Dad said and took his plate into the kitchen.

As I listened to him clean up, I considered that maybe he and I were doomed. If *Dad* + *me* = *y*, then *y* = *battle*. We'd have to learn to love each other anyway.

He came out on the deck. "You don't slouch anymore."

"Remember how Mom used to say we'd kill each other if she wasn't around?" I said.

"I do."

"I'm sorry I keep hurting you," I said.

He tilted his head.

"I'm sorry for the things I've done," I said. "For right now. For the things I'll do. It's our equation."

Dad clamped his lips and sighed out his nose. He squatted beside me, pulled my head close, and kissed my forehead. "Me too."

Just as he started down the steps, Gage curved around the pines on his snowboard. Dad paused, looked back at me with eyebrows raised, and walked to him. "Hello, Gage."

"Hey, Mr. Briggs."

I waited for Dad to say, "Aren't you supposed to be in school," but he just nodded to Gage and headed to ski patrol's headquarters.

Gage turned to me. Under his arm was my parka. I shot to my feet and bounded down the steps.

"How did you get this?"

His face fell. "I thought you'd left it. A sign, you know, after standing me up and not calling for *seventeen* days."

Sign, indeed. "Where was it?"

"Next to my back door." Gage looked at me knowingly. Anyone familiar with him knew he used the back door to access the slopes and village.

I held out my hands and he passed me my parka. I pressed it to my face and smelled a perfume of smoke, yellow grass, and horse. As he unbuckled his board's bindings, I unzipped my parka's pocket and pulled out my phone. Dead, of course.

"Is that why you haven't answered my texts?"

I raced inside and plugged it into its charger. If my Súmáí had died ... how could my parka have gotten here?

My mind ran through scenarios. Maybe my Súmáí had come on another visit but was scarred from burns and worried he'd seem hideous to me. Maybe he'd grown old and had been trying to get the parka back to me for years. Or maybe he was giving *me* a sign, telling me to move on, to make a life with the person he'd become in my time, in this world.

No matter what, it meant he'd survived.

I slid on the parka, lifted the collar, smelled it again, and dove my hands in its pockets. In the other pocket was something pencil-shaped. I pulled out the white bone tool he'd used to draw our picture.

"You all right?" Gage stood in the open doorway.

"When did you find it?" I said.

"Night before last." He leaned against the doorjamb, silhouetted by the bright light outside. He was taller, yet how he held himself was totally Súmáí. As he stepped to me, I let myself see the hurt in his face, and I forced myself not to step back. He reached out, took a lock of my cut hair, and rubbed it between his fingers. I pressed my forehead to his chest, and he hugged me.

We'd made out plenty of times in our year together, but we'd never really hugged. Now, the way he held me was so like Súmáí, it sent a tear straightlining down my cheek.

We pulled apart, looked at one another, and laughed, a little embarrassed. I pulled off his hat, slipped his hair behind his ear, and ran my finger over its tip.

Me + my ski-patrol family = 8, but *Súmáí + Gage + me = ∞.*

Inside felt confined, so I led Gage onto the deck. I leaned on the rail and he leaned beside me, our arms touching. I traced my scar necklace as I peered to my right, down the valley to Emerald West, where Mom and Dad had said their vows. Beyond, to the barely discernible highway where she'd died. To the spot nearby, where Súmáí's people had wintered for eons and his brother had been killed. I scanned Platinum and Gold Bowls and saw Mom reading to a different me on a blanket, Mom as a bear on the edge of Always. I held the bone tool Súmáí had used to draw us, pictured our drawing in the Silver Bowl drainage, and felt the line where my arm that had broken against the spruce met Gage's. Everything seemed to lift and swirl on the air around me—my past, my present, my future, and places there weren't words or equations for. Yet.

"Someday," I said, and sent my promise into that crowded air.

Glossary of Ute Names

- Súmáí—to remember
- Chief Úwápaa—rainwater
- Túwámúpúch—nighthawk
- Mú'ú'nap—windmaker
- Panákwas—lightning

Acknowledgments

There are many people to thank in the making of this book. Oliver Compton for explaining Calculus, and Steve Gordon for checking my Spanish. I worship World Science University (http://www.worldscienceu.com) for their fascinating and accessible courses on math and science. Huge thanks to Goldin Wall and his family at the Ute Mountain Ute Reservation for their critical help with, and perspective on, Ute culture and history. Thanks also to the Native American Cultural Center at Colorado State University.

My Beaver Creek Ski and Snowboard School bosses, Mike Blakslee and Pete Petrovski: I have such gratitude for your kindness and grace when I had time constraints, and for allowing me the space to pull this whole book together. Nicole Magistro of The Bookworm of Edwards, you always remind me that a writer cannot exist only in her tunnel of imagination. Credit to my trusty readers Sue Staats, Liza Alrick, and Rick Attig. Praise to Brian Farrey-Latz and Sandy Sullivan for excellent editing of the highest standard. Secret Agent Bri: not sure what I'd do without you. As always, thanks to Ross and Sydney—my first readers, sounding boards, bullshit filters, and fellow geeks.

Katherine M. Schmidt

About the Author

Heather Sappenfield's first novel, *The View From Who I Was*, was published in 2015. Her short stories have won numerous awards and finalist positions, most notably the Danahy Fiction Prize and the Flannery O'Connor Award. She has also received a Pushcart Nomination.

Heather lives in Vail, Colorado, with her husband and daughter. In her spare time, she loves to ski, trail run, bike, or watch her daughter play soccer. Visit her online at www.heather sappenfield.com.